GHOST CATS

GHOST CATS

human encounters with feline spirits

Dusty Rainbolt

THE LYONS PRESS
Guilford, Connecticut

An imprint of The Globe Pequot Press

The Lyons Press is an imprint of The Globe Pequot Press.

10 9 8 7 6 5 4 3 2 1

Printed in the United States of America

Designed by Sheryl P. Kober
ISBN: 978-1-59921-004-9

Library of Congress Cataloging-in-Publication Data is available on file.

I dedicate this book to

Weems and Alta, who understand,
Wendy Christensen, who made it possible,
And especially Maynard, for taking time from his
busy schedule to say good-bye.

You can never lose anything that really belongs to you,
and you can't keep that which belongs to someone else.

—EDGAR CAYCE

contents

acknowledgments

I want to express my deepest appreciation to everyone who made this book possible, especially my editor, Holly Rubino—you're the best! Thanks to Kate Epstein—the bad-cop agent to my good cop, Linda Gorsuch—a wealth of wisdom and information, as well as a wicked proofreader; Wendy Christensen, who recommended me for this project; and my husband, Weems Hutto—who put up with all the inconveniences associated with important projects.

Thank you to Margaret Rainbolt and Mary Anne Miller, for reading and making suggestions; Al Chewning, for helping get inside information about the Cavalier Hotel; and Diane Samsel, Sue Darroch, Carol Gurney, and Steve Rusher, for sharing their knowledge.

And also a huge thanks to friends, communities, and list managers for helping me get the word out, including the Cat Writers' Association; the Cat Fanciers' Association; Katherine Hopper; Karen Hooker; Ghoststudy.com; unexplained_world@yahoogroups.com; realghosts@yahoogroups.com; Mythi and the PsychicAnimalCommunication@yahoogroups.com; WillCountyGhostHuntersSociety@yahoogroups.com; Ed Shanahan and the unexplained_world@yahoogroups.com; Anita Billi, author of *After Life From Above: Healings of a Paranormal Nature*; Nicki Modaber; and Phyllis Galde, editor/publisher of *FATE* magazine.

And of course, my gratitude to all of you who are mentioned within the pages of this book, for having the courage and generosity to share your amazing stories with me and the world.

introduction

I want all of you to know without a glimmer of uncertainty, that all of our pets, and animals of every kind, live on the Other Side, also known as "heaven" or "the afterlife" . . . It goes without saying then, that when an animal dies, its soul goes Home just like ours.

—SYLVIA BROWNE, PSYCHIC AND SPIRITUAL TEACHER

Most of us have had the misfortune, at some time or other, to say the final good-bye to one of our cats. The feeling of loss can be overwhelming; the sudden change and subsequent hole in our routine can make us feel empty and alone.

While some people believe that the end of a cat's life is simply that— the end—others feel and hope that they and their pets will meet again. Until that time, you wonder if the pain you feel will ever ease.

Maybe you think you catch a glimpse of the cat you recently lost out of the corner of your eye near the food bowl. Or you hear his unique voice. Or you swear, in the middle of the night, that you feel him jump on the bed and take his normal place down at your feet as if nothing has changed. Naturally, when you look there's nothing there. After all, he's no longer on this earthly plane. You chalk up the voices, visions, and sensations to your imagination, wishful thinking, or just to the fact that you've become accustomed to the cat's presence in your life. You may begin to question your sanity.

But you're not crazy. And you're not alone, either.

If someone had told me ten years ago that I would write a book about human encounters with feline spirits, I would have laughed. I wrongly be-lieved people who had experienced ghosts in any form may have had one too many mind-altering experiences in the 1960s and '70s. Then, one night, everything changed. I had my own brush with the fantastic, the very brief return of a foster kitten named Maynard; I was the recipient of one such priceless paranormal gift.

When my husband Weems and I first started working with orphan kittens, we raised a sweet little one named Maynard. Clad in a tuxedo, he even had a coat with a white bow tie and gloves and a pair of white boots. Baby boomers may remember the character Maynard G. Krebs from the sixties sitcom, *The Many Loves of Dobie Gillis*. Maynard had a Krebs-style goatee, big copper eyes, a huge head, and a tremendous problem. We learned when he was six weeks old that he was hydrocephalic. Because he was active and happy, we decided against our veterinarian's recommendation to euthanize him and instead homeopathically treated him. He responded very well to the treatment. Every night he jumped up on the bed, walked across the mattress, and lay down on my ankles. I always thought it couldn't possibly be comfortable for him, but he claimed my ankles as his space.

At Thanksgiving, Weems and I went out of town for a couple of weeks. During our time away from home, the pressure against Maynard's brain suddenly started to build. Thanksgiving morning I found myself on the phone giving my best friend, Debbie, permission to put him to sleep.

What-ifs plagued me. While surviving eight months is nothing short of a miracle for a hydrocephalic cat, I still dwelled on the idea that Maynard might still be alive if only I'd stayed home. If only I could have told Debbie where to find the medicine. If, if, if . . . I didn't even get to say good-bye.

Once I was back at home, despite the comforting presence of our other cats, I had a huge hole in my soul.

About two weeks after we returned home, I had just climbed into bed, but hadn't settled in yet. Suddenly, I felt the familiar sensation of a cat jumping up on the bed, the paws padding across the mattress and flopping down on my feet. While cats jump on the bed all the time, this one settled into Maynard's special corner. Enough light seeped through the curtains that I could see there were no cats on the bed. I felt the weight but knew there was nothing down there.

Prior to Maynard's return and my very first paranormal encounter, I truly believed that ghosts didn't exist. At that moment, with his six pounds of body weight pressing against my feet, I realized the folly of my prior beliefs. I felt at peace and forgiven. I didn't dare move for fear of shattering the moment. I wanted to relish it. I prayed it wouldn't end. Eventually, I slipped off to sleep.

In the morning, the weight against my feet had vanished. It would never return, but for one brief happy moment I'd had little Maynard back. I didn't mention Maynard's return to my husband—or anyone else, for that matter—for over a year. I knew people would think I should be committed to a mental hospital. And I must confess that for a while, I even questioned my own sanity. But I finally accepted my experience. From then on, people who confessed to having seen or experienced a ghost no longer seemed insane.

I treasured that moment. I had experienced a bona fide ghost, something beyond death. It changed a couple of things in my life. It affirmed what my faith had said for years: There is life after the body fails. It confirmed what my mother had told me when I was little. "Your pet will be in Heaven with you."

I don't know whether Maynard came back of his own accord or whether he was sent, literally as a comforting messenger, but I do know I was given a priceless gift—one of closure and comfort. Almost like a fairy tale, my little cat returned for just that one night. He came to say good-bye and to give me the same opportunity. While I wished he could have stayed forever, I happily settled for that one visit.

At the time, I believed my experience to be solely unique, and that I *was* chosen. Well, I was chosen, but it was hardly unique. As a matter of fact, when I mentioned I was writing this book, I expected most people to laugh at me or roll their eyes. Quite the contrary; folks often responded with, "My cat came back," or "I had a ghost cat." I joined some special-interest online communities and mentioned that I was looking for stories. Some of these communities were interested in paranormal phenomena; others were people who bred and showed cats; still others were writers' organizations. Strangers were so interested in the project that they posted my request in places I have yet to uncover. I couldn't believe how excited cat lovers and ghost hunters got over my book! I easily had a hundred responses, and they are still trickling in. I was amazed to discover how many of the stories were similar to mine.

It surprised me, the range of people who responded; I heard from physicians, ministers, lawyers, authors, and even middle school–age kids—all of whom spoke openly about their experiences. There's even a story from a woman whose faith defined paranormal activity of any kind as demonic. She knew that what jumped on the bed at night was no demon, but her beloved tabby.

Although a few owners enjoyed repeated visits from their pets, most of the encounters only happened once. It seemed as though the cats came back just to say good-bye. Universally, people reported that the brief meetings gave them closure, allayed guilt over adopting a new pet, and gave them permission to get on with their lives. Sometimes there's the promise that they will meet again in the afterlife, as imagined in the well-known story of the "Rainbow Bridge"–a mythical place based on a poem originally published in the mid-1980s. In the poem, the soul of the beloved pet goes to a happy meadow where it romps and plays until it is reunited with its owner in death. The pet senses its owner's arrival, and there's a tearful reunion, after which human and animal move on to Heaven together.

Of course, skeptics—you know, people who accused me of using mind-altering substances in the 1970s—think that my own experience was merely wishful thinking. I have had pets since the day I was born, and have raised hundreds of neonatal orphaned kittens, many who didn't make it. With all those pets that I dearly loved coming in and out of my life, my experience with Maynard was the only one I had with the ghost of a pet. Had I the ability to will a cat back from death even for a short time, I would have had many paranormal kitty visits. This wasn't mind-induced. If it were, my mind would have produced Maynard during my deepest grieving rather than weeks later. Had I been able to produce the apparition on my own, I would have chosen other cats to return as well.

Like me, some of the people who had these experiences had never believed in the paranormal prior to their rendezvous with their cat's ghost. That brief exchange brought comfort to the owner, because he or she now knows that not just the cat's essence continues; they now feel re-assured that their own spirit will also endure.

Many owners find themselves suddenly facing the unexpected death of their pets, whether from disappearance, a short catastrophic illness, or sudden death from an accident. The owners weren't given a chance to say good-bye, and many of them harbor toxic guilt. "If only I hadn't let him out that night . . ." "If only I had taken him to the vet sooner . . ." "If only I'd looked under the car hood . . ."

Unfortunately there aren't any redo's. As much as we would like to, we simply can't go back in time. We can't even apologize for our mistakes. But sometimes our cats give us a rare and priceless gift—the gift of being in their presence just one last time.

Friends of mine tell me they have been visited by parents, siblings, or spouses who have passed. Their sudden appearances were frightening. It's ironic that even experienced ghost hunters have been shaken by brushes with human ghosts, but with rare exceptions, most cat owners come away from a visit with their recently departed cat with a sense of relief and joy.

I thought I would uncover lots of frightening stories—even planned to have a whole chapter devoted to them—but soon discovered that such scary tales are quite rare. Instead, I heard about real-life experiences; about love, home, comfort, gratitude, bonding, and forgiveness. Although we are different species, humans and cats have more in common than we realize.

So why does the appearance of a loved human apparition often invoke fear, while a cat spirit brings tears of comfort and allows a sense of closure?

Sue Darroch, co-director of the Toronto Ghosts and Hauntings Research Society, believes that most of our fears surrounding ghosts are based in popular culture and media. Fictional accounts and horror movies are meant to frighten us. While malevolent human ghosts factor heavily in fictional stories and Hollywood films, ghost cats are seldom represented.

We are taught to fear the unknown, the afterlife, and our fellow humans, but for the most part, we are taught to trust the household cat. So when confronted with the apparition or spirit of a cat, we are far less likely to feel fear, particularly if it was a beloved pet.

Besides, in real life, running into someone unexpectedly in your home is terrifying, no matter who they are. It's the kind of fear you feel when you bump into someone in a dark alley. Who are they? Are they going to hurt you? Whether they have kind or evil intentions, the potential for danger with human spirits is there. And you can't clobber a ghost with a bat or shoot them to protect yourself. You feel utterly powerless.

Karen Duban, who shares her story in these pages, also shared this perspective: "It's not surprising that domestic cat ghosts would have more to do with positive interaction than scary or creepy stuff. The creepy stuff is in our heads—not theirs. They are 'domestic,' after all; in other words, associated with the home."

Another common theme among the stories people shared with me was their easy acceptance of the occurrence. With the exception of the Demon Cat of the nation's capitol in Washington—which I discuss later in the book—and visitations to children, few people felt threatened or disturbed by the dead kitty's appearance. People usually felt blessed and happy about their cats' spiritual return, while they might have gone into a complete panic had a dead parent or spouse shown up instead.

Of course feline spirits aren't scary. Ghost cats are the friends you had when they were alive.

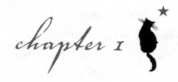
Didn't You Just Leave Me?
WHY GHOST CATS EXIST

*Science tells us that nothing in nature, not even the
tiniest particle, can disappear without a trace. Think
about that for a moment. Once you do, your thoughts
about life will never be the same.*

— WERNHER VON BRAUN, GERMAN PHYSICIST
WHO HELPED DEVELOP THE U.S. SPACE PROGRAM

Our cats seem to live in that mysterious realm between the natural and
the transcendental, betwixt the living and the dead. There is so much passion shared between cats and their families in those few allotted years.
Then all too quickly, the flame of light is blown out and they are gone
from our lives—we fear—forever. But the passion between cats and humans, like the cats themselves, can transcend death. Sometimes a cat finds
a way to reach through that thin veil with her paw. In the blink of an eye,
you see her, and then she is gone. For a short moment you hear her voice.

So what is it that you've really experienced?

WHAT IS A GHOST?

The truth is, if you query fifty people about the definition of ghost, you'll
get fifty-five different answers. The terms ghost, spirit, and apparition, as
well as entity and specter may all technically have different definitions,
but they are often used interchangeably. Basically, these words refer to
the energy or soul or personality of a person who has died but remained
on earth after its death.

But what of animal souls? Are there really ghost cats? In his 1913 book, *Animal Ghosts*, Elliott O'Donnell says, "The mere fact that there are manifestations of dead people proves some kind of life after death for human beings; and happily the same proof is available with regard for a future life for animals; indeed there are as many animal phantoms as human—perhaps more." While there were brief mentions of animal apparitions in journals and books in the late nineteenth century, it appears that O'Donnell's collection of animal ghost stories was the first examination and acknowledgment that ghost cats do exist.

There have been many other reports of animal specters recorded throughout history. The most common stories revolve around cats, dogs, and horses. This could be because of the close bond humans have developed after living so closely with these animals over thousands of years.

A human ghost can be felt, heard, seen, or even smelled. In this book, people who shared their stories have shown that cat ghosts have the potential to be experienced with these same senses.

In 1970, parapsychology researcher Raymond Bayless published his analysis of animal ghosts throughout recorded history. He examined reports of both spontaneous appearances, like the ghost cat jumping on the bed, and apparitions seen—or ones that materialized—as a result of a medium; that is, a person who can receive or channel messages from spirits.

Bayless concluded that as with their human counterparts, animal ghosts at times show obvious purposeful, intelligent behavior. In these cases, they are more than just recordings of the animal. "It can be said, then, that animal phantoms are vehicles of individuality and consciousness . . ." Bayless writes. He concluded his book with this: "Animals do survive death, and on occasions are capable of manifesting their continued existence through apparitional and 'haunting' phenomena."

In much of Western culture, those who "believe" consider ghosts to be restless souls lingering on Earth. Paranormal experts say that a human spirit returns (or never leaves) for a number of reasons, but primarily stays behind because it is stuck or doesn't realize death has occurred, or has some kind of unfinished business.

Although a cat may not have a similar agenda, she may still have important business left to do, usually revolving around her unconditional love and loyalty for her human. Often she returns simply to say good-bye—especially if there was no chance for closure before death, perhaps because the cat disappeared, or died mysteriously or unexpectedly.

She may have become "stuck" because she doesn't realize she's no longer in her body. If the death occurred so quickly, the cat may not know she's been hit by a car, or attacked by a coyote, according to animal communicator Carol Gurney. A cat who is stuck in that way will go about life as if she were still in her body. She would go through the old familiar actions: eat, sleep in her owner's bed, and play with her toys, for instance. In a story that follows in these pages, a family's ghost cat even answers the call of nature. On occasions they can smell a phantom litter box.

A deceased cat may really like his old body and simply not want to leave. Gurney says once your cat has entered the spirit world, he can do whatever he wants to do and come and go as he wishes.

You may notice that several people in the book seem to attract cat spirits no matter where they move. There are people who are "sensitive" to ghosts; that is, someone who, in varying degrees, has the ability to sense the presence of a spirits. It's believed that spirits both feline and human are drawn to sensitive people in the same way that good listeners attract a lot of friends. Sensitivity often runs in families, but in some cases, a ghost's presence is so strong, anyone can see or sense it.

TYPES OF HAUNTINGS

Not all ghosts are created equal. When a cat specter returns, it is usually as one of two types of hauntings. A residual haunting occurs when the cat repeats the same motions over and over again, but doesn't appear to have any intelligence, like an image on a DVD. She doesn't interact with her environment or pay attention to anyone around her. The cat's image is placed into the setting by either a sudden or traumatic event. Some believe that the energy of specific actions can be repeated so frequently that it is absorbed by the room or the surroundings, again resulting in a playback of the action. Laura Underwood's story, "The Tigger Beat" in Chapter 3, is a perfect example. The cat behaves like a recorded image, repeating the same action without intelligence.

Then there's *intelligent haunting*, in which the spirit interacts with the environment, people, and even the other animals around her. She curls up on her owner's pillow, swats at a toy, or knocks a knickknack off of a bookshelf, and even teases the family dog as happens in "A Little Game of Cat and Dog." You may notice a cat toy that disappears and then reappears for no reason.

A cat specter can manifest itself in a number of ways. You may experience cold spots, prickly or chilling sensations, or feel the cat jump up on the bed. (Those cold spots are believed to be caused by the entity drawing energy from the atmosphere and causing a significant drop in temperature.) You may see something out of the corner of your eye. A cat-size shape may appear transparent, silvery, shadowy, misty, foggy, or dark. It might look like a little orb of light. You may be able to hear sounds produced by the ghost. Some cat specters manifest their presence by meowing, ringing a collar bell, or ripping at a favorite scratching post (or chair arm).

So if after the loss of your cat, you see a familiar shape in your peripheral vision or hear his collar bell or find his catnip toy suddenly in the middle of the room, you're not crazy; consider yourself blessed.

How Do You Know If Your Home Is Haunted by Your Cat?

Simplistic as it sounds, the most certain way to know if you are being haunted by the spirit of a cat is to actually see the apparition. If your cat had a daily routine such as curling up on a bed, or rattling her food dish, or playing with a favorite toy, and these events appear to be repeating themselves after the cat's passing, through sound, smell, or touch, this probably indicates a haunting. And finally, for those who are sensitive to it, it might be a feeling that the cat is still with them.

Often the cat returns for a single brief encounter, but if you suspect that your cat is hanging around for a longer time, theoretically you should be able to utilize the same investigative methods used by paranormal researchers (or if you prefer, ghost hunters) to find their human counterparts.

Here are some tools of the trade you might use:

Camera: When you "feel" the presence of the cat, snap a picture. You may find a ball of light known as an *orb*, or *ectoplasm*, sometimes referred to as *ecto* (which looks like a mist or fog), or a transparent image of the cat, or even a solid presence. Purists prefer 35mm cameras, but it can cost a fortune in film and developing before you catch anything. Digital cameras are inexpensive to operate, but many ghost hunters question whether orbs captured with them are really spirits or just dust. Don't forget to try your video camera. Sometimes you can catch voices or moving orbs with a standard video cam.

Electromagnetic Field Detectors (EMF meters): These meters detect disruptions in electronic fields, which many believe can be caused by ghosts.

Dowsing rods: The world's oldest ghost-detection device is also the cheapest (providing you occasionally take your clothes to the dry cleaners in order to replenish your supply of wire hangers). Get a pair of wire coat hangers and shape them into identical "Ls." Hold the short end loosely in each hand with the long ends pointing straight ahead. Mentally instruct the rods to cross when you find a spirit. If you pass over a spirit's energy source, theoretically they should cross.

Thermometer: A digital thermometer should tell you if there's a sudden drop in room temperature, often associated with the presence of ghosts.

Here are other ghost-hunting terms you should be familiar with:

Orb: In photos your cat's spirit could appear as an *orb*. An orb is condensed spirit energy that takes the form of a ball of light. It usually shows up in pictures, but sometimes can be seen with the naked eye. You may see it as a brief flash or as a sustained sphere of light.

Ectoplasm: Made famous by the movie *Ghostbusters*, this is a semi-physical substance that looks like a vaporous cloud, mist, fog, or smoke. According to paranormal researchers, *ecto* is a spirit's energy trying to materialize.

Cold spots: Ghost hunters should also look for these, usually indicated by a drop in temperature of at least ten degrees.

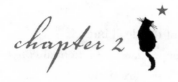

chapter 2

From Deity to Devil
THE SUPERNATURAL LORE OF THE CAT

In ancient times cats were worshipped as gods;
they have not forgotten this.
—TERRY PRATCHETT

The cat veils her soul in deepest mystery. A near relative of the king of beasts, she gives her affection only to whom she pleases, and likewise, withholds respect from those she deems unworthy. Contrary to a feline's nature, a dog is very eager to please. He needs your company, and wears every joy and every fear on the tip of his tail.

But the cat's trust and love must be earned. For those who don't understand her, she keeps her thoughts close to her fur. She appears distant, enigmatic, and oftentimes unreadable, lost in deepest thought. Who hasn't looked at a cat's dynamic golden eyes and wondered what she was thinking? As she stares unblinking at something visible to her and her alone, you may wonder whether she's communing with God, or if she is hearing acolytes' prayers herself. That inability of humans to read the mind of the cat has led to both her ascension and her near destruction.

Throughout human history, cats have been considered supernatural. This is linked not only to their mysterious nature, but also to the fact that their predatory prowess saved new civilizations from starvation. In some centuries people adored them as gods, building magnificent temples to honor them. Witches and other pagans have kept them both as pets—showing the loving, domestic side of the animal—and as animals of the night— "familiars"—the cunning predator and protector. The cats' own nature set up the duality of how she was perceived. Others, especially since the European Middle Ages, have reviled the cat as a vessel of the devil himself.

Egyptians were one of the first to fully appreciate the potential contributions of small cats. When the Egyptians first started pioneering agriculture, they stored their bounty in granaries. Unfortunately, that was the equivalent of putting out a sign written in Rodent that says FREE LUNCH. Mice and rats were fruitful, and multiplied exponentially.

However, this was also a boon for area felines who were lured away from the harsh desert by the possibility of their own free lunch—a smorgasbord of all the prey they could kill. It was like eating rats in a barrel. Domestic cats are one of the few animals who will continue to hunt in the absence of hunger, so farmers bribed them to stay around by offering them milk and fish heads. The cats saved the grain without asking for so much as a nibble of grist. Everyone but the mice benefited. The Egyptians named the little predators *miu* (some books say *mau*) because of the meowing sounds they made.

Because *miu* delivered Egypt from the jaws of famine, Pharaoh elevated her from adorable pest control to demigod around 2000 BC. Enter Bastet (sometimes called Bast). With the body of a woman and the head of a black cat, she was the daughter of the sun god Ra, and the goddess of motherhood, fertility, grace, and beauty—and of course, cats. You will notice that I refer to cats throughout the book as 'she' unless discussing a specific cat or quote because they are so closely associated with the feminine.

Although Americans and a few other cultures associate black cats with evil, most of the world believes just the opposite. The association of the black cat with good luck is believed to have begun with Bastet. It is said that Egyptians courted her favors by keeping black cats in their homes. They believed that she would merge with their pet cat and bless the home with riches and prosperity.

The Egyptians also thought that cats captured the setting sun in their eyes, protecting it until sunrise. In part to protect the rising sun, it became unlawful to kill a cat, or even for anyone outside the royal court to own one. Thousands of mummies bear silent witness to Egyptian adoration of the cat. The royal tombs contained food not only for the mummified ruler, but also for the mummified cat. Obviously, the Egyptians expected to see their beloved pets in the afterlife.

SEAFARING FELINES

Cats were also highly valued by ancient mariners for many of the same reasons the Egyptians revered them. From early seafaring days, ships have always had at least one cat on board, not only for rodent control, but also for companionship and good luck. Sailors believed if the ship's cat approached them, it promised them good fortune. If the cat walked toward them, then changed her mind and went elsewhere, the sailor could expect trouble. A cat running ahead of a sailor to the pier assured a prosperous future, but if the cat crossed his path, it was a sign of bad luck to come. The liveliness of a ship's cat predicted the strength of winds they would encounter when they put out to sea. While any hue of cat provided a vessel with good fortune, a ship's black cat (with no white hair at all) blessed the ship and everyone aboard it. Carrying a black cat on board promised to bring Yorkshire fishermen safely home from the seas. Japanese sailors preferred calicos as the best charm against spirits and wouldn't set sail without one.

Cats as lucky charms extended well beyond the ship. Sailor's wives always had an ebony feline as a house pet, to keep their husbands safe. A shortage of black cats at the height of the fishing-industry boom spawned a black-cat black market in the village of Yorkshire, England in the 1800s. Fishermen's wives had to keep constant watch on their valued raven cats for fear that racketeers would snatch them and sell them to another fisherman's wife.

Mariners' wisdom warned that the deliberate drowning of the ship's cat would be fatal for everyone aboard. Other legends decreed that the perpetrator would be repaid with a sudden violent storm at the very least, and a lifetime of bad luck if he survived.

In the port of Suffolk, England, the eyes of cats were thought to dilate and constrict with the ebb and flow of the tide. European sailors also highly treasured their ship's cat because, if all else failed, they thought the cat knew the way home. Since kitty couldn't tell them to turn "Twenty degrees starboard," they attached great meaning to where she slept, believing she would always bunk in the section of the ship closest to their homeport. In the event the cat's luck failed them and the men had to abandon ship, the cat was never left with the derelict vessel, but taken on the lifeboats alongside her companions.

For safety's sake, ancient mariners used cats to predict the perils of impending voyages. Welsh sailors knew that if the cat cried, they could expect a dangerous journey. A widely held belief warns that a ship's cat will desert a vessel about to depart on a doomed voyage. Wary sailors refused to sail following the desertion of the ship's cat.

In an account mentioned in the 1903 book, *Rabbits, Cats and Cavies,* C. H. Lane illustrates the cat's ability to predict disaster. One morning in the late 1800s, the English destroyer, the HMS *Salmon,* was lying alongside of HMS *Sturgeon. Salmon* had two cats, the special pets of the crew, who had never shown the slightest inclination to leave the destroyer. On this particular morning, both cats seemed determined to jump ship to the *Sturgeon,* but the sailors managed to stop them. When the *Salmon* weighed anchor, the cats made one last spring as the vessels separated, and landed on the deck of the *Sturgeon.* The destroyer *Salmon* and all hands were subsequently lost at sea.

Although the case of the *Salmon* was an obscure one, a more famous ship, the *Titanic,* had a cat who foresaw the impending disaster. While docked at Southampton the day before departing for New York, Jenny, the *Titanic's* mouser, picked up her four kittens and carried them one by one down the gangplank to the pier. Coal stoker Joe Mulholland, who watched the queen's determined effort, told another coal stoker, "That cat knows something." He packed his seabag and left the most prestigious and well-paying job an uneducated Irishman could hold. In his latter years he told reporter, Paddy Scott, that he owed his survival to a mother cat and her four kittens.

Not only could a sailing cat foretell disasters, she could also predict the weather, vital information for anyone trekking through unpredictable seas. Sailors' lore holds that a cat who passes her paw over her ear signals an oncoming storm. One rain prophecy stated, "When puss washes behind her ears, we'll soon be tasting heaven's tears." Dr. Erasmus Darwin (father of naturalist, Charles Darwin) confirmed this in his well-known poem, "Signs of Foul Weather," in which he describes natural indications of coming storms. "Puss on the hearth, with velvet paws, Sits wiping o'er his whiskered jaws." The same action is also discussed in Melton's *Astrologaster*. As with other lore about cats, this belief may have some scientific foundation. Allen Moller, a severe-storm forecaster at the National Weather Service, said that electrical fields completely surround a thunderstorm and, while there have been no scientific studies to support cat ears as barometers, it's logical to assume that cats are reacting to the approaching squall. The cat may be attempting to discharge uncomfortable static electricity from her inner ear by running her paw over the external surface.

NOAH'S CAT

According to different legends, the sailors' love affair with the ship's mouser may have begun with the Great Flood. Several versions recall that Noah had a breed of cat called the Turkish Van aboard the ark. Also known as "The Swimming Cat," today's Vans appear the same as they were depicted in Bronze Age carvings on Hittite jewelry sometime between 1600 to 1200 BC: a white cat with a red-ringed tail. That physical evidence shows Turkish Vans roamed the Lake Van region of Turkey not far from Mount Ararat, where it is believed that Noah's ark came to rest. Even today, wild descendants of the cats roam the Van Lake area.

An ancient Arab naturalist wrote this account of the cat's voyage on the ark: "When, as the Arab relates, Noah made a couple of each animal to enter the ark, his companions and family asked, 'What security can you give us and the other animals, so long as the lion dwells with us on this narrow vessel?' Then Noah betook himself to prayer, and entreated the Lord God. Immediately fever came down from heaven and seized up the king of beasts.

"But soon thereafter, the single pair of mice brought aboard the boat did what mice do and increased to plague proportions. They began raiding the food stores and soiling the ark.

"And so Noah renewed his supplication to the Most High, the lion sneezed, and a cat ran out of his nostrils. From that time the mouse has been timid and has hidden in holes."

In another version, two solid white cats accompanied Noah, but when they left the ark, the door accidentally shut, mashing their tails. The tails turned fiery auburn. God felt sorry for the cats and their aching tails. He blessed them, touching them on the foreheads. Where His fingers brushed their fur appeared two auburn patches that matched their tails. The cats made their way down the mountain to Van Lake, where they found plenty of fish to eat. The cool waters of the Van gave the Turkish Vans a place to wade, fish, and swim in the buoyant salty water, where the small soft-finned *darekh*, a freshwater fish that has adapted to Lake Van's saline environment, thrive.

Still another version of the Flood described two white cats with their flaming red tails held high, surviving the journey on Noah's ark. They made their way down Mount Ararat into what would eventually be called Mesopotamia. The auburn spot on some Turkish Vans appeared where Allah placed his fingertip while blessing the cats as they left the ark. Even today a Turkish Van still carries this "Mark of Allah" as a colored thumbprint.

PSYCHIC CATS

Since the cat first graced man with her company, she has come across as all-knowing. When she emerged from the sandy desert, Egyptians greeted her with open arms and soon worshipped her as a goddess. Then later during medieval times, the Catholic Church began demonizing her as a familiar of the devil. She may indeed have supernatural powers—extrasensory perception. And though her mystical abilities should never be discounted—as seen with the miraculous escape from the doomed ships *Titanic* and *Salmon*—much of her power to see into the near future is linked to her predatory nature and might be more accurately called supersensory perception. After all, she can see in the dark, hear sounds we can't hear, detect vibrations we can't feel, and smell scents undetectable to us. Sometimes it seems like she can even read our minds.

Compared to our meager human sensibilities, her ability to glean information from her surroundings seems to give her supernatural awareness. As a small predator, and at the same time prey for larger carnivores, she needs that edge to survive.

Contrary to popular myth, the cat cannot see in absolute darkness, but she can see in light so faint it would appear to us to be dark—a seemingly superhuman ability. Being a night hunter, she requires only one-sixth the light humans need, partly because her pupils can dilate to 90 percent the size of the eye. The cat possesses the added advantage of that ghostly yellow glow you see in the dark when light strikes a cat's eyes. It's a reflective layer of cells called the *tapetum lucidum*. Those amazing cells reflect incoming light, bouncing it off of the cones, and recycling and magnifying available light. Unfortunately, this eerie glow has also identified the cat with satanic forces. An additional otherworldly aspect of the cat's eyes is the shape of the pupil. In full sunlight the iris constricts into little slits. The alien shape of the pupil made the cat appear all the more unnatural—and evil, to those who didn't understand her exquisite design.

The cat also uses her extraordinarily sensitive whiskers to help her hunt in low-light conditions. The whiskers work like flexible probes to help determine the location of prey or help her ascertain the size of an escape opening. Her sensitive paw pads allow her to move in virtual silence and to detect static in the atmosphere or faint vibrations in the earth.

A cat's ears are essential weapons in her hunting arsenal and protection against predators who would like to invite *her* to dinner. She can hear sounds a full octave and a half higher than you can (even higher than dogs can hear), so she can pick up the high-pitched squeaks of her own potential mouse meal, or feel vibrations of movement around her.

Don't let that cute little nose fool you. Your cat can sniff rings around you. Cats have 200 million odor-sensitive cells in their noses compared to about the 5 million in yours. She uses her sense of smell in the same way humans read the paper to learn what's happening in their world. She nasally reads the latest news: traffic reports (which cats and other animals have moved through her territory), food ads (nearby prey), the personal columns (potential mates), weather (rain), and the pollution report (smoke and gases). The cat uses all of her senses to detect subtle changes in atmospheric pressure or ground vibrations to help her predict severe weather and other catastrophes.

The belief that animals can predict earthquakes has been around for a millennium. In 373 BC, historians recorded that huge numbers of animals, including rats, snakes, and weasels, fled the Greek city of Helice a few days before tremors nearly destroyed it. Prior to the 1975 Haicheng earthquake, Chinese officials ordered the evacuation of the city with a population of one million people, just days before a 7.3-magnitude quake struck. Authorities based the evacuation in part on the observation of strange animal behaviors.

In a January 2005 *Agence France-Presse* story, Alan Rabinowitz, director for science and exploration at the Bronx Zoo–based Wildlife Conservation Society in New York, said, "Earthquakes bring vibrational changes on land and in water while storms cause electromagnetic changes in the atmosphere . . . Some animals have acute senses of hearing and smell that allow them to determine something coming towards them long before humans might know that something is there."

Even as recently as Christmas 2004, the Indian Ocean tsunami demonstrated that animals in general use their superior senses to protect themselves. An earthquake that measured between 9 and 9.3 on the Richter scale, and the massive tsunami that followed, claimed over 229,000 human lives, but few dead animals were found, supporting the idea that animals somehow sensed impending disaster. Although there are no scientific studies to back up the theory, it appears that seismic activity prior to earthquakes and volcanic eruptions causes behavioral changes in animals. Other ideas suggest that they detect electrical changes in the air or gas released from the earth. Cats who are normally outgoing and active often hide or run away before a disaster.

So cats can predict disasters—but what else can they sense? Cat owners are quick to say their pets are sensitive to both their moods and physical discomfort, as well as perhaps the ability to do something about it. Folklore has long maintained the healing abilities of cats. Stroking a black cat's tail supposedly cures a sty, and rubbing a black cat's tail over a wart during the month of May will make the blemish go away. Another cat proverb declares, "Brother, put away your groans, bring a black-cat charm to mend your bones."

Many of the people interviewed for this book have suffered through a wide range of ill health resulting from horrific accidents, life-threatening illnesses, and even bouts of depression. One common thread that ran through so many of the stories was how the cat sought out its ailing owner, lying next to them or actually on top of them and purring in an apparent attempt to comfort them. Perhaps the owner's positive response isn't simply improvement as a result of the moral support. We may now have scientific explanations of the cats' healing power, which wouldn't be news to the ancient Egyptians, who relied on their healing ability. In 1999, studies conducted by Dr. Clinton T. Rubin and his associates discovered exposure to sound frequencies between 20 to 50 hertz caused accelerated healing of injured bones. Other studies have determined that vibrations between 20 to 140 hertz are therapeutic for pain relief, difficulty in breathing, bone growth and healing of bone fractures, swelling reduction, wound healing, and muscle and tendon repair. Different feline purrs fall within that range. It looks like nature has provided cats with a self-healing ability via the endearing purr. So when people say that their cat made them feel better, it's very possible that she did.

While it was once forbidden to bring cats into human hospitals, now it's just what the doctor ordered. Other studies have confirmed that stroking a cat will help lower blood pressure and help ease depression. Today, feline physicians are often brought into assisted-living homes and retirement centers to visit with the patients. Who knows? In the future your doctor may actually say, "Take two cats and call me in the morning."

Sacred Cats

Cats aren't just good for the body; they've had a longtime connection to the soul, as well. Long before mankind began recording events on temple partitions, he scratched paintings on cave walls. Stone Age art discovered in sacred caverns depicted lions being slain, possibly in ritualistic fashion for religious purposes. According to C. J. Conway, in *The Mysterious, Magical Cat*, such hallowed caverns "were symbolic of the body of the Great Goddess, the resting place between death and rebirth."

While the Egyptians' love of cats is legendary, they weren't the only ancients who held the creatures in high esteem. The Romans portrayed the goddess, Liberty, with a cat at her feet. According to Finnish folklore, black cats carry the souls of the dead to the afterworld, while the Celts believed black cats were reincarnated beings with the ability to foresee the future. Followers of the Roman goddess Diana deemed the cat divine because Diana once assumed the form of her brother's black cat. She, too, was considered the protector of cats.

Although Muslims don't worship cats, the Prophet Mohammed had a beloved tabby cat, named Muezza, who fell asleep on the sleeve of his robe. When he answered the call to prayer, he cut off his sleeve rather than disturb her. Supposedly the cat saved his life when a snake crawled into his sleeve. In appreciation for protecting him, Mohammed blessed the cat. Tabbies wear the 'M' on their foreheads in remembrance of Mohammed's blessing, and three dark lines on their backs where he stroked the cat's fur.

Christians interpret the 'M' differently. Their legend says that baby Jesus laid in the manger crying and shivering from the cold when a cat laid next to him, warming him. Mary thanked the animal by petting her. 'M,' for Mary or Madonna, appeared on the cat's forehead. Another version of the story says the cat killed a poisonous serpent sent by Satan to bite Jesus in his crib.

Three of today's most popular breeds are descended from cats that were worshipped by ancient societies. Abyssinians, Birmans, and Siamese were either revered as gods themselves or as vessels sent to accompany human souls to Heaven.

ABYSSINIANS

While her origin is veiled in mystery, today's Abyssinian cat has more than a casual resemblance to the elegant cats depicted in Egyptian bronzes and paintings on display at the British Museum, as well as the mummified remains of cats found at Egyptian burial sites. The objects and artifacts portray cats with muscular bodies, arched necks, large ears, and almond-shaped eyes. Abyssinians are similar in frame and color to the cats who once guarded the Egyptian granaries. While the Abyssinian is one of the oldest breeds, there's no definitive evidence that they are direct descendants of ancient Egypt's venerated cats. However, it wouldn't be much of a stretch to believe that Romans exported them to different corners of their empire to protect their own food stores.

The name "Abyssinian" was given to the cat because the cats first shown in England in the late 1800s were imported from Abyssinia (Ethiopia), not because they originated from that country.

BIRMANS

According to a legend attributed to Sir Russel Gordon, a nineteeth-century Englishman who studied Birmans, long before the time of the Buddha, one hundred yellow-eyed cats with long, pure-white fur guarded the temple of Lao-Tsun. A golden goddess with sapphire eyes lived within the temple and watched over the transmutation of souls.

The head monk, whose beard had been braided with gold by the enlightened one, often knelt in meditation before the golden goddess. At the monk's side was a beautiful temple cat, Sinh, who often gazed up at the goddess's blue eyes. One night, Thai marauders killed the monk. When his master died, Sinh leapt upon his master's body and gazed into the sapphire eyes of the golden goddess and gave a wordless appeal for his master's soul. When the monk's spirit passed into Sinh, the cat's white fur was instantly misted with a golden glow and his head, tail, and legs changed to the velvety brown color of the monk's robe. Where his feet touched the holy man's robes, they remained pure white. The cat's eyes became the same color as the goddess's. Sinh never left his master's body. On the seventh day, poor Sinh died and carried the soul of monk with him into Nirvana. Since that day the priests have guarded their sapphire-eyed cats, believing them to hold the souls of priests. The legend states that each Sacred Cat of Burma (Birman) carries the soul of a priest or a special person on its final journey to Paradise.

SIAMESE

Siamese cats originated from Thailand, the country formerly known as Siam. Illustrated poems called the "Tamra Maew" provided evidence that the blue-eyed cats protected temple altars from barbarian raids in Siam's capital, Ayutthaya, as long ago as AD 1350.

These cats were held in such high esteem in their native country that no one except the king and members of the royal family were permitted to own them. They were originally known as "Royal points."

The people of Siam believed that these cats had the power to act as intermediaries for a person's soul. When royals or people of high status were dying, they chose a cat to receive their souls. That chosen cat lived out its life in the temple surrounded by opulence and being pampered by monks and priests. It was thought that the temple cats had special powers of intercession on the behalf of the person whose soul it held.

CAT TOTEMS

Cats are also important in Shamanistic belief systems. Often people use cat totems to help them, in a sense, become a more complete person. An *animal totem* is a symbolic creature many people use to get in touch with the specific characteristics found in the animal that the person needs. Each animal has its own unique power and wisdom to impart. According to the belief, the animal totem chooses its person, not the other way around.

Mayan and Tibetan and Native American traditions, among others, embrace Shamanism and celebrate animal totems. In different traditions the meanings of the animal qualities may vary. In these traditions, people believe that the cat's energy field rotates in an opposite direction to that of humans, giving felines the ability to absorb energy that affects people negatively, and aiding the cat in her ability to help heal people.

Contrary to the evil reputation thrust upon them during the Middle Ages, the cat totem was believed to ward off evil.

Because they are creatures of the night, shamans consider cats to be indispensable allies in dealing with the supernatural and the unknown, and in helping people work through their fears. The cat totem's valuable characteristics include independence, protection, meditation, seeing the invisible, love, resourcefulness, able to defend himself when necessary and fearlessness.

BLACK CATS, GOOD CATS

While Americans are notorious for their fear and distrust of the black cat, much of the rest of the world believes there is a deeply spiritual connection between humans and the gentle couch panther known as the domestic black cat. With her patent-leather fur and her eye on a warm fireplace on a cold night, she has a dual identity. She's been the omen of doom to some and the salvation of others. But despite all the power that black cats supposedly possess, they are simply cats who happened to be born with black fur. Most of the time they don't represent a particular breed. The Bombay is the only exclusively black breed of cat in the world's largest cat registry, the Cat Fanciers' Association.

All over the world, black cats are associated with luck, both good and ill. Whether a black cat represents good fortune or bad luck depends on what part of the globe she lives on. Unfortunately, black cats have frightful reputations in the United States, Spain, and Belgium, where they're considered portents of destruction associated with witchcraft and the devil, bad luck, and evil. In the U.S., humane societies and rescue groups struggle to find homes for friendly black strays because of their unearned reputation for evil and wreaking havoc.

Fortunately, the rest of the world has a more optimistic opinion of the lap-size panthers. In Egypt, Great Britain, Australia, and Japan, owning or encountering a black cat will bring good fortune. In these countries, people believe that if a black cat enters a home, she should be welcomed. Chasing the cat away assures that the luck will leave with her. Indeed, some believe that whether the cat abandons a home or ship of her own accord or someone chases her off, a great disaster will soon follow.

A series of cultural beliefs and proverbs have specifically extolled the virtues of black cats over the years. One old English charm promises "Black cat, cross my path—good fortune bring to home and hearth. When I am away from home, bring me luck wherever I roam." An early sixteenth-century British tradition encouraged visitors to kiss the family's coal-colored feline, presumably for good luck, while another adage suggests that kissing a black cat is good for one's health: "Kiss the black cat, and twill make you fat. Kiss the white and twill make you lean." Some British proverbs have even linked black cats with luck in love, proclaiming, "Whenever the cat of the house is black, the lasses of lovers will have no lack." Another maxim from southern England advises that a bride whose path is crossed by a black cat will have a happy marriage—which no doubt caused many a bride to arrange just such an encounter.

King Charles I owned a black cat who he believed to be lucky. He so feared losing his pet that he placed a twenty-four-hour guard around him. The day after the cat died, Oliver Cromwell's troops arrested the king. In 1649, Charles was beheaded.

Winston Churchill, a well-known cat lover, believed in the power of the black cat. His black kitty, Nelson, reputedly had his own chair at the Cabinet. During World War II Churchill made a point of stroking any black cat he found. He allegedly attributed his wartime success to this practice.

Buddhist tradition respected cats of all colors, but the home of a dark cat would be blessed with gold, while a light-colored cat attracted only silver.

From a health perspective, black cats may be luckier than their fairer-haired counterparts. The dark coat actually affords "survival benefit." Ebony fur not only provides the night hunter with the perfect camouflage, but a genetics study released in 2003 also indicates that the same gene that gives cats the black coat also makes them more resistant to some diseases.

Look Who's Really in League with the Devil

In ages past, it would seem that no other animal was quite so entwined with the spiritual life of humans as the cat. The connection was fraught with conflict, however. Although Egyptian priests waited on her, popes condemned her. The poor creature had quite an identity crisis.

While cats themselves weren't worshipped in the Norse tradition, they were held in high esteem. The most important goddess of the Scandinavian culture was Freyja, the mistress of magic called *Seidh*. Freyja's personal mode of transportation was a chariot drawn by two magnificent black cats. The cats often transformed themselves into black horses. Needless to say, Freyja revered cats, and she wasn't the only one. Norse farmers, in order to assure a bountiful harvest, left offerings to her cats. This legend would eventually come back to haunt the cats—and women—of Europe in an apocalyptic way.

While the Dark Age for humans were officially dated prior to AD 1000, a truly dark period for cats came during the European Middle Ages. Prior to that period, the Catholic Church didn't have an opinion on cats one way or the other. Monasteries often had mousers for companionship. A ninth-century Irish monk even wrote a loving and humorous poem in honor of his cat, Pangur Ban. Had he been born centuries later, both he and Pangur Ban could have been burned alive for the relationship.

As Catholicism became the dominant religion in Europe and the Middle East, the status of feminine-based and goddess-based faiths dropped off drastically. With their downfall, the decline of the cat began. Since many of the same pagan, goddess-centered religions also revered cats, the creatures became vilified by the Catholic hierarchy as being against God and their religion. This is called *syncretism*.

Once people converted to Catholicism, the church spun Freyja's image. Suddenly, the goddess of love was transformed into a witch, and her beloved changeling cats became possessed by the devil.

Toward the end of the sixth-century, Pope Gregory the Great had a pet cat of whom he was very fond. Ironically, the low point in the annals of the cat began in AD 1232, when Pope Gregory IX, looking for a scape-goat to distract attention from food shortages and the spread of disease and war, declared the cat as a diabolical creature. He asserted that cats embodied the devil and were a symbol of heresy. Suddenly, anyone who had a cat, especially a black cat, was accused of being a devil worshipper. It's hard to say in retrospect whether the cats themselves or the Catholic Church was more feared.

Everything about the cat's nature condemned her. She loved the night, as did Satan. Witch hunters interpreted the eye glow that helps the cat see in near dark as "night shine," which was lit up by the fires of hell. It was a sign that cats roaming the streets of Europe were the devil's harbinger. Their fur stores static electricity, which when stroked produces a small shock and sends tiny sparks flying, seen as more evidence of her collusion with the devil. This fiery-sparkling tendency and the static shock of the coat, combined with the cat's stealthy movements and somewhat furtive lifestyle, probably led the superstitious medieval people to regard the un-fortunate creature as either Satan's companion or some sort of evil spirit.

The cat's unblinking stare gave people the impression that she could read human minds. Even today, cats are sometimes accused of sucking the breath out of a baby (although most of these unfortunate deaths are at-tributed to Sudden Infant Death Syndrome). English author Sarah Hartwell writes that "stories of infants being harmed by cats are usually exaggerated" and are extremely rarity.

Because of her association with witches, the cat was dubbed the "furred serpent." The real evil visited on Europe didn't come from the "witches" or their feline familiars, however, but instead, from those who had been charged by God to protect His flock. Needless to say, God had nothing to do with the unimaginable torture hoisted upon the accused women and their innocent pets; during the last century of the Medieval Age through the Renaissance it was primarily the Catholic Church and its own evil minions who were at fault.

No one was exempt from charges of witchcraft; not even children. The Church exterminated the most vulnerable persons in Middle Ages society—usually women—including widows and spinsters; the infirm, mentally ill, and the poor; and women with cat companions. They also targeted midwives and women who used herbs to treat a variety of ailments. Who better to persecute than those who might use their herbs and potions to cast spells? Cats suffered right along with their mistresses. Thus marked the beginning of the near-total extermination of cats and their vulnerable owners. Such demonization seems to occur when a patriarchal culture assimilates a goddess-centered culture.

The domestic cats of Europe stood on the precipice of extinction. But justice was soon to visit all of Europe, pound for deadly pound. Whether delivered by Bastet herself, or the God of Moses, human and feline suffering was repaid in kind.

By the mid-1300s, the domestic feline population of Europe had been reduced to almost nil. The cats had either been brutally killed or driven away from the villages. At the same time, trading ships from Asia brought a deadly menace along with their cargo: rats that were infested with bubonic plague–carrying fleas. They delivered these rats to a continent with no immunity, and with virtually no cats to control the rats, the rodent population exploded. The pests gorged themselves on the food stores and fouled what they didn't eat with their waste. Statistics vary, but with no women left who were skilled in the healing arts, between 1347 and 1351, the Black Death claimed between one-third to one-half of the population of Europe—approximately 34 million people. It's believed that 90 percent of the French people and half of the English succumbed to the disease.

Though the mid-1300s was the most catastrophic period for cats, their demonization and annihilation continued for many centuries. In 1486, Pope Innocent VIII upped the ante and issued the *Malleus Maleficarum*, ordering that all cat owners should be tried as witches.

In 1618, an interdict was issued in Flanders prohibiting the festive ceremonial annihilation of cats during a Lenten celebration. It wasn't until the eighteenth-century that cats were once again welcomed into villages and homes. Ironically, the plague in its most virulent form disappeared from Europe during that same period. Finally, in 1835, the English Parliament came to its senses and passed a law that forbade the mistreatment of any animals.

While cats may not have saved all of mankind from extinction, it's fair to say they did save Europe by once again controlling the scourge of rodents packing deadly hitchhiking parasites. Were they God-sent? Perhaps. But regardless of whether their part in saving Europe was planned or not, they did what they have done since they first walked out of the desert into our lives: They have loved and protected humans.

Today, thanks to medical science, the bubonic plague can be treated with antibiotics. But cats are still there to protect our barns, bestow good luck, and grace us with their affection. And if we're fortunate, when they have shed their earthly fur, they may come to us a last time or two with the precious gift of a final good-bye.

Strange Footprints in the Night
EERIE ENCOUNTERS WITH FELINE PHANTOMS

From ghoulies and ghosties and long leggety beasties and
things that go bump in the night, Good Lord, deliver us!
    —SCOTTISH SAYING

Most people, especially kids, find it hard to resist a good ghost story. We love the tingle we get in our stomachs and the knots we feel in our chests. We want stories that send shivers up our spines. We want to feel that adrenaline rush when the foundation settles and creaks, knowing we have to look over our shoulders when we get up to go to the bathroom.

There's a mystery and a tension that comes with cat entities when you never knew that cat in life. I selected these tales for their strangeness. In most cases, the people featured in the stories were visited by ghost cats they'd had no connection with. Why did these cats come back? Did they select the people to haunt, or were they simply trapped in their place of death?

When I started working on this book, I planned to include a section of scary stories. I had expected terrifying black-cat stories similar to "The Demon Cat at the Capitol," which you'll find later in this chapter. The reality is, the zombie black cat in Stephen King's *Pet Sematary* and Poe's "The Black Cat" are sensational stories, just like all horror stories, but they have no association with the reality of feline spirits.

It's time to dim the lights, get out your flashlight, turn your fog machine on high, and hide under the covers. We're going to read some ghost stories.

WHITE CAT IN THE CLOSET

In August of 2000, Cari and her family were moving into a rental home in Las Vegas. After a long day, Cari's husband and his friend left at about eight o'clock to retrieve a last carload of stuff from their old apartment. Cari felt exhausted. She had set up her son Dakota's new room, but still hadn't had a chance to put her daughter's bed together. Cari, her daughter, and Dakota all sat together watching TV until Cari's husband returned to help finish assembling the bedrooms.

Suddenly, Cari felt suffused with a really hostile feeling that overwhelmed her. She instructed her children to move away from her. She wrote it off to stress, since she's always hated moving—and moving with two small children was the stuff of nightmares. But not the only stuff.

The next day, she sensed the same hostile feeling in the room. Believing it only existed in her head, she tried to ignore it. A few weeks later, Cari was sitting on the couch watching television in the living room before bedtime. Her big cat, Luna, lay beside her. About the time the local news came on, her four-year-old son let out a bona fide horror-movie scream. She found him crying and holding his face. He told his mother that a small white cat had come out of the closet and scratched him. Cari examined her son's cheek. Yes, those two or three little lines trickling beads of blood were definitely from a cat scratch.

While Cari had experienced a great deal of paranormal activity on her own, she wasn't ready for it to be part of her young children's lives yet. She looked around, thinking a stray cat had somehow managed to sneak into the house. Despite her thorough search of both Dakota's bedroom and the house, she found nothing. It couldn't have been Luna. It was impossible for her son to confuse their thirty-pound black cat for a small white cat. Besides, Luna had been asleep next to Cari in the living room when Dakota had screamed.

Cari put on her detective hat and began asking questions. When she asked her son exactly where the cat had come from, Dakota pointed to the top of his closet. But that was impossible. A real cat could never have reached that high, unless he climbed up on something, and there was nothing for him to climb on. If Luna had attempted a climb like that, the room would have been in shambles.

After that, the ever-present feeling of hostility intensified. Cari could feel it surround her whenever she was putting Dakota's clothes away. Despite the angry presence, the cat never attacked the boy again. Instead, the presence began concentrating its anger on Cari in more subtle confrontations. When Cari went into her son's room to clean or put something in the closet, sometimes she would struggle to breathe. One day Cari had grown angry and tired of the games, so she verbally took the ghost cat to task, yelling aloud that she wanted him to leave, but if he was going to stay he had to deal with the fact that her family lived in the house now.

Even Luna sensed the white cat's presence. He didn't venture into either of the kids' rooms much, and preferred to sleep on Cari's husband's lap. Sometimes Luna would sit in the living room and stare at something with the same intensity he would devote to watching a mouse or a bird. He would follow an unseen motion with his eyes. A few times, Cari found Luna on the end of her son's bed, staring into the closet—not with his ears back or dilated pupils as if he were threatened, but simply staring with interest at something in closet. After a while he'd hop off the bed and trot back to the living room.

Cari asked her father, who was sensitive and had helped others with problem spirits, to bring over some sage so she could spiritually cleanse the room. She thought because of his past experience with paranormal events, her dad might be able to help where she had been ineffective. The smoke of the burning sage is said to have healing or cleansing properties, and it is sometimes used to help a stuck spirit cross over, or to remove negative energies from a home or possessions. Cari's dad placed the sage in the burner, then literally ran out of the room, closing the door behind him. He warned Cari not to let her son stay in the room for at least a day. The next day, she discovered to her dismay that the sage cleansing hadn't worked.

She still felt the presence, and it felt angrier than ever. Even with the hostile presence, Dakota liked his new room and wanted to sleep in there.

Since the night he was scratched, the unfriendly presence of the cat had left Dakota alone and focused on Cari. Uneasy about her baby sleeping around the hostile entity, and not willing to share all her concerns with Dakota, Cari only allowed her son to sleep in his room with the door open and the lights on.

"I told the spirit that it didn't have to leave, because it was there first. I respected that, but if it was going to stay, it had to respect the fact that we were there to stay, too." She warned the ghost cat that if the physical and mental attacks didn't stop, she would find a way to get rid of it.

Friends believed that the white cat had died in the house—that it might have been abandoned there. It is not unusual for animals abandoned inside homes to die of starvation before they are discovered by landlords. This lonely little creature may have continued to wait for owners who would never come back for it. The entity wasn't evil, but rather angry and lost.

While the cat's hostility gradually dissipated, Cari continued to feel its presence. She could feel it lurking in the closet, simply watching them, for the next three years. But instead of feeling threatened, Cari began to feel a little sorry for the ghost. Ever since her family moved to a larger home nearby, she still thinks from time to time about the unwanted cat. She doesn't really worry about the new tenants, but she often wonders how the old white ghost cat is doing.

THE WITHERED ROSES

With Halloween fast approaching, industrious employees had set up a display of grinning pumpkins atop hay bales outside the local grocery store in Sweet Home, Oregon. The jack-o'-lanterns with their carved grins provided a unique early-morning greeting as Marianna Love entered the store to buy a few things for dinner.

When the electronic doors *whooshed* open, two small black figures darted into the store, shot under her feet, and slid underneath the line of shopping carts. As little as these figures were, Marianna first thought they were mice.

That's when she heard a faint meowing from under the carts. She knelt down on the tile floor. Looking underneath the long line of carts, she could make out four golden eyes peering back at her. Slowly, she laid on the floor on her belly, calling, "Here kitty, kitty, kitty . . ." She could hear people gathering behind her, curious to know why anyone would even entertain the notion of lying on a grocery-store floor unless they had been clonked on the head.

A little boy crawled down beside her. "Whatcha lookin' at?" he asked.

"There are kittens under there." She pointed.

"Kitties," he squealed, and again louder "*Kitties!*"

Much to her dismay, the kitties backed away further into the corner where the darkness swallowed them up. Hauling herself to her feet, she grabbed the nearest person, demanding they not allow anyone to move the carts and risk crushing the kittens. Then she raced to her familiar haunt, aisle nineteen, the cat-food aisle. She grabbed up a tin of Fancy Feast and raced back to the gathering crowd.

She again lay on her belly, squirming under the line of carts. She popped open a can, scooping food out on her fingers, and waited. Smelling the food, the kittens inched forward, but not far enough. She had lain under that cart so long, her arms were becoming numb, but eventually she felt the first contact as a kitten nudged her fingers and began to lick the extended treat. Soon the second kitten joined in. Very carefully she pulled them out and popped them in her purse.

Explaining that she would be back in a few minutes to pay for the can of cat food, she retrieved a cat carrier from her trunk. Soon the kittens were eating from inside the safety of the carrier, and she was dishing out sixty-five cents for their food.

The two kittens were very tiny and undernourished. Both were females; one had long gray fur, and the other was a tuxedo kitty. Christened Squirrel and Tazzy respectively, the kittens were welcomed into Marianna's home, growing up happily alongside all of her other rescues.

One morning when Tazzy was five years old, Marianna was outside washing the litter pans in the industrial sink when she noticed Tazzy crawling into the yard under the fence. Once she had cleared the underside of the fence, she continued crawling. Marianna scooped her up, only to find to her horror that Tazzy had been severely injured. After an examination, the vet broke the news to Marianna: Tazzy had been hit by a car. Her front leg had suffered nerve damage that might heal on its own. However, she had other extensive injuries that needed emergency surgery. Marianna signed the forms with shaking hands and sent her off to surgery. The operation would take some time, and the vet recommended that Marianna go home. He would call when he had news. As he suggested, Marianna left immediately and prayed all the way home.

At three in the morning, she got the call that Tazzy would be ready to go home the following afternoon. Grateful that she had pulled through, Marianna brought Tazzy home and gave her cat twenty-four-hour TLC.

While her other injuries healed slowly, Tazzy still refused to put any weight on her front leg. A new X-ray revealed she had a break above the scapula. There were only two options: euthanasia or amputation. Marianna chose the latter.

When Tazzy came home again, she was fine physically. But over time, it became clear that she wasn't right mentally. She became aggressive with Marianna, her husband, and the other cats, to the point of drawing blood on her victims. She reverted to a near-feral state. Tazzy would rarely sleep, and when she did, she had what Marianna called "night terrors." She became increasingly hostile by the day, and adding insult to injury, her body started shutting down. There was nothing else Marianna could do for Tazzy.

Quietly, Marianna gathered Tazzy up, wrapped her in a sweater, and drove to the vet. He examined her; sadly he informed her that after six months of fighting the good fight, the battle had ended. Apparently she had suffered brain damage during the collision, much like shaken baby syndrome. Reluctantly, she agreed; it was time to put her to sleep.

They buried her in the garden and planted two trilliums on her grave. Marianna drove to the local florist shop and bought a dozen red roses in a vase. The roses were set on her grave as well. Two weeks later, although they hadn't watered the roses, they were as fresh as the day Marianna bought them—as if Tazzy's life force had seeped up from the dirt to keep the roses alive.

The fourteenth night after Tazzy's death, Marianna and her husband lay in bed, still crying over the loss of such a special cat. In the far corner of the bedroom, Marianna noticed a glowing light. The light bobbed in the darkness, like a helium balloon caught in a gentle breeze. Neither spoke as the globe of light grew larger; soon, it hovered over their bed. Finally, the orb came to rest several feet above them. In the center of the light, they saw their Tazzy-girl; just her head, like a disembodied Cheshire cat from *Alice in Wonderland.* She wasn't grinning; she was just there, her face staring down intently at them. Then, suddenly, as if the balloon had been popped, she was gone.

When she could move again, Marianna turned on the lamp. Her husband was visibly shaken. He had also seen the apparition, and his mind was still processing the encounter.

"Do you think she was mad at us?" Marianna whispered.

"I think she came to say good-bye," he answered. They spent a restless night, neither one willing to sleep or brave enough to douse the lights.

The next morning, they walked to Tazzy's grave. The roses, which only a day ago were fresh and fragrant, had all withered and died.

THE TIGGER BEAT

Laura J. Underwood, an author of science fiction and fantasy novels, has a leg up on other writers of the fantastic since she grew up with what many would consider a fantasy. When her family first moved into their new house in the 1960s, they had no cats—no living cats, that is. But practically from the first day, everyone noticed a cat sitting at the top of the stairs just off the bathroom door. When the cat saw someone approach, she would arch her back, bolt into the back bedroom, and then vanish.

The family assumed the strange cat, marked with tortoiseshell oranges and blacks and accented with tabby stripes, was a stray cat seeking shelter in the vacant house. They figured she'd somehow squeezed in and out through a hole in the attic. But each time the cat disappeared into the bedroom, they could never find her.

This cat-and-mouse game continued for years, even after the family had adopted flesh-and-blood felines. They finally decided the house's original cat was a phantom when they realized the cat was repeating the same motions without change.

A silver point Siamese named Ben, whom Laura acquired about nine years later, had no problem finding the home's earlier resident. When he first arrived at the Underwood home, Ben would go to the head of the stairs, staring at empty air, and hiss. Despite Ben's attempt to chase it off, the cat would still appear from time to time.

Once, after her sister's boyfriend had used the upstairs bathroom, he asked when they had gotten the new cat. The sisters looked at each other and shook their heads. They admitted that it was probably the ghost cat. The boyfriend refused to ever go back upstairs again.

Although several decades have passed, Laura still catches a shadow fleeing for the back room. Laura's current resident cat, Gato Bobo, doesn't mind the ghost the way old Ben did. He spends a lot of time hanging out in the back bedroom.

The calico ghost now has a companion, as Laura believes her mom's orange tomcat, Tigger, has returned to his old stomping ground. Not long after they moved into the house, Laura's mother received the orange male cat as a gift. At night he'd patrol the home. He'd roam from room to room, jumping up on the foot of the bed, walking the length of it, and sniffing the slumbering person's face. Then he'd go and check out his next stop—a feline version of rattling doorknobs. They always said he was just making the rounds to ensure his family was safe.

Tigger was a classic predator. He was fierce when it came to defending territory, and he fathered a heck of a lot of orange cats in the neighborhood. Basically, he was all tomcat, king of the house and a mighty hunter, and he used to scare the "bejeebers" out of Laura's mom by trying to open the doors. He wasn't much of a play kitty, but he did love to be petted. When Tigger died at the age of fifteen, his death left the home cat-less.

Not long after he died, Laura felt the *whump* of a cat landing on the bed, walking its length, and the whiskers of a cat brushing up against her cheeks. When she opened her eyes, there was no cat there. This happened several nights in a row, but Laura didn't mention it to anyone. Finally, her mother told Laura that she had felt a cat walking on her bed, but when she'd looked, there was nothing there.

After that, her brother and sisters all confessed to the same experience. Although the family admitted they had an invisible pet, they never spoke about it to outsiders. Yet over the years, when guests have stayed in the spare room, they have also reported feeling something walking up the bed.

Selina Rosen, Laura's publisher at Yard Dog Press, also experienced Tigger's patrols. The night before they left for the World Science Fiction Convention in Boston, Selina spent the night in Laura's guest room. Because Selina is allergic to cats, Laura warned her that if she didn't want Gato Bobo in the bed with her, she needed to close the door and brace it, which she did.

That night Selina had just drifted off to sleep when she felt something tugging on the covers, like a cat trying to climb up the sheet onto the bed. At first she suspected that Gato Bobo had somehow snuck into the room. She turned on the light and checked everywhere. There were no cats in the room. On the way to the bathroom she saw the live cat sleeping soundly on the landing. She returned to her room, checked GB's whereabouts one last time, and closed the door. Again she felt the yanking at the sheet. Exhausted, Selina knew the creature wasn't belligerent, so she simply went to sleep.

The next morning on the road to Boston, Selina asked Laura, "Do you have an animal ghost in your house?"

Clearly, even after all these years, Tigger still wanders the rooms at night, making sure everyone in the Underwood home is sleeping safely in their beds.

Laura had another experience with a ghost cat at a different location. While settling her late great-aunt's estate, Laura brought along her dog Rowdy to stay at the aunt's home. She noticed that Rowdy occasionally stared into the hall. One day, Laura observed a black-and-white cat with gray patches slinking into the living room. Laura knew that her aunt didn't have a cat when she died. Since all the living-room furniture had been sold and the room was empty, the cat should have been in plain sight. It had simply disappeared.

Laura saw the cat slip in and out several times over the months that followed. She finally remembered that her aunt had once owned a cat named Riddles. Could this be Riddles returning for a final farewell?

Later, a friend who was hanging out with Laura in the living room asked, "When did you get a cat?" She described the cat from head to tail. Laura told her it was probably Riddles's ghost. Apparently, the friend had been standing in the kitchen when she turned and saw Riddles running for the living room. She was quite amazed, as she had never seen a spirit before. Laura assured her that she herself had been seeing animal spirits most of her life, and that they were quite harmless.

Now that the home is in the hands of another family, Laura occasionally wonders if they enjoy their new pet or if Riddles has joined her great aunt on the Other Side.

THE HEADLESS CAT

When you're a kid, those carefree hours of summer vacation tend to blur. But for Keri Sweeney, one particular night will stand out in her memory as long as she lives. She was just a teenager that bizarre night when she first saw the cat in her front yard.

Keri grew up in a typical three-bedroom house in Tempe, Arizona, with a stay-at-home mom who created a loving environment. Her house always felt warm and safe. In the evenings the place was filled with the aroma of a home-cooked meal simmering on the stove. Keri's room—her personal domain for as far back as she could remember—was like that of many teens growing up in the 1980s. She had covered her walls with posters of her favorite stars, including the summer's latest heartthrob—*Miami Vice* star, Don Johnson. She would have preferred Metallica, but her mom wouldn't permit it. Wall-to-wall hunks hid the real wallpaper, that flowery visual abomination that appealed to parents, but turned the stomachs of the "in" group. Her bedroom offered sanctuary during hormonal moments and after arguments with her parents. It was the perfect space for Keri to do homework, watch television, listen to music, and just be alone.

On a warm, clear night in 1987, however, Keri's feeling of safety was ripped away as she got ready for bed. She was gazing out the window at the lone oak tree that dominated the lawn. When she was little, Keri had played with its broad leaves; back then, it was barely big enough for her to climb its branches. In some ways she looked at the tree as an old friend; it had grown along with her. On this night, Keri noticed that a dark tabby cat was lying at the base of the tree like a small sphinx, with his paws stretched out in front of him. The tip of his tail swished casually back and forth. There was something odd about the stray, but in the darkness, she couldn't pinpoint what it was.

Suddenly, she realized this was no ordinary cat.

His head was missing. Looking up, she saw his head floating up in the tree. He gazed down her at her with a penetrating yellow stare. At first she thought she was just imagining the cat, but then he meowed at her. He looked okay; no visible injuries or trauma. Other than the fact his head was hovering six feet above his body, he looked normal.

A soft *Whoa!* escaped her lips. She was trembling. As she blinked and rubbed her eyes, the cat disappeared.

In those first few moments, the cat spirit had just given her the chills—then, as what she was witnessing sunk in, it terrified her. She was not afraid of the cat himself, but horrified at the sight of his disembodied head floating up in the tree.

Keri didn't recognize him; as far as she knew, he didn't belong to any of her neighbors. Her family had owned dogs off and on over the years, but they had never owned a cat. She hadn't seen the dark tabby before, not even hanging out with the neighborhood strays. There had been no rumors of missing cats or bodies found after accidents or ritual sacrifices. She believes he may have appeared to her because she is sensitive to spirits.

Keri never figured out who the cat had belonged to, and as far as she knew, the cat never came back. Of course, she never really knew for sure because she never looked out of her window at night again, for fear she'd see the cat or even more frightening images. For all she knows he might still be waiting for her under her parents' tree.

Scamper's Specter

It was about ten o'clock on an October night in 2004, when a young man dumped a little gray kitten out on a quiet road in the Hill Country of Texas. The abandoned waif was still a baby, no more than a month old, way too young to be on his own. He needed a good meal of mother's milk. Terrified, the kitten sought help from the human voices he heard nearby.

Across the street Renee Leppard had just opened up the doors and windows of her home to clear away paint fumes from a recent renovation project. Renee suddenly noticed the tiny kitten, wandering in from the pampas grass. Scared, hungry, and crying, he ambled up to the front door and announced his presence. Renee, who owned several cats already but could never resist a kitten, scooped him up. Within a few minutes, the little guy found himself in front of kitten-size dishes of food and water. He ate a bit, and drank a lot. He immediately found a nearby litter box, used it like a perfect gentleman, and then proceeded to explore the rest of the house.

Renee took him to their bedroom while her husband, Mike, went to the store for kitten milk formula and kitten food. She laid the kitten on her chest so he'd feel safe, and so she could keep an eye on him.

The small, bedraggled kitten sported a gray tuxedo—a gray coat with a white muzzle, white chest, and gloves. He resembled Tom of *Tom and Jerry*. His ribs showed, and he was crawling with fleas. Despite his problems, he could have won a Mr. Congeniality contest. Renee immediately fell for him.

Mike kept telling the kitten, "You're quite the little scamp," so he earned the name Scamper Doodles. From that night on, Scampers slept with Renee and Mike. In the middle of that first night, Scampers woke Renee up with his playing—not the kind of play a kitten does by himself, but the rambunctious roughhousing games he'd probably played with a buddy in his short past. This time, however, the buddy was invisible. Scampers tumbled around the bed and waved his paws, mewed, and purred. He jumped up, swung around, reacting to invisible counterattacks, and chased . . . something. Renee didn't know who the invisible companion was—a ghost cat, fairies—maybe nothing at all.

Two years later Scampers still wakes Renee up playing with his unseen friend. Sometimes Renee can even see the bed covers sink under the weight of the ghost cat. Renee said she and Mike don't get scared about the visitor. Occasionally, Scampers will carry on conversations with his pal, meowing playfully like he's sharing the latest cat gossip. Since Scampers discovered the invisible cat, a new Russian Blue kitten named Ember Blu has joined the household menagerie, bringing the headcount to six. He's also joined in the fun and games with the invisible cat.

Sometimes Scampers and the ghost friend play together for only a brief moment; other times they can carry on for close to thirty minutes. As Renee calls it, the "Whisker 500" starts about five in the morning and can last until six or later. As many as six of Renee's cats have emerged from all over the house to join in the excitement. It's something to behold when the cats begin to chase the invisible cat in different directions, leaping, stretching, and vocalizing, no two kitties running in the same direction. Renee used to think the melee was the cats' morning wake-up call for their breakfast, but rarely are the food dishes empty when this occurs. Now, she believes the ghost cat gets them stirred up.

Lady Isis Greydawn, Renee's six-year-old Egyptian Mau, also sees and plays with the "fey." She has done this since she was a kitten as well. In spite of being quite round, she still plays and chases the ghostly friend. The only two who don't play as often are Her Royal Highness Princess Penelope Anne Powder-Puff and her brother, Traveller John Little-Love. Traveller is very shy and timid—the absolute definition of "scaredy cat"—whereas Penelope is just a plain "Hissy, Prissy Missy."

Scampers, now two years old, doesn't discriminate, nor does his ghost buddy. He will cavort with anyone who is willing to play with him. Renee said she and Mike don't mind the additional "pet" that seems to have tagged along when they adopted Scampers. After all, what's one more?

YELLOW EYES

Nicki Olson doesn't remember a time in her short life when Sebbe wasn't around. Sebbe, short for Sebastian, was almost nine years old when her parents brought baby Nicki home from the hospital, about ten years ago. From the very beginning, the registered Blue Persian was fascinated by the noisy little bundle his humans had brought to their North Texas home. When Nicki was just a few weeks old, Sebbe jumped up into her bassinet and laid down on top of her. With her new baby's bed next to her own and her new mommy-radar on full power, Robbi Olson immediately noticed that her daughter's breathing sounded distressed. Dad discovered Sebbe and snatched him up as Robbi grabbed Nicki. While no harm was done, Sebbe found himself exiled from the bedroom. Nevertheless, Sebbe still loved his baby.

The Sebbe-Nicki love affair took a downturn during those terrible twos, when Nicki's desire to yank on a tail or pull the fur just couldn't be resisted. Nicki said they became friends again when she got old enough to understand that if you do mean things to a cat, it's going to come back and bite you . . . or rather, scratch you.

Sebbe graciously endured the humiliation of being dressed up in teddy-bear clothes and pushed around in a doll carriage. If it fit him,

Sebbe wore it. Nicki loved everything about her little best friend: his gentle nature, his long, pewter-gray fur, and his enormous yellow eyes, so bright they almost seemed to glow.

Sebbe had a long life, free of the health problems often associated with being a purebred Blue Persian. While smaller than most cats, he had a protruding nose, so he never suffered from sinus or eye problems often linked to the breed. However, his age finally caught up with him. He became incontinent and couldn't make it all the way to the litter box. Robbi bought puppy housebreaking pads to help him out.

When Sebbe was nineteen, the family came home from Christmas shopping to find that he was slipping away. Needless to say, Sebbe's death, just two weeks before Christmas, put a damper on the holiday.

A few months later, ten-year-old Nicki awoke in the middle of the night because her bedroom suddenly felt icy cold. She turned off her fan and then headed for the bathroom. From there she heard crunching, like the sound of their black Chow dog, Brutus, munching on dry dog food. But through the faint light Nicki could see Brutus sleeping soundly on the other side of the room.

Over by the food bowl, she saw a dark, cat-size blob. When it turned its head to face Nicki, she found herself caught in the stare of two huge, glowing yellow eyes. The eyes rose a few feet in the air and began floating toward her. Her brain told her to run to the safety of Mom and Dad, but she couldn't move. Her brain said scream, but her voice wouldn't work. She stood there paralyzed, with her eyes transfixed on the glowing stare that was gliding ever closer. Nicki thought she was going to die. The eyes came to within a foot of her own face. They blinked slowly. As the glowing orbs opened, they slowly faded away; she felt a cold breeze, and then they were gone.

At first she had no idea what she had encountered. Suddenly she could move, and she ran back to her bedroom and pondered what she had seen. She said nothing to her parents because she knew they wouldn't believe her. A few days later she figured out that the ghostly figure was her best friend, Sebbe, because those huge yellow eyes were Sebbe's eyes.

And the shape had been about Sebbe's size, as well. Nicki kept quiet about her experience; she didn't tell anyone, not even her parents, for six months.

When Nicki encountered Sebbe's spirit, her mind had told her to run, scream, or do something. Now she's glad she didn't. She knows that Sebbe died before they had a chance to say good-bye to him. She has since learned that a slow blink is one of the ways that cats communicate affection—sort of a kitty kiss. Even at her young age, Nicki understands that her childhood friend came by one last time. Had she called her parents, he might have disappeared immediately, and he wouldn't have had time to bid her farewell.

Nicki feels like her cat is her guardian angel. Shortly after his visit, things started going better for the youngster. She made friends more easily. She says she's happier. And she wouldn't mind if Sebbe returned for another visit.

CAT IN THE RAFTERS

Mary Anne's neighbor has not had kind thoughts about her ever since he returned from work one evening and found her two legs sticking out from under his porch. As he reached for his cell phone to dial 911, she emerged, covered in Lord knows what, restraining a spitting, pregnant feral cat by the scruff of her neck. Mary Anne quickly wrapped the cat in a towel. She had been trying to catch the queen for weeks so she could offer the expectant mom an indoor birthing room complete with free midwife. The neighbor scowled at her, mumbling something about "trespassers being eaten by pit bulls," but since he only had a black Lab, she didn't worry. She apologized before taking the feral mama home to a cat room that had been prepared just for her.

A few days later, Funny Face—so named because there was a streak of white that artfully split her black face in half—gave birth to six kittens; four males and two females. One of the kittens had muted calico markings and the tail of a Manx. She called the calico kitten Callie.

Callie showed her independence early. While her brothers were content to stay inside, she joined her mom and her sister, Hissy, in the barn. Callie soon grew to be an accomplished mouser. She would run proudly across the pasture, bolt up the steps, and lay her latest trophies on the mat at the back door. As Mary Anne played with the kitten, Callie would wrap her little legs as far around Mary Anne's neck as she could reach.

When Mary Anne opened the door to gingerly accept the gift of a dead rodent, she would keep the door open, hoping Callie would come into the house. But, a true feral spirit, she preferred to remain outdoors.

Callie had a distinctively patterned coat. Wide stripes of orange, black, and gray ran down her sides and legs, layered onto a creamy-white coat. She wore a raccoon mask around her eyes, the black-and-gray circles standing out in stark contrast with her almost pure-white face. She loved to walk on the rafters in the barn and sleep in the hayloft. In the mornings as the horses ate breakfast, Callie would leap from the top rafters in the barn, right into the hay trough, and settle down for a nap. The horses never minded her; they just munched their hay contentedly. When Mary Anne walked into the yard, Callie would come running to her, fall over on her back, and invite Mary Anne to rub her black-and-white belly.

As she grew, Callie picked up the habit of walking across the back of one of the horses, a mustang named Racer. While the horse was pretty bombproof, he would spook on occasion. Mary Anne feared he would throw the kitten across the fence. But Racer seemed to like this feline massage, and he would stretch his neck out as she quietly walked up and down his back.

Callie never strayed off the property. She would fish in the creek and run into the woods behind the house, but the sound of the door opening called her home to dinner on the porch as surely as an electric can opener would most inside cats.

When Mary Anne's husband, Mike, worked in his knife shop, Callie would leap up on his work table and catch a nap on the newly sharpened knives. They would marvel at how she could sleep so soundly on such sharp objects, yet she never hurt herself.

Even after Callie turned eight, the pile of trophies at the back door continued. She had a new game now; she would run up the walnut tree and claw at the walnuts. When they dropped down to the ground, she would race down the tree and bat at her new toys.

Then one morning, as they were returning home, Mike turned the truck into the driveway. They both spied a still shape lying in the road. It was a familiar form with fur of black, gray, and orange on white. Mary Anne screamed. It was too late; Callie was gone.

Mike went out to the road, gathered up the kitty in a towel, and brought her to Mary Anne. She would have given anything if this lifeless cat hadn't been Callie, with her short bobtail and her distinctive blend of colors. Her body was still warm to the touch, but her spirit had departed. They both cried as they buried her beneath the walnut tree that she'd loved.

The next morning started, as every morning did, with Mary Anne's sunrise feeding of the horses. Things were somehow different that day. Despite the presence of all their pets, the yard felt empty. But the horses were pawing at the gate, and life goes on. While she was preparing Racer's breakfast, Mary Anne heard a noise overhead. Looking up, she thought she saw Callie slipping into the darkness. In one of the stalls she heard a very familiar *plop*. She looked up, and there was Callie, standing in the horse feeder. Slowly, she walked over to the cat, and picked her up. The cat that looked like Callie nuzzled Mary Anne's chin and wrapped her paws around her neck.

In disbelief, Mary Anne's knees gave way; she sunk down to the ground, hugging Callie tightly and sobbing. Thoughts of Stephen King's *Pet Sematary* ran through her head. In that novel, the cat was killed by a truck, only to return from the dead after he was buried. *Did we bury a cat that was alive?* she wondered. There were no wounds; no dirt under her claws; and her coat was bright and shiny. By then Mike had come out to start his day. When he saw Mary Anne with Callie, he stopped short.

"Callie's alive," she whispered.

Mike took the cat from his wife. Callie wrapped her paws around his neck, nuzzled his beard, and leaped on his shoulder. He, too, was stunned.

Suddenly, Callie leapt off Mike's shoulder, landed on the ground, and took off running to the creek. They quickly ran after her, but she scrambled over the culvert and vanished into the woods that surround their property. They rushed over to the old walnut tree to check on her grave. To their shock, the new dirt mound lay undisturbed, just as they had left it the day before.

THE DEMON CAT OF THE NATION'S CAPITOL

Although most feline apparitions are friendly and comforting, there is a famous entity with an ominous reputation. The most feared of America's feline specters resides in the basement of the nation's capitol in Washington, D.C.

In the nineteenth century, when caretakers of public buildings kept cats around for rodent control, the U.S. Capitol Building maintained a thriving population in its depths. Now that pest control has been handed over to beings with just two legs, only one cat remains in the bowels of the Capitol. He's one cat that no one in their right mind wants to tangle with. He's known as the infamous Demon Cat of the Capitol, or D.C. for short.

Unlike other spirits who appear randomly, the Demon Cat reputedly materializes with the selective precision of Julius Caesar's soothsayer, as if to say, "Beware the Ides of March." Just as the soothsayer warned of the death of a leader, so, allegedly, does D.C. He usually makes his appearances in the basement of the Senate near the catafalque storage room. The catafalque is the raised ceremonial platform on which a president's casket rests when the body lies in state in the Rotunda. It's kept in the crypt beneath the Capitol Rotunda with the other funereal items. (There is a similar, but less widely circulated legend about the Demon Cat in the basement of the White House, probably due to confusion between the two buildings.)

It is alleged that the cat was spotted by a security guard prior to the Lincoln assassination, the week before the 1929 Stock Market Crash, and again just before President Kennedy was assassinated in 1963. However, there has been no report of the cat in recent decades, even prior to catastrophes such as 9/11 or Hurricane Katrina. And there have been sightings with no devastation following. But that was probably of little consolation to D.C.'s victim.

The possibility of running into D.C. makes the basement a place where both angels and security guards fear to tread. Being a watchman takes a lot of nerve under the best of circumstances, but it requires undaunting valor to patrol the shadowy depths of the Capitol's basement. At night the cavernous structure comes alive with echoes and hints of the supernatural. Add to that creepy environment the threat of encountering a massive black cat with a nasty disposition and you have one of the world's scariest jobs during the late 1800s. The sight of even the most innocent stray black cat wandering the basement could make a professional lawman tremble like a frightened toddler. Large paw prints cast into the concrete act as a permanent reminder to guards that the black cat may lurk just around the next corner.

A story about a guard's encounter with D.C. appeared in the *Philadelphia Press* on October 2, 1898. It didn't name names, but the article stated that the attack of the cat scared the watchman "out of his wits." It also mentioned the cat's first terrifying appearance in 1862. At that time one of the watchmen shot at it as it vanished before their eyes. Not all of D.C.'s victims emerge from the catafalque storage room unscathed. A few actually showed up with impressive domestic cat scratches. Oral accounts reported a black cat prowling the shadows of the basement. The cat waited until his victim was alone, then attacked.

In the 1898 incident, the guard walked alone through the basement, making his way from door to door, rattling doorknobs. He stopped suddenly, frozen by a vague sense of alarm, though he couldn't see or hear anything out of the ordinary. He listened for anything that might be causing his dread. He knew it was pointless. No doors had opened, so it wasn't human. And as for cats . . . Well, cats were silent as the tomb.

After another couple of steps, the guard froze, as if encased in plastic. His heart beat so fast it felt as if it were going to explode; he'd spotted a little black kitty walking toward him. With yellow eyes glowing, the cat appeared to develop and swell, all the while drawing nearer. He grew to the size of a large dog. Still unable to flee, the man stared helplessly as the Doberman-size panther charged. By the next step, the cat had grown to the size of a lion, and the next, a bull. Finally, when he was just a short fathom away, he swelled to the size of an elephant—feet extended, fangs and claws brought fully to bear. The guard, still paralyzed, watched the cat spring toward his face. He hoped it would be quick. Then, when it was so close the man could see inside the beast's snarling mouth, the guard gained his wits and pulled his weapon. As he fired in the creature's general direction, the enormous black cat simply vanished.

The guard closed his eyes. His breathing slowed, as did his pulse. He holstered his weapon, then wiped the sweat from his brow with his sleeve. Finally, his legs quit shaking and he could take a step. As he made his way up the stairs, he paused a moment for a final look back.

He wondered what tragedy awaited the nation. He shrugged and continued up the stairway.

For months he scanned the Washington papers, expecting to read about the death of a dignitary or the first shots of a new war, but the anticipated disaster never came. The guard then surmised that D.C. had to practice every now and then just to keep in shape for the next time an ominous omen really was required.

The Guardian Angel

Andrea Shurmard was new to ghost hunting just a few years back. One night, close to Halloween of 2002, she tried to talk some of her friends into going with her to check out an abandoned house. She couldn't find anyone who would brave the creepy building near Wilmington, Illinois. While folks in the area claimed the building was haunted, Andrea remained skeptical. Nevertheless, she was curious—and she wanted to look for ghosts. Screwing up her courage, she climbed into her car and headed south on Route 102. She didn't really know what to expect. She hadn't been on many ghost hunts yet; as a matter of fact, this was only her second one. Andrea had always had a sense for spirits, and wanted to see what she could find. She'd heard rumors about mysterious and possibly paranormal noises, lights, and people coming from the deserted building, and she wanted to see for herself if the activity in the house lived up to the hype.

As she pulled up to the curb, she stared at the old prairie Frank Lloyd Wright–style house. Its beautiful stone walls were washed in a combination of late afternoon sunlight and lengthening shadows. While others found the dying dwelling creepy, Andrea found it had a unique beauty.

Time had been cruel to the once-stately home. By the time Andrea visited it, the shrubs were overgrown, outside lights were broken, and grass grew unfettered in crevices of the broken sidewalk. Vandals had broken windows and stolen everything that could be hauled off. Personal belongings of all ilk had been scattered everywhere. Someone had told Andrea that the elderly man who once lived there had died, and his family had no interest in his belongings. The fact that the place had been neglected and abused gave it a tragic feeling.

While she strolled about the exterior to inspect the structural integrity of the building, Andrea heard something. Not the kind of sounds that can be explained by air blowing though a vent or a salamander scurrying away, or even a whisper in her ear by an unseen spirit, but rather the crunching of autumn leaves as something stealthily mirrored her movements. When she turned around to see where it came from, a cat trotted up to her. The orange tabby was smaller than most, with sleek fur and big yellow eyes. She didn't pay much attention to him. He appeared to be simply a neighborhood cat that was curious about her.

She entered the building, and found that the interior was comparable with the exterior. The few pieces of furniture that remained had been destroyed; the good pieces had probably long since been stolen. As she moved from room to room, she thought, *Why would anyone allow a place with this much architectural interest to become such a dump?*

She took some stairs down into the home's largest room. Descending the third step, she saw small red windows lining the tops of the picture windows, providing her with a clear 360-degree view of the yard outside. Through the windows she could see a wooded area that was shaded and cool.

For such a large house it had a small kitchen, but a set of double doors opened to a nice covered porch. A second set of double doors revealed a set of stairs leading down and outside. Inlaid among the bricks in the staircase walls were old tombstones. She followed the stairs down to a bathroom; or at least it appeared to be a bathroom. Unlike a normal toilet with a holding tank or flushing device, a white, toilet-shaped basin stuck out of the floor. Above the basin was a small-scale lookout tower, similar to something you'd expect to see in a castle. Not far away the cat sat quietly, his eyes glued to Andrea.

She ventured back inside the house, finding a normal bathroom with a marble shower stall. There were also three bedrooms—two were unremarkable, but the last bedroom had a natural stone wall with three-inch-tall diamond-shaped windowpanes looking out to the strange basin room. In some ways, the room felt oddly normal—men's shoes were still lined up inside the closet.

She found an empty room with a hardwood floor with nothing in it. Other than some dust, it was basically clean. There was also a narrow set of stairs next to the wall, which appeared to lead to an attic. Her orange shadow stood quietly in the door.

She then decided to check out the basement. Although she anticipated a trove of discoveries, it was surprisingly small and uninteresting. As she kicked around the basement, she realized that the cat hadn't followed her down the stairs, but instead remained at the top landing, his eyes still watching her every step.

She climbed the stairs, leaving the basement behind, and decided to head outside. She walked over to the garage and entered through the rickety side door. She discovered that the garage had uncharacteristically thick walls. There was a small opening just big enough for her to squeeze through. She found wooden stairs leading to an opening in the ceiling. After great effort she pushed the opening loose, revealing the same empty room she'd entered from inside the house. The opening wasn't a door, but a movable piece of the floor.

Andrea never figured out what this room was used for, but a large area rug in the center of the room would have disguised the opening's presence. Unlike the rest of the house, this room felt heavy and oppressive. Suddenly, she became anxious and wanted out of there.

As she was exploring each room, her orange shadow was trailing behind, just barely out of reach. He'd stop every now and then and groom something unsavory from his paws, but mostly he sat and observed—the way cats do when they are amused by the antics of humans. Throughout her quest, the cat behaved as though he belonged there, not skittish like she'd expect a longtime stray to behave. He acted friendly, yet he kept his distance. He never rubbed her legs or asked for scratch like most friendly cats would.

With her tour complete and curiosity satisfied, she climbed into her car to leave. Not far away, the cat sat on a broken piece of sidewalk and watched her drive away. It later occurred to her that this was no ordinary cat. He had acted as if he were actually a protector—her guardian totem—as she made her way through the house.

THE NEWBORN KITTEN

Maggie Bonham is a dog person from the tips of her fingers that hold the mushing gangline to the bottom of her feet. She owns a kennel full of racing sled dogs—Malamutes and a couple of mutts. These dogs aren't just pets and friends; they're also transportation. Maggie is a dog expert, and has written twenty-two books about dogs and dog care.

But everything changed when this steadfast member of the Dog Writers of America Association attended a Cat Writers' Association (CWA) conference. This wasn't an arbitrary move. Many members of DWAA also write about cats and attend the conferences. Maggie became fascinated by the mysterious little creatures. After being around cat writers, who were enthusiastic about their pets, and seeing cats at the cat shows, Maggie was ready to get a cat.

At a local shelter Maggie was drawn to a six-year-old tortie with a tuxedo named Hailey. She fell in love with Hailey immediately because, along with the cat's affectionate nature, Hailey acted very doglike. She soon became the house's resident mouser and the official bed warmer. Since adopting Hailey, Maggie has written an award-winning cat book and joined the Cat Writers' Association.

Early in 2005, the author had just finished writing her latest novel and headed to bed for a well-deserved night of sleep. She left Hailey downstairs, but kept the bedroom door open so the cat could join her up-

stairs when she was ready. Hailey liked spending part of her nights en-
gaged in the world's best and cheapest feline entertainment: watching
moths fluttering around through the outside window.

Maggie climbed into bed around midnight, but wasn't tired quite yet.
Just a few minutes after she'd turned off the lights, Maggie felt Hailey
jump up on the bed. Hailey curled up and laid down on Maggie's feet. At
the same time something else jumped up on the bed, walking between
Maggie and her sleeping husband, Larry. Whatever it was, it was much
lighter than Hailey's thirteen pounds.

For a moment Maggie panicked, fearing that Hailey might have been
in a particularly benevolent mood after a successful hunt. She was afraid
her friend had brought a live mouse or, God forbid, a rat, to bed. With
some trepidation Maggie looked over and in the faint light saw a kitten
within a foot of her face. It wasn't a normal kitten. It appeared to be a tiny
tuxedo, with that typical newborn look: large head, closed eyes, stubby
sealed ears, and a pink nose. It had a black or dark-gray face with a white
muzzle in the shape of a pyramid, little white mittens, and an all-black tail.
This kitten would have fit into her hand; she guessed it was about five
inches long, not counting its tail.

"The moment I felt it, I was sure I was going to see a rat," Maggie said.
"It didn't compute."

More so than by the strangeness of a tiny kitten suddenly appearing
in her bed, Maggie was puzzled by the fact that he seemed to be a bit bigger than an average newborn. Upon closer examination, Maggie wondered if the kitten might be blind with sealed eyes, or perhaps it had a
birth defect.

She stared at the kitten helplessly for several seconds. When she
moved just a tad, the kitten backed up a little and just faded away. When
he moved, he didn't use his legs, but she still felt him taking tiny little
strides. Hailey was lying next to Maggie, staring at the place where the kitten had just been. The entire encounter had lasted just a minute or two,
and her husband had slept through the whole thing.

After the kitten disappeared, Maggie lay in bed and wondered what she should do. *What the hell just happened?* she thought. *Kittens aren't supposed to be scary . . . but this little guy scared the bejeebers out of me!* Maggie wasn't taking any medication that would have led to hallucinations.

While she couldn't explain where the little ghost kitten had come from, she had some suspicions. "We have a lot of ferals around here," she said. "This area is a dumping ground for cats." It's not unusual for Maggie to see frightened cats scurrying around outside. When she tries to help them, they usually just run and hide.

"You'd think a little cat would be concerned with all the dogs in the house," said Maggie. "With a little ghost cat, I guess it's a moot point. He could have been a kitten born to an abandoned cat in the nearby woods that later died."

Maggie has another theory. Her odd three-story house up in the mountains of Colorado had been built in 1970. According to a neighbor, the original owner purchased two old farmhouses scheduled for flooding because the U.S. Army Corps of Engineers was building a dam. The man bought the homes, tore them down, and rebuilt Maggie's current house with the remaining antique farm materials. Maggie said there's not a right angle in the whole house (but then, she'd heard the truck driver who built it had had no prior construction experience).

Perhaps the kitten was the pet of the truck driver who built her home? Or maybe it had lived briefly with a family who had lived in one of the demolished homes, and its spirit had lived on in the lumber used to construct her house.

Maggie said she'd be curious to see the kitten a second time. "I didn't feel threatened, but it was unsettling. If I saw him again, I'd be more mentally prepared, and perhaps I'd try to touch it."

Why did the kitten visit her?

"Heck if I know," she says. "To be honest, I always attract animals, be they pets or wildlife, so why not a ghost cat?"

Of course, it's just possible the little kitten wanted a little snuggle from someone. Who better than a reformed dog writer turned cat lover?

A Cat Named Miracle

Steve Rusher, of Fordsville, Kentucky, loves his exotic cats. Until recently, he had six: two Savannahs, three Jungle Cats, and a Mystery Cat. In 2005, he purchased Miracle, his special girl, a registered Savannah queen. Savannahs are hybrids of the Serval and domestic cats.

At one time Steve considered buying a full-blooded Serval, but after doing considerable research, decided against it. While majestic cats, Servals are too large to keep in the house. And when they mark territory, it's like turning on a fire hose. The cat would need a six-foot-square area— and that was just the sandbox. Besides, Servals are wild animals, and like their cousins, cougars and tigers, don't make good pets.

Then Steve began to modify his desire and consider the Savannah hybrid. They're bigger than a Maine Coon, weighing in at eighteen to twenty-five pounds without being stocky or fat. They've been compared to the Egyptian Mau except that they are larger.

Steve traveled to The International Cat Association (TICA) cat show in Washington, D.C., to see the Savannah cats firsthand. There, he fell in love with the large, leggy felines. His research led Steve to a year-and-a-half-old Savannah. He purchased her as his foundation female for his new breeding program, rescuing her from a neglectful, even abusive, situation. The previous owner was scared stiff of her huge cat and sold her to Steve with a stern warning about the cat's vicious nature. The woman kept the nearly thirty-pound cat locked up in a three-by-three-foot cage and even had to wear mesh gloves to feed the animal because, according to her, the Savannah would attack her without warning.

The poor Savannah had never known the slightest bit of freedom or affection. She was a grayish-brown cat with black spots on her body, similar to a cheetah. Steve named her Miracle, a name that would later prove to be prophetic. After he brought her home, Steve never saw the aggression the former owner had warned him about. Within two weeks Steve could go inside the cage and pet her. A week later, he let Miracle out in the house with the other cats.

True to her breed, she was very independent and kept much to herself. Steve looked past her distrust, seeing her as a sweet-natured cat. He tried to broaden her horizons and socialize her with people and other cats. Unlike her previous owner, Steve met her on her own terms instead of making her meet on his.

"I was patient and it paid off in silver dollars," he said.

In their favorite game, she jumped on his shoulders and he carried her twenty-seven pounds around the house. Steve gave her a segment of a heavy knotted power cord that she'd toss around. Miracle liked to play ball by herself. And like most any cat, she loved to play with the twist ties from bread packages.

Miracle spent all her time in the living room. She never ventured into Steve's bedroom, despite his cajoling her, preferring to sleep on the back of the bar. She never woke him up. In the morning she always went to the kitchen to wait for Steve, because she knew she'd find some special hors d'oeuvres like tuna or turkey in her dish, a snack for her to enjoy before Steve served her a breakfast of wet food.

Then one morning as he was waking up, Steve felt Miracle climb onto the bed. *Great!* he thought. *She's finally in the bed.* He reached over to pet her. He felt her soft fur between his fingers as he scratched her ears. Miracle meowed, and then hopped off the bed. Steve felt the bed move as it always did when a cat jumped down to the floor. She trotted out of his bedroom and headed toward the living room. Out of the corner of his eye he caught a glimpse of her slipping under the couch. After he got up, Steve went to feed her, but she wasn't waiting for him in the kitchen. He couldn't find her anyplace else, either. Then he remembered the image of her crawling under the sofa.

He looked beneath the couch and found her lying there, motionless. He picked up the couch to move it, and stared in disbelief. Obviously, rigor mortis had already set in.

Steve clenched his fists and screamed.

"I freaked out because she was such a sweet cat," Steve said. He'd become very attached to Miracle in the year he'd had her. "Then, I realized that she'd been in my bed only minutes before. How could it be possible that rigor had set in so quickly?"

Steve immediately switched into emergency mode. He didn't have time to grieve. He feared she might have died as a result of something contagious or toxic. He had to protect his other cats.

"You have to do the right things," Steve said. He took the body to the vet for a necropsy. According to the pathology report, the two-year-old cat had not been exposed to anything poisonous, but had died of natural causes: deformed kidneys.

But there was one more shock in store for Steve Rusher: Miracle had died about twelve hours before he had found her body.

His friend later asked him if he had considered the possibility that he had seen a ghost that morning. "Yes," Steve replied quietly. He now understands that Miracle came back to lead him to her body.

Miracle—he had named her well, not realizing the miracle she would give him just minutes before he found her. Steve is consoled by the fact that in Miracle's last year of life, she felt both freedom and love.

"I feel she came back to tell me that she's OK now, and to thank me for loving her so much."

ZIGGY'S INVISIBLE FRIEND

Growing up, many children have invisible friends; these friends are usually little boys and girls, or sometimes, friendly adults. Many experts in the paranormal believe that what adults brush off as a make-believe friend could actually be a ghost or an angel who befriends the child. In Karyn Vanderburg's home, it's not a kid who has an invisible friend, but her cat. Her young male cat, Ziggy Too, talks to his "special friend" every night between eight and nine.

Ziggy Too came from a litter of feral kittens that were born inside Karyn's bathtub. At the time, she lived in a mobile home. Somehow Ziggy's mother had found a hole on the underside of the trailer that she could squeeze through. So she gave birth to her kittens in the hollow area between the fiberglass tub and the floor. Karyn could hear the kittens crying but couldn't get to them, or even see them. She used to talk to them while she took a bath. When the kittens were about six weeks old, and had their mom's permission to venture out of the interior of the mobile home, a neighbor caught them and kept them in her bedroom until Karyn could find homes for them.

Ziggy was the largest of the babies, but also the shyest. Karyn sometimes calls him "her bashful, barefoot baby boy." Since two of her elderly cats, Ziggy and Melly, had recently died, she kept Ziggy and his brother, J. B. Ziggy's name changed from "Bashful" to "Ziggy Too" because he was similar in appearance to her older cat. The first Ziggy was a large silver tabby, whereas Ziggy Too is a smaller, brown tabby. While he may have had different coloring, they had the same face with beautiful copper eyes.

Karyn has since left her mobile home and the old bathtub behind. She now lives in a single-story, three-bedroom ranch house in Cincinnati.

Quite the conversationalist, Ziggy has a wide variety of vocalizations when he talks, including meows, chirps, and trills. His personality has blossomed, and he's turned into a social little guy who gets along well with all of the other cats. Most of Karyn's cats are Ziggy Too's relatives: J. B., his littermate, and three other cats from his mother's other litters. Naturally, Karyn couldn't abandon such a conscientious mother. She kept the mom, as well. Ziggy Too likes running-and-romping games with the other cats, and prefers not to play alone.

Karyn has loved cats for many years, and has a curio cabinet with a special shelf, which holds the urns containing the remains of her ten deceased kitties: Polly, Shadazzar, Cuddles, Nifty, Gianetto, Melly, Ziggy, Chester, Kiki, and Patsy. The urn of Karyn's own mother, Lillian, is also in the same location.

A year ago, shortly after they moved into the house, Ziggy Too began running around every night between eight and nine, looking up at the ceiling and vocalizing the entire time. It's as if he's talking to an invisible friend. He becomes especially chatty when he is near the shelf where she keeps the urns. He'll stand on top of the small curio cabinet, reaching up toward the ceiling, chattering continuously. As he carries on these conversations, he uses the complete range of his vocalizations. His discussions can last from ten minutes to an hour.

Karyn said the only thing above this cabinet is an unfinished attic with an electric light. She's checked, and there's never been anything or anyone in there. Some evenings he'll run to the front door, jump up to the peephole, and then try to open the door with his paws, all the while chatting with something on the other side of the door. Since Ziggy refuses to go outdoors even when the door is open, Karyn assumes he's talking to someone outside. Karyn always tells him that his "friends" can't come in the front door. She has no clue who or what Ziggy Too has been talking to. She doesn't believe his friend is any of her "urn kitties" because they had already passed when she moved into the house. She learned from neighbors that while the previous owner of the house had not been an animal lover, she had once owned a large orange-and-white cat.

Although another possible candidate for the friend at the door is the ghost of Karyn's first cat, Kiki, who died in 1996, long before Karyn moved into the house. One night, Ziggy was banging away at the linen closet door, yelling for all he was worth. Karyn told him that his friends would have to stay in the closet. She placed a heavy sculpture in front of the door to keep the cats out. When she woke up the next morning, the sculpture had been moved, the door to the linen closet was standing wide open, and the sheets were on the floor. Karyn wonders who helped Ziggy move the sculpture. Kiki had been fond of napping in a linen closet; Karyn thought perhaps Kiki had been in there, and then decided she wanted out.

Ziggy's conversations usually don't bother Karyn. When people ask her what he's doing, she tells them that he is talking to his special friends. Karyn and her friends have started referring to Ziggy as the "Cat Whisperer."

Karyn said the only time his activities spook her is when he jumps from the floor to the level of the front-door peephole, like he's trying to see who's there; then he tries to turn the doorknob with his paws. Thank goodness he doesn't have an opposable thumb! Although she doesn't sense anything evil about these incidents, she does admit it's creepy to imagine that Ziggy might be trying to let something—or someone—unknown into her home.

"Now *that's* a bit disturbing," she said. Karyn comforts herself because she personally believes that a vampire can't come into your home unless he's invited. Fingers crossed, she hopes the same is true of ghosts.

PHANTOM AT THE VET'S HOME

Several years ago Emily and Russ Youngreen moved into a beautiful historic house that had been the home of a veterinarian and his wife, both now deceased. Not only had the vet lived there, but he had also had his practice on the site.

For the Youngreens, living in the hundred-year-old home was like a fairy tale. Bright petunias, pinks, and herbs grow in window boxes. The living room in the stately three-story home has two picture windows with an enviable view that overlooks Kootenay Lake in southern British Columbia, Canada. A long hallway leads to a very unusual laundry room, which was once the animal hospital's surgery unit. The laundry room has a beautiful stonework birdbath just outside the west-facing window, built solely for the purpose of occupying a cat's attention while it was being cared for. Guests enter the home through the enclosed sun porch that leads into the kitchen—a perfect place for cats, both living and not, to catch a few rays.

Long after their deaths, the reputations of the old vet and his wife live on. Ask any of the locals and they'll tell you they were a loving and caring couple. Animals were their life. The vet, a kindly old man, was semi-retired, treating pets for only the cost of medications.

Emily said the home is a happy place for animals. She believes that quite a few animals have been laid to rest around the yard, both the vet's own pets and some of his patients' pets too. Even when the Youngreens first moved in, their pets responded happily to the loving atmosphere. Normally, when they moved into a new house, the dog and cat would hide for a week. This time, the pets immediately seemed to act perfectly at home, not bothering with the previously obligatory game of hide-and-seek. Their elderly dog instantly loved his new surroundings, even though he was quite ill and near death at the time. He had a very happy final two weeks there before he died. Neither he nor the cat required any settling-in time at all.

But before long, Emily started noticing movement out of the corner of her eye. She often spied the brief image of a black-and-white long-haired cat near the door of what used to be the vet's surgery—except they didn't have a black-and-white cat. The cat appeared solid—solid enough that Emily thought it must have been a stray cat running loose in the house.

Recently Emily saw him run across the doorway to the studio. Emily's own orange tabby was close behind, almost as if she were chasing it. Another time, she saw the black-and-white cat leaping across the hallway. When they first moved in, she once saw a long-haired orange cat, but she hasn't seen that one since the first few weeks they lived there.

Even today, Emily sees things when she least expects them. For a while she wondered if the apparitions' visits fit a pattern. Over the two winters they've lived there, Emily made check marks on her calendar whenever anyone had a paranormal encounter. Her research showed that they usually appeared around the full moon, especially in the late fall. According to her calendar, the family sees phantom cats once or twice a month.

Emily also catches a rare and unexpected glimpse of an unidenti-fied woman in their flower garden. When she turns for a full view, the apparition disappears. Sometimes they see her as a reflection on the entry-porch window, causing Emily to run to the door several times, expecting someone to be there. Even their new dog will bark before Emily sees the woman.

Fortunately, there's nothing scary in this haunted house. They've all been friendly hauntings. On one occasion, Emily was outside repotting plants. As she squatted to fill the pot with soil, a cat rubbed up against her backside so hard he almost pushed her over.

The Youngreens' home is a happy, comfortable place for yesterday's cats as well as today's. After all, they learned from neighbors that the vet's wife used to cook prime roast beef for their own cats and dogs. With that in mind, Emily asked, "Why would they ever want to leave?"

THE SPIRIT OF THE HOUSE

On a hot, summer day in San Benito, Texas, just before she entered the ninth grade, Ginger Quezada's best friend, Bethie, had to show her something cool she had just bought. Excitedly the two teens flipped through the pages of a book about conjuring spirits. A particular page featuring a spell for conjuring the spirit of the house caught their attention, and they immediately had the same idea: "Let's go conjure up something!"

In no time they were standing in the front yard of a vacant house in their neighborhood. The 1920s vintage two-story home was like many of the homes in far south Texas, with its striking red-tile roof and arched windows. The white, Mission-style stucco house had stood vacant for at least ten years, maybe twenty—certainly as far back as Ginger could remember. Ginger had always loved the old house and secretly wanted to buy it and move in when she grew up. But there were those nasty rumors—vague ones—that the abandoned abode harbored spirits. The girls didn't really expect to see a ghost. Like many teenagers, they had tried communicating with spirits using a Ouija board on a couple of occasions. Nothing had ever happened. But they looked forward to that exhilarating fear of the unknown, like a wild roller-coaster ride.

As they explored the structure, they learned what a toll the years had taken on the aging building. Layers of dust that had taken years to accumulate caked every surface. It smelled musty and old. Although it had a solid roof, vandals had knocked out windows throughout the home, adding to the creepy ambience.

After fifteen minutes spent canvassing the whole house, Ginger and Bethie walked upstairs to the kitchen, bizarrely located in the center of the house. They sat down and Bethie pulled out her recently acquired *Crone's Book of Spells*. Thinking themselves spiritually wise, they planned to contact the spirits of the abandoned house. Together they read a spell aloud. Being a good Catholic, Bethie held the book in one hand and a crucifix in the other (believing this precaution would save them if they happened to encounter an evil spirit).

To their combined disappointment and relief, nothing happened. They waited, not breathing. Still nothing. So they repeated the spell.

This time the crucifix flew out of Bethie's hands and plummeted to the floor. They screamed. At that same instant, a black cat appeared out of thin air, leapt down onto the old dust-covered stove, and bounded out of the kitchen. He was a small but solid adult cat with short hair, basically the stereotypical Halloween cat. Despite the ruckus he had caused, he didn't make a sound.

They looked around the kitchen to see where the cat had come from. Although they found one set of paw prints where the cat had landed on the stove, they could find no others to indicate where he had gone. They couldn't find where the cat had jumped from. There were no cabinets near the stove. Surely, they thought, it couldn't have just come out of nowhere! But all the evidence led to exactly that. Despite a thorough search of the house, they could find no more paw prints or the cat. Upon the realization that maybe this cat was the spirit of the house, the two girls couldn't get out of that house fast enough. Ginger took the book from her friend so she wouldn't try any more spells. She still has it hidden away, almost thirty-five years later. The two friends have sworn off Ouija boards, as well.

"I've never opened that book again, and we've never spoken about what happened to us that summer day—until now."

Both of the teens loved cats, and today, they have cats of their own at home, but this black cat gave them the willies. Ginger doesn't think the cat was evil, but believes his sudden appearance was more of a warning . . . a warning to stay away from things they shouldn't play with—like books about conjuring spirits.

A Little Game of Cat and Dog

Christine and Jeff live in a century-old farmhouse that has been completely encapsulated by encroaching suburbia in Washington State. When it was first built around 1910, it stood in the middle of a hundred-acre potato farm. Today, instead of being surrounded by crops and plowed fields, a new housing development envelops the home, and an elementary school lies across the street.

Christine had been living there with her husband, Jeff, a ninety-eight-pound Golden Labrador named Jaxon, and a Golden Retriever named Rosie. Then one day about six years ago, a child came to live with them. Despite the fact that the little blond boy belonged neither to Christine nor to her husband, they needed no legal papers regarding his residence, nor a formal adoption. He was literally a free spirit—that is, a ghost who had come to stay. Christine researched the house's history, and found nothing about the blond boy who had taken up residence with them. He never bothered to keep his presence a secret from anyone, appearing before Christine, Jeff, and even their guests. The boy looked to be about ten years old with blue eyes, and he had a sweet but sad face. When he first moved in, he wore an old-fashioned white shirt and trousers with suspenders. The youngster had a good sense of humor and liked to play harmless pranks on guests. After Jeff's earthly children had moved back in with their mother, the spirit boy became the new adopted son. He liked to move things around. Sometimes on cold nights, while Christine and Jeff slept, he'd remove the blankets from their feet.

After the little ghost boy had been there for about two years, he did what many little boys do: he showed up with a calico cat. He and the cat had at least one thing in common. She was deceased, just as he was. He gave Christine one of those looks, as if to say, "She followed me home. Can I keep her?" Christine nodded okay and the ghost cat was there to stay. In the beginning the calico looked as though it had lived a hard life. As time went on, however, Christine noticed that the cat looked sleeker and appeared healthier, just as a hungry stray would look after a few weeks of regular meals. Thomas seemed to be taking good care of his new kitty. (Although Thomas had whispered his own name in Christine's ear shortly after his arrival, he never gave any hints as to his cat's name; the family simply referred to her as "Kitty" or "the cat.")

Like his master, the cat had no fear of revealing her presence to others. Christine and Jeff, their family, and their friends all saw the cat. Something of a chameleon, the cat's appearance changed depending on who saw it, according to Christine. Often appearing transparent, a couple of friends will say the cat is black; another says she's white. Once, a friend reported that the phantom cat appeared to have "blue" points on her ears and six toes on each foot. Regardless of the cat's color, she was always a short-haired cat. She made typical cat noises, meowing and purring frequently, and her progress across the hardwood floors was marked with the sounds of scratching and periodic thuds.

And as with any spirit's presence, both Thomas and the cat always created cold spots.

The cat also had Thomas's sense of humor, and loved to tease the dogs. Christine's two large dogs saw the cat as well. Sometimes Christine would hear the ghost cat meowing from somewhere in the house. This was not lost on the dogs, who would go in tandem from room to room on a quest to seek out the crying cat. The sound would shift around the house as if the dogs were "It" in a frustrating game of hide-and-seek.

Christine and her husband became used to many interesting sounds once they knew they were sharing the house with a feline spirit, in addition to Thomas. They soon came to ignore them. However, a target that moves around was entirely too provocative for the dogs, who felt the need to investigate every shifting sound.

Like many living cats, this calico seemed to enjoy teasing the dogs. She'd attract their attention, and before you knew it, the hunt was on. Once the dogs were committed to a full-speed chase, the cat would vanish into a wall or a closed door, thus causing the pooches to smack full-force into very solid objects. After about six months, the retrievers became accustomed to the new pet and learned to ignore her.

Christine's friend Karen has also seen Kitty. The two friends get together at least once a week to work on craft projects or to play Renaissance music, with seafaring and tavern songs thrown in for good measure. The women have been friends for many years, visiting each other's homes without anything extraordinary happening.

All that changed one afternoon as they were standing in the kitchen talking about nothing in particular. The early-twentieth-century kitchen had light-colored wooden cabinets that gave the room a bright airy feeling and the illusion of greater size. On this particular day they had been working on craft projects. As they chatted in the kitchen foyer, near the garage and the back door, Karen noticed a pretty little calico cat walking purposefully between them.

At first Karen didn't pay much attention to the cat. Although she loved all animals, Karen knew Christine was a full-blooded dog person and had a couple of pooches running around the house. So Karen was a little surprised to see a kitty—and a transparent one at that— in Christine's house. The cat acted as if she owned the house, as did many of the cats Karen had known. The cat ignored Karen and Christine and stayed pretty much to herself. Suddenly, Karen realized the cat had walked right through the wall that led into the garage.

She stared for a moment and then told her friend what she had seen. Christine hesitated. She explained to her astonished friend that although the calico ghost kitty was a frequent visitor to their home, they didn't usually discuss her with other people because some of their friends have become upset about being in the presence of a ghost, or they don't believe them.

Although she has visited the home many times since that day, Karen has never again seen the ghost calico.

Recently Christine and Jeff started raising rabbits that live in cages in the backyard. Occasionally, Christine would hear the bunnies screaming like they had seen a ghost. On investigation, she found that they had. Kitty had introduced herself to the rabbits and, true to her mischievous nature, was harassing them. The poor bunnies screamed and scrambled around trying to get through the tiny holes in the cage wire to get away from the predatory specter. It only happened a few times. When it did, Thomas always acted contrite, as if he had done something wrong.

For a while after the bunnies arrived, the cat disappeared. Christine didn't know if Thomas had gotten tired of his pet, or if he was worried about the rabbits. Then, about six months later Kitty returned. Recently Christine has seen the cat again out with the rabbits. But she's no longer teasing them. When Christine lets the rabbits out in the backyard to get some exercise Kitty hangs out with them, jumping around and almost mimicking the rabbits' movements. It seems they have all learned to co-exist.

After all, there's no place like home. And Christine and Jeff's place is Kitty's home, dogs, bunnies, and all.

CAT IN THE ATTIC

When Tasha Slone was eight years old, the school bus driver's wife gave her a kitten. The black-and-white puff of fur was so young, she could fit in the palm of Tasha's tiny hand. Tasha named her new best friend Dozier, because like a bulldozer, she was determined to get where she wanted to go.

Although the family had other cats, Dozier belonged to Tasha, the first kitty that was her very own. Dozier loved Tasha. They played together all the time, and she followed her little mistress around like a puppy. Tasha's parents allowed some of the cats to come inside, and Dozier was one of those privileged few, but all the cats slept outside.

Dozier was very playful and friendly, with above-average feline intelligence. Tasha and her mom even taught Dozier to play tag. Mom would run and Dozier would try to tag her with her paw. Then they would reverse the game and chase Dozier.

The family had a problem with the cats sneaking into the attic, so Tasha's dad nailed up boards to block the holes. More clever than the rest of the cats, Dozier still managed to slip past her dad's best efforts. On one of her attic excursions, Dozier discovered a small rectangular opening in the ceiling of Tasha's room. They spent countless hours teasing each other with paws and fingers. If Tasha had any food in her room, she would slip some of it through the gap in the ceiling. Little Tasha couldn't help but smile whenever she'd see that black-and-white paw stretching toward her.

Dozier grew up and had a litter of kittens, but sadly, only two of them survived. Two weeks after giving birth, Dozier disappeared. While Tasha and the rest of the family were at the store, her grandfather had found Dozier dead in the road, obviously hit by a car. Instead of burying her, Tasha's pragmatic granddad decided to throw the body over the hill so the kids wouldn't see it. That evening, Tasha's mother told her about Dozier's fate. The child was devastated; she simply couldn't believe that her grandfather hadn't bothered to bury her beloved pet.

The job of raising Dozier's two surviving kittens fell to Tasha and her mother. They tenderly bottle-fed the two kittens, which brought comfort to Tasha. Several days after Dozier's death, Tasha was sitting in her bedroom doing homework when she spied a familiar black-and-white paw poking through the hole in her ceiling. Instinctively, Tasha went over to the beckoning paw, teasing it and petting it, just as she had always done. Tasha waved a piece of string in the air for Dozier to play with. The cat stuck her face through the hole, and Tasha stroked the pink nose with her fingertip. The furry foot felt so real and so normal that for a few minutes, Tasha forgot that Dozier was dead.

When she reached around to sneak her a nibble of something to eat, it dawned on Tasha. Suddenly her joy turned to terror. Tasha fell flat on the floor trying to get away from the ghost, and she smacked her head on the floor. The throbbing didn't bother her, probably because she was in shock. She looked back up at the hole. The paw still waited, flexing and wiggling. Dozier was still there, waiting for Tasha to bring her something to eat, just as she had always done. As she ran to get her mother, Tasha began to wonder if perhaps her grandfather might have mistaken another cat for Dozier.

Tasha didn't tell her mother what she had witnessed. She just urged her to come to her room and look. Tasha's mom, seeing her daughter's ashen face, knew that something was wrong, but she was all the more confused by Tasha's next request: to call all of her cats on the porch. Once the cats had congregated, both mother and daughter raced upstairs to the bedroom. Neither could believe what they saw: The little black-and-white foot, the paw belonging to the dead cat, still awaited the treat it had always, up until that moment, received.

Despite her fear, Tasha understood two things: Dozier had come back to say good-bye, and that her friend was not at rest.

The next day on her way home from school, Tasha walked over the hill where her grandfather had thrown Dozier's body. She scoured the weeds and finally found what was left of her beloved cat. She returned with her dad's small shovel to bury her friend. With a child's perseverance and love, Tasha buried Dozier in a grave on the hill. She laid rocks and boards over it so no other animals would dig her up. That afternoon, Tasha bid farewell to her best friend. She returned several times to make sure nothing had disturbed Dozier's grave.

"So I put her soul to rest, and she was satisfied," Tasha said. "She had no reason to come back again. Seeing a ghost is one thing, but *touching* one is something you never forget. The reason that so many ghosts try to reach the living is because they want us to help them reach the Other Side."

Since that afternoon, Tasha has never seen that little paw again.

THE SCARLETT SIGHTINGS

Orange tabby males can be found at almost any animal shelter, but red-headed female cats show up only rarely. Nonetheless, Steve and Muriel Finkel and their kids rescued an orange female kitten at a pet store. She was the runt of the litter, and the other kittens were beating her up. When the Finkels brought the orange kitten home, Muriel, a classic-movie fan, dubbed the little bundle of fur "Scarlett," because of her beautiful orange fur, and also after the timeless character in Gone with the Wind. It wasn't until Muriel took her to the vet to be spayed that they discovered Scarlett should have been named Rhett. By that time the cat's identity was established. Scarlett, despite the boy parts, remained Scarlett. From that point on, Steve and Muriel considered their cat a girl, even referring to Scarlett as a "she."

As often happens with kittens who were taken away from their mothers too soon, Scarlett had some issues. She suffered from a serious case of species confusion. She liked to nurse on the family's spayed Scottie-mix pooch, Belle. The Finkels often had to rescue the dog from involuntary motherhood by making her get up and leave the confused kitten behind. The best of buddies, Belle and Scarlett slept together and suffered through children dressing them up in doll clothes. In addition to wearing the clothes, Scarlett also allowed the kids to wheel her around in a doll carriage. And she answered to her name. Scarlett became an integral part of the family. As time passed and the kids matured, Scarlett had to endure fewer humiliations. When the kids had reached their mid-teens she was able to live out her senior years in peace.

One afternoon in 1994, the Finkels came home from work and found Scarlett dead on Muriel's side of the bed, the victim of kidney failure after eighteen long and happy years of life. After Scarlett's passing, family friend Sue Smith, of rural Ohio, began visiting the Finkels in their big-city Chicago home. On one of those visits, Sue happened to hear a cat meowing behind her. Sue was sitting in a big green leather chair in the family room, watching *Deadwood* on television. Out of the corner of one eye, she saw a cat streak across the dining room.

"I didn't even know they'd had a cat," Sue said, recalling the night she first met the departed Scarlett. She turned around to see if maybe there was a cat at the door, but there was nothing there.

Sue's next sighting was in the upstairs bedroom. That night Muriel and Steve had given Sue the upstairs guest room that had once belonged to their daughter, Jennifer. It was a comfy, spacious room with a dormer; the hardwood floors had been carpeted to keep noise levels down. Sue spent an uneventful first night in the upstairs bedroom—that is, it was uneventful until early the next morning.

As she lay awake in the strange surroundings, Sue heard a meow. The cat cry was so vivid and so distinct, it made her look around, but she couldn't find the cat who had made the noise. The second time she heard it, Sue looked under the bed—still, no cat. She tried to brush it off as her imagination, but Sue knew what she'd heard. After all, she raises and shows Russian Peterbalds and Oriental Shorthairs. This wasn't just her imagination. She told her invisible audience, "If there is a cat in this room, get in bed with me." No one obliged.

She was fully awake by this time, when she heard another cat meow. She looked over both sides of the bed to see if there was a cat hiding somewhere far beneath the bed. Nothing. For some reason, she wasn't afraid.

That morning at breakfast, she told her hosts that she'd heard a cat meowing in her room. Muriel and Steve just stared at each other, then told Sue that she was not the first to have a "Scarlett Sighting," as they lovingly call their cat's return visits.

On another visit, Sue heard the cat at the French door behind her. She thought, "There must be a cat out there." But still, she didn't see anything. This time, she smiled, chalking it up to another Scarlett Sighting. Still later in the dining room, Sue actually spied Scarlett as she raced under the dinner table.

The fraternity of Scarlett Sighters has many members. Steve and Muriel and their grown daughters have all seen their kitty. Only after Muriel had seen Scarlett several times did she break the ice and mention her sightings to Steve; several months later, their daughter Audrey mentioned her own Scarlett encounters to her sister.

It's been twelve years now since Scarlett died. Muriel says the cat's appearances have dwindled, and they no longer have the same visual clarity. However, they sometimes hear her moving around in the upstairs bedroom, and they have occasional sightings in the kitchen, where her feeding bowls are.

"We never put her bowls away," Muriel confessed.

Maybe she's just waiting for them to feed her.

CAT IN THE BASEMENT

In 1989, when Dana Ludeking was only nine years old, her sister's family moved into the home of her great-grandpa in Janesville, Wisconsin. Many families had lived in this home over the years, and many had mysteriously moved out in the middle of the night. Prior to her grandparents moving in, there were rumors circulating around the neighborhood of a homeless woman who had died in the basement bathroom.

As is usually the case, moving day was chaotic. This box goes in the kitchen, not the bathroom. This one rattles and it shouldn't. They stored some of boxes in the basement until they had time to put items away in their proper places. Among the things they didn't move into Grandpa's house were pets. In fact, neither family had any furry companions.

The basement would become a popular hangout for the family. They planned to set up a little bar down there, so the adults could enjoy their drinks while the kids would play darts. A set of exercise weights would help keep Dana's brother-in-law in shape. While unloading boxes in the basement, Dana's sister spied a black kitten, about nine months old. Not knowing where the cat had come from or who he belonged to, Sis tried to catch him. She didn't want him to get trapped down there. Later, when the tired moving crew had a few spare minutes, they all scoured the basement for the little black kitten. He had simply disappeared; everyone assumed he was hiding behind a box or stuck in a cranny. Before long, someone spied the cat. They chased him into the bathroom. Not having time to deal with him, they closed the door.

Hours later, when they opened the door to let him out, they discovered that he'd vanished. Obviously, someone else must have set him free. They finally decided the kitten must have been a stray or a neighbor's cat with an undiscovered secret exit. Once in a while, when someone spied the stealthy kitten, they still made an attempt to catch him.

Little Dana spent a great deal of time visiting her much older sister at the new house. In fact, Sis often babysat for Dana. The little girl had a gift with animals; people marveled at how easily Dana caught creatures like wild cats, chipmunks, even birds. At the age of nine, she could catch anything. Sis figured Dana could just as easily catch the kitten and take him back with her to live in the country. Not surprisingly, no one else had had any luck with the black kitten—until Dana came along. Dana believed that like any kitten, this one didn't trust any of them because they just kept leaping to catch him rather than trying to coax him gently.

Finally, after Sis had lived in the house for four months, seeing the kitten intermittently, Dana was able to catch the little creature by patiently coaxing him to her. He felt a little different from other cats, but not so different that she thought he was anything but a real live cat— he was extremely light, but she could feel his paws press against her skin. As she pet him, his fur felt like fluffy static, tingling against her little fingertips. During the short time that Dana's sister had lived in the home, Dana was able to catch and hold the kitten on several different occasions. A few times, he let Dana hold him for as long as fifteen minutes.

A month later the family started to become suspicious of the kitten in the basement. After all, in that length of time, he should have grown, at least a little—but he hadn't.

Sis was amazed that Dana could handle the shy kitten. Once, when Dana wanted to show Sis how friendly the little guy was by placing the cuddly animal in her sister's arms, the kitty suddenly slipped clear through her arms and disappeared. So did Sis. After standing frozen for a moment, Sis ran upstairs as fast as she could, screaming, "That cat's a ghost!"

From then on, the adults forbade Dana to go down into the basement alone, but when no one was watching, Dana would steal down there anyway to play with the cat. She would also visit the people she called the "Elder Spirits" as well—two nice women and the kindly man she encountered there. She didn't feel threatened by the different spirits; she knew they were friendly. Dana believes the kitten was attached to the spirit of the old homeless woman who had died in the basement bathroom before her grandparents bought the place. She said the kitty would hang around with the woman the same way most any cat would shadow its loving owner.

The spirits regularly rolled the fifty-pound weights around the basement floor. While Sis and her husband were able to look past this, the day he witnessed something invisible lifting his 350 pounds of weights was the limit. They moved out of the house shortly after this incident.

APARTMENT FOR RENT: GHOST PETS WELCOME

To Sue Darroch, the paranormal is normal. She is a co-director of the Toronto/Ontario Ghost and Haunting Research Society. She considers herself a pararesearcher and documentarian, so she usually feels comfortable with events and happenings that may be difficult to explain. But she says it's different somehow when they hit closer to home.

Sue and her husband, Matthew, were really enjoying their new apartment. But shortly after taking up residence, something surprising happened. One evening, about three weeks after they had moved in, she opened the front door and a medium-size cat raced past her, down the entrance hall corridor, and darted into an adjacent room. When she looked for the cat, it had disappeared. Rather than automatically tagging it as being of paranormal origin, Sue assumed the cat had somehow snuck back out of the house unobserved. After a thorough search, however, she was still unable to find the cat, and decided it was impossible for the cat to have gotten out without being spotted. She finally wrote it off as simply a shadow, a trick of the light, and a fatigued brain. She didn't tell anyone about her experience because she didn't think she'd seen anything worth talking about.

A week later, her husband mentioned that he'd seen something odd in their kitchen: a large black-and-white cat sitting by the refrigerator, waiting for his noontime feeding. When he approached to get a better look, the cat was gone. Like Sue, he wondered how the stray had gotten in, and when he couldn't find the cat, he assumed there must be a logical explanation, like poor lighting. When Matthew told his story, Sue rushed to tell him that she'd seen a shadow of a cat as well. A short time later, a friend who visited the house asked about "their cat." They didn't have a cat at the time; at least, not a living one!

They did some research and found that the fellow who lived in the house before them did have a cat, but as far as they could figure, Puss had no reason to stay behind as he'd been alive and well when the man moved out.

"Who knows how many cats have come and gone from this apartment?" Sue says. "This cat could be from any era or time frame." After all, the building is more than eighty years old.

Others have also witnessed the Darrochs' phantom cat. As a matter of fact, Sue was even confronted by the building superintendent over her new pet.

"Oh, I see you brought in a cat," he said.

When Sue denied it and said they didn't own one, he quickly changed the subject. The cat the super had described sounded just like the feline apparition Sue and Matthew had both encountered in their home. They had no idea why the super hadn't seen him before they had moved in.

In addition to actually seeing the cat, Sue and Matthew have also experienced some feline-related poltergeist activity. Odd little things happen all the time, they say. Once, after the family had adopted two cats of the flesh-and-blood variety, Sue had set a cat brush out in the open. She remembered vividly that she had left it in a certain place. When she returned, it had been moved to a stack of library books. Sue was positive it wasn't there when she had left the house, and Matthew insisted he hadn't moved it.

Sue said she hears stories of people who are terrified of ghosts, but she finds them kind of comforting. Sue believes that the ghost cat hangs around the eighty-year-old apartment because of a past attachment of some sort. She feels that as old as the building is, it could be completely natural for the cat to be present. She said human spirits tend to haunt locations where they spent their earthly time. Why should it be any different for the spirit of an animal?

"They don't hang around cemeteries. They hang around the places where they played, loved, and worked," Sue said.

The ghost cat has almost become a member of the family. They call him Tom and always refer to the cat as a "he."

"When my husband, Matthew, comes in, Tom is sitting in the window sunning himself. It's as if he's wandering around, going about his business," said Sue.

Sometimes Sue sees the cat as a blur of movement; at other times, it's a perfectly solid cat. Sometimes Sue finds the ghost cat just sitting there in the kitchen area where they now keep the living cats' dishes. "It's a neat experience," she said.

She believes her living cats are aware of their ghostly brother simply because they seem to respond to things that Sue and her husband cannot see. The cats' response isn't fear, but curiosity. She speculates that because the ghost cat was there first, they view his presence as normal, similar to the way a new live cat would view the resident cat of a household.

The ghost cat sticks mainly to the hallway, kitchen, and living room. They can always recognize him at a glance because he's twice the size of their female cat. The living cats don't seem to mind sharing their food bowl with a specter. As a matter of fact, they don't appear to be bothered by his presence at all.

Although it's been a couple of months since either of them has seen the cat, he has appeared sporadically for three years. Every time he disappears for a few weeks, they wonder if he's left for good, but until now he has always returned. Although Sue is not sure whether the ghost cat will keep coming back, she still often wonders who he was and who he belonged to. Her favorite theory is that if he has moved on, it is because he has accepted the Darrochs as the new family living in his home. She believes that perhaps because he has been acknowledged, it's his time to go forward—his own time here on this earth being done.

THE HURRICANE CAT

The folklore of ghosts and hurricanes are oddly fused together. There are several legends in which spirits walk before the arrival of a hurricane. One of the most famous is the tale of the Gray Man of Pawleys Island, South Carolina. This benevolent spirit, who is carrying a hurricane lantern and is dressed in old-fashioned gray clothes, appears before the arrival of a hurricane, warning residents to leave the island. Supposedly the Gray Man has appeared to someone before every hurricane to hit the island for the past hundred years.

Just down the Atlantic coast in the northernmost corner of Hurricane Alley lives Serena Fusek. Since 1972, she has lived off the coast of Virginia near the North Carolina border, an area vulnerable to hurricanes.

Serena has been through a score of hurricane watches over the last decade and a half. In the last eight years, she's been through five hurricanes, one of them Isabel, which did a great deal of damage. Hurricanes have played such a role in her life experiences that she even named her cat after Hurricane Bonnie, which visited her in 1998. Prior to that, she and her husband, John, had lived in the American colony in Bad Godesberg, Germany. While there, a neighbor's black cat gave birth to a litter of four kittens. Serena adopted the largest kitten, who it turns out was also the best eater. He had short black fur except for a few white hairs on his chest. They named him Maverick.

The tiny kitten grew to a strapping fourteen pounds in his prime. He had a Siamese apple-shaped head and a sleek coat. His eyes glowed a beautiful golden green. When he sat at attention, he resembled a statue of the Egyptian goddess, Bastet. Despite his regal appearance, Serena thought of him as something of a clown. If she let him sit in her lap while she ate, he would steal food off of her fork on the way to her mouth.

Serena admitted Maverick wasn't the world's calmest cat, but he was very loving, and took their many moves around the world in stride. Had airlines offered them at the time, Maverick would have had more frequent-flyer miles than most people. Born in Germany, he was later shipped to New Jersey, and then moved on with Serena and her husband to Virginia. Maverick handled what would have been an incapacitating trauma for many cats without much fuss at all.

Serena considered him an ordinary cat, except for the fact that she was able to call him to her just by thinking of him. "He'd come even faster if I mixed the thought of him with the thought of food," she said. "I would think to myself, 'It's time to feed Maverick,' and he'd appear in the kitchen from halfway across the yard. I'd think, 'Time for lunch' and he'd show right up."

Until he was three and moved to America, he was not allowed outside. Therefore, he enjoyed his newfound freedom in this new land. He never went far (although like many outdoor cats, he would disappear once in a while, returning a day or three later, hungry and tired). In his later years, he spent much of his time lying under the front hedge, watching the world go by.

During his hitch in Virginia, Maverick had the pleasure of mostly calm weather. He went through a few hurricane watches, but he never endured worse than the remnants of category-two or -three storms. Like everything else, Maverick took them in his stride. He spent those stormy afternoons sleeping on the couch.

Then came that terrible year, 1983. Serena was plagued with deaths, illness, and fires. Her first loss was the center of her cat family, fourteen-year-old Maverick. His kidneys had shut down and she had to have him put to sleep. Within months of his death, her sixteen-year old cat Tabitha died, followed by one of her younger kitties who also died unexpectedly. That ended the first generation of her cats.

A year after Maverick died, the warming Atlantic waters gave birth to a storm that would become Hurricane Gustav. A strange storm that formed much farther north than most, Gustav hovered off the coast. While this new tropical depression was growing in the Atlantic, something else strange happened. At Serena's home, a spirit walked. While preparing dinner one evening a week before Gustav formed into a hurricane, Serena sensed Maverick approaching her from out of nowhere. Out of the corner of her eye, he appeared as a patch of darkness that simply "felt" like Maverick. This was how she often caught a glimpse of him when he was alive. It seemed natural, real. For a moment she'd forgotten he had died. But when she turned to look at him straight on, she only saw empty space.

The next day, Maverick just walked into the kitchen and sat behind her, waiting for Serena to acknowledge him. Several times Serena got the impression that he wanted a piece of cheese, one of his favorite treats. He has appeared five times in that week. Serena felt no fear during these visits; after all, he had always been a loving cat, who never gave her a reason to fear him. She has no fear of ghosts, and she certainly didn't fear an animal she had loved.

The final time Serena saw him, Maverick appeared in the kitchen from the living room. At first, Serena thought it was her new cat, Snow Boots, but then Snow Boots came running into the kitchen from outside. At the sight of Serena's new cat, Maverick's shadow simply faded away, and never appeared again. That was the same afternoon the National Weather Service elevated Gustav from tropical storm to hurricane. Gustav never made landfall. Serena wonders if the atmospheric conditions out in the Atlantic may have caused her to see Maverick, and while there have been more hurricanes, Maverick has not returned.

THE PHANTOM INVASION

Three years ago, while Kimberly and her husband, John, were loading the car for a one-week vacation, they noticed a stray ginger kitten hanging around their garage. The little six-month-old had an outgoing personality and a coat of milky yellow with white stripes. The kitten immediately started a campaign for adoption; she ran up to Kimberly's two boys, rubbing up against their legs and begging for affection. Because she was so sweet, Corey, who was fifteen, and Justin, who was ten, fell ears over tail in love with her. As Kimberly put their suitcases in the trunk, she heard a chorus of "Can we keep it?"

She told the kids that if the little cat was still hanging around when they returned from their trip, they'd keep her. A week later they found her lying on the back patio as if she belonged there. They dubbed their new kitty Linxy.

Before long, gentle Linxy became pregnant. One day during her pregnancy, Linxy was lying on the floor by Kimberly's feet. As Kimberly rubbed Linxy's tummy full of kittens, she heard the cat tell her telepathically, "I have five kittens, and one is just like me." Kimberly understood this to mean a ginger-yellow cat like her. When Linxy's time came, Kimberly had to help her deliver the first kitten, and then rushed her to the vet clinic because she was having difficulty with the rest. The vet said she would be fine, and thought she would have four more. Indeed, she did deliver the rest on her own over the next hour: a litter of five, just as Kimberly felt she had been told. Linxy's litter was an artist's palette of kittens: a gray, two gray tigers, a black, a black-and-white, and a pale yellow kitten who looked just like Linxy. Unfortunately, two of the kittens died within the first twenty-four hours; then, one by one, the others passed away, until the only baby left was the ginger kitten. They named the Linxy look-alike French Fry—or Fry, for short.

The day after the kittens died, the family began hearing kittens crying in their home. Pathetic little kitten mews could be heard in the living room, dining room, and the master bedroom. Linxy never looked for them or reacted to their phantom cries. Kimberly believes Linxy could ignore the ghost kittens bacause she abandoned them, as mother cats sometimes do, because there was something wrong with them.

Of course, there were no kittens left, except for Fry, and Kimberly was holding him in her hands when the mews began. Fearing Linxy may have had other kittens they didn't know about, Kimberly frantically searched for the source, but as soon as she began scouring the room, the pitiful meows abruptly stopped. Kimberly tore her entire house apart searching for the kittens—it looked as if a tornado had ripped through. Even with the whole family hunting, they found no signs of the babies. The phantom kittens remained silent until the next day. The pattern continued for three days, and then the kitten mews stopped permanently.

They kept Fry, and the following year Linxy became pregnant again. Just before she delivered her second litter, Kimberly found the pregnant ginger cat on the bedroom floor, dead. The day after her death they began hearing the cries of a single kitten. Just as it had happened a year earlier, when she started to look, the meows ceased.

Kimberly thought Linxy may have had a kitten and hidden it before she died. Again she ripped the house apart, yanking every drawer from its dresser, looking through every stitch of clothing and shoes from the closets. Not one solitary spot went unsearched. And just as in the search a year before, there were no kittens to be found.

From that point on, the family began seeing phantom cats all over the house. Most of the time, they appeared very lifelike—but in the blink of an eye, they would disappear. To this day, almost anyone who visits or lives in the home encounters the ghost cats, including John, Kimberly's husband, her youngest son, Kimberly's sister, and a family friend.

Kimberly's husband even saw the doggy door (that leads from their dining room into the garage) swinging as if an animal had just gone through it. When he searched, he found no animal anywhere.

The phantom cats move through rooms and jump up or down from the dining-room table. They walk around on the coffee table and rub their bodies around doorjambs the same way a live cat would head-mark a table leg. One evening while Kimberly and her sister, Regina, watched television, Regina started looking on the floor between the sofa and the coffee table. She said she was looking for a yellow cat she had just seen walk by with its tail sticking up. Yet there was no cat. Fry, their living yellow cat, is an outside cat, only coming in through the doggy door in the mornings to eat and lay around for a little before he's out tearing up the neighborhood.

Kimberly would every so often see the late Linxy jump from the table to one of the chairs or the floor. Throughout the house she would see a short-haired black cat. She saw him so frequently she named him Spooky. She has seen Spooky rub his body as he rounds the doorway, then he just disappears.

With all the ghostly comings and goings, Kimberly only became alarmed when she saw a headless cat—a brown tabby—walking through the foyer and disappearing as if he had walked through an invisible doorway. She had no idea who that cat was.

Even her son, Justin, has seen a cat standing by a laundry basket. The cat looked so real that Justin went back to pet it, only to discover the cat had vanished.

When Kimberly's mother came over for a visit, Kimberly entered the living room to find her mother talking to an invisible cat. At first she thought her mom was talking to the family's new kitten, Moody, but Kimberly found him lying on the rug in front of the television. A little while later Kimberly saw a white cat she didn't recognize saunter toward the spare room.

A few weeks later they had another sudden burst of phantom-cat activity. In the course of three days, Kimberly saw two different adult cats, one black and one a yellow ginger. One evening she was sitting in

John's recliner and her peripheral vision caught a black cat jumping on the dining-room table. Thinking Moody may have escaped the bedroom, she went to retrieve the kitty and take her back to the bedroom, but found no cat there. She sat back down. A few seconds later she saw the same cat jump off the table and onto the chair, and then to the floor. When she checked the bedroom, Kimberly found Moody snoozing on a green chair. She walked to the bathroom, and the same black cat ran right in. This time, she caught a full view. It was semitransparent, and as it casually walked from one floor tile to the next, it disappeared as if walking through an invisible wall. She watched as this almost-clear black cat vanished. The following night she didn't experience a single sighting of the cat.

A few days later she had a similar experience with the ginger cat. Kimberly believes it might be Linxy, but she's never been able to look at the cat long enough to be sure.

Although Kimberly isn't really sure who the phantom cats are, the spectral kitten mews started right after Linxy's first litter of kittens died. However odd their presence may be, she said there's a certain familiarity about them. She's often wondered if the strange ginger cat may be Linxy, and the others are the grown kittens that Linxy lost.

Kimberly wishes she knew why these poor animals remain. Her religious faith tells her that animals don't haunt, but go straight to Heaven. She often wonders if the entities she sees aren't ghost cats at all, but some other sort of negative energy source *imitating* cats, and wanting her to believe that's what they are. But she has a few other theories, as well. She says the veil between our world and the dead is so thin that someone who is sensitive like she is, can often see right through that veil into the other realm. Or maybe they're simply ghosts of animals that have yet to cross over, because their unaware they've died.

While the phantom cats don't really bother Kimberly, she'd be happy if they went away. She said there's really no benefit to them being here, and it's very awkward having to explain to visitors about these phantom animals in their home.

SMOKEY AND TONI

Big Spring, Texas, is a quiet community. Nothing very exciting happens around town. The same can't be said of the Big Spring home that Toni Reese and her husband, Greg, bought six years ago. When some previous resident of the two-bedroom house moved away, they apparently left something precious behind. The home came equipped with its own ghost cat.

When they first moved in, Toni noticed that their pets were behaving oddly. In the beginning the cats acted uncharacteristically skittish. The male stayed under the house and yowled for the first several weeks. When Janice, the female, finally trekked into the bedroom, she jumped up to the foot of the bed, looked across the bedroom floor, and hissed at something unseen. Eventually she came to an agreement with the source of her aggravation, and ignored it. Even their small dog (named Kitty) seemed to be playing with something that wasn't there.

Toni and Greg just wrote these peculiar occurrences off to the new environment. However, the pets weren't the only ones who "saw" something extraordinary. Toni's thirteen-year-old daughter, Amanda, kept saying that she saw a strange cat in the house. A bluntly honest girl and oh-so-serious about what she saw, her parents had no reason to question her. They assumed a stray had somehow snuck in. The family scoured the house looking for the cat, but they found nothing.

As time passed, they all caught an occasional glimpse of the little cat darting from room to room. This inspired more pointless full-scale home searches. Over the years they began to see the cat more often and for longer periods. Smokey, as Toni now calls the mystery cat, began to show herself more frequently and more clearly to her "new family." She (Toni feels the cat is a she) appeared translucent most of the time. Over the last few years, they were able to see her plainly enough to tell that Smokey is tall and lean with short gray fur.

Everyone has been startled by Smokey in the laundry room at one time or another. Smokey has a special affinity for the clothes dryer. While someone is distracted, loading the dryer, the cat will suddenly materialize to check out the human activity. She stands up on her hind legs and puts her front paws on top of the dryer, and takes a good, long stretch. Then, *poof*, she's gone again, vanishing like the smoky mist her name implies. Toni never knows when Smokey will drop in; day or night, there's just no way to predict. Sometimes she disappears for weeks or even months at a time, only to reappear suddenly one day.

They have witnessed her playing with a variety of household objects. A bedside lamp covered with crystal prisms and spears makes an exciting interactive cat toy for the ghost cat. After all, when tapped with an invisible paw, it jingles and sometimes even tips over. When they hear the clinking of the crystal, they know it's playtime for Smokey.

"It will drive you nuts after a long day," Toni said.

Last winter, after many sleepless nights, they had to move the lamp to the living room. Their ghost cat had been playing with their blanket and the lamp, waking them throughout the night. From then on, if Smokey wanted to play with the lamp, she'd have to do it without the benefit of an audience.

The little phantom makes her presence known all over the house, including out on the Reeses' deck. In the early morning hours, when Greg goes out the back door on his way to work, he often sees the gray cat streaking across the deck, leaping up and disappearing in midair. Sometimes Greg can see her rush around under his feet before she disappears. When opening the back door, Toni said they will often sense that something is running out of the house between their legs, and a long gray tail can be clearly seen. Then suddenly, she is gone.

The outside cats simply look briefly at the specter and then ignore her. When the dog, Kitty, was younger, she often played for several minutes with an invisible animal. Toni assumes it was Smokey. But as the pooch has gotten older, she just perks up her ears and stares at something invisible from time to time.

Despite the fact that their friends think they are "bonkers," the family has become attached to Smokey. They almost consider her one of the family—although they do admit it can be unnerving when she's been on sabbatical for a while, and then suddenly returns and runs between their legs or in front of them.

Like any young live kitty, Smokey seems to have an excess of energy; she's never just lying around. "We believe she doesn't know she's dead," Toni said. "She's always having such a good time. She seems to be a happy cat."

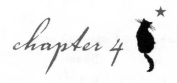

chapter 4

Fear Not, My Friend
COMFORTING ENCOUNTERS WITH BELOVED COMPANIONS

No heaven will not ever Heaven be
Unless my cats are there to welcome me.
—AUTHOR UNKNOWN

During their lives with us, cats act as our companions, caretakers, nurses, counselors, and even entertainers. And after that all-too-short life comes to an end, their absence leaves a huge hole in our lives. Nothing will ever be the same. You feel incomplete, empty.

But that spirit who loved you so unconditionally in life continues to love you despite that vast invisible gulf that divides you. Even in death, cats occasionally continue to play the role of the comforter when they return briefly for a formal good-bye, and sometimes even to give you permission to share your love with another cat.

Sometimes their return inspires their owner to develop a closer bond with God. Regardless of your faith, there's a close relationship between spirituality and death. Many of us believe, but we all hope, that something awaits us when we die. Some people believe that animals have no souls, and once they have shed their mortal shells, they cease to exist.

But in stories such as "Grungy's Greeting," some people come to understand firsthand that this is not true. They learn that their family's beloved cats are patiently waiting for them on the Other Side.

Warm up your tea and get out your tissues. It's time for some comfort and joy.

THE MOUTH THAT ROARED

Felicia was a born charmer. A seal point Siamese, she had stunning blue eyes and a voice that could penetrate a bank vault. Even though she was a petite girl, those who loved her often referred to her as "The Mouth that Roared." She would not be ignored.

She never met a person she couldn't bewitch with those hypnotic orbs. Her human owner, Maggie, often hired a handyman named Al. Every time he came over to make repairs on the air conditioner, he would say with a deep Southern accent, "Ma'am, can I have your cat?" Naturally, the response was always the same: No way. But Maggie couldn't blame Al for his infatuation with Felicia. He said she was the sweetest, prettiest cat he'd ever met. Whenever he left, Maggie practically had to frisk him and search his toolbox to make certain he didn't try to take her special cat.

Then one day Maggie noticed that Felicia's breathing appeared extremely rapid. Maggie put her in the car and rushed the cat to the animal hospital. Felicia's vet immediately put her in the oxygen cage. While the vet suspected allergies, an X-ray revealed scar tissue buildup in her lungs from feline asthma. Although Felicia visited her vet regularly, the absence of any classic outward symptoms, like coughing and difficulty in breathing, allowed her condition to go undiagnosed for some time.

They tried several treatments, but finally settled on AeroKat, an asthma inhaler especially designed for cats. It made her comfortable and happy for several years. Eventually Felicia's gorgeous eyes went dim and she went blind. The vet explained that Felicia was fighting not just the asthma but also her advancing age.

After doing some research, Maggie learned that most house cats actually adapt to loss of vision very well, provided no one ever moves the furniture or the items stacked around the room, as a change in layout will confuse the cat. Blind cats need predictable paths and a constant routine so they can find their way around. Everyone who knew Maggie found it amusing that it was Felicia who finally spurred Maggie on to keep a neat and tidy house (since Maggie had been known as something of a clutter bug over the years).

Felicia didn't face her blindness alone. She had a seeing-eye cat and bowl-sharer named Lola Felina, a twenty-four-pound red Maine Coon with six human years to her girth. When Felicia lost her sight, Lola began a new feeding routine. Maggie would put the food bowl down on the floor. Lola would have a two-bite appetizer of cat food, then go to the entrance of the kitchen and let Felicia in to eat as much as she wanted. Lola would then head off to the porch or the bedroom to wait; only when Felicia had eaten her fill would Lola return to finish her own meal.

Despite their obviously special relationship, Felicia had a little sanctuary called a Kitty Kube. It didn't matter whether or not Felicia occupied her Kube; Lola knew better than to try and venture inside. It was as if Felicia had put up a virtual off-limits sign. She never permitted Lola inside the Kube—ever. That didn't stop Lola from pushing Felicia's buttons. Lola would pass by while Felicia was napping, and with her large Maine Coon paw smack Felicia on the head. Poor blind Felicia would wake up, get her bearings, and wonder what the heck had happened. It appeared to give them both a "meow moment." Lola would always look at Maggie as if to say, "Hey, Mom, I didn't do anything." Lola just wanted Felicia to come out.

Felicia's little body finally gave out in early 2006. Three days after Felicia passed away, Maggie noticed Lola still going through the same feeding routine. Even today, Lola follows what Maggie believes has become ritual. Lola continues to take her two bites and waits by the entrance of the kitchen until an invisible Felicia has finished. Only then does Lola approach the food dish.

When Lola sits at the kitchen entrance, she follows something imperceptible with her eyes as she moves to the bowl, and her eyes continue to follow unseen Felicia as she leaves the kitchen for other parts of the house. Even though she's been gone for many months, Felicia still refuses to share her Kitty Kube. Lola continues to bully the phantom with a quick swipe to an invisible head. Maggie doesn't question or interfere on that one! She says simply, "It's beyond me."

A short time ago, a still broken-hearted Maggie finally healed enough to put out a couple of photographs of herself with Felicia. Until recently, she couldn't bear to even look at a picture of her beloved kitty, much less put out constant reminders of her. Still unable to look at her when she walked past the desk, Maggie placed a frame holding a photo of Felicia behind a framed photo of her nephew's wedding. That way it would be out in the open, but not in her face.

One day, while Maggie was having her morning tea, she realized that she was sitting face-to-face with Felicia's photo. Maggie's only roommates are her two cats, one living and one beyond the veil. After finding the picture out in front for the third time, she gave up and left it there. Even in death, "The Mouth that Roared" won't be ignored.

KOCHKA'S RETURN

Tricia Erickson was the last person in the world who expected to have a visitation from her departed cat. A self-proclaimed skeptic and a woman of faith, she boasts a degree in physics from MIT, has a responsible managerial position, and sits on corporate boards. She is the model of a person grounded upon rational, explainable events of this reality. She'd always dismissed other people's paranormal experiences as the result of an overactive imagination, or perhaps even an unstable mind.

Tricia grew to dearly love her cat, Kochka, whom she'd had for nearly seventeen years, but their relationship had started on a much more utilitarian level. The area mouse population had adopted the bedroom of then pregnant Tricia's home in the country. For weeks the mice had scurried around her bedroom, keeping her from sleeping. Tricia said it sounded like they were roller-skating on the uncarpeted bedroom floor. After two weeks of mouse conventions and sleepless nights, she decided to hire a pest-control expert. When she spoke to her Polish-speaking grandmother about getting a cat to control the mice, Grandmother said, "*Dastan kochka*," meaning, "Get a female cat." Tricia also wanted a kitten who would not have sense enough to be afraid of her three-foot-tall Great Pyrenees dog, Chuko.

Down at the Newport Animal Shelter in Newport, Rhode Island, Tricia scanned the assortment of sad faces looking back at her through the bars of their cages. A certain little tortoiseshell tabby with white feet caught her eye. Everyone in the shelter adored the kitten. She had such a sweet disposition that the shelter staff discouraged Tricia from even looking at other cats. The volunteer even convinced her that the kitten was younger than her actual eight months. Tricia named the tortoiseshell "Kochka" after what her grandmother had told her to get.

The kitten fit into the new family like the final piece of a jigsaw puzzle. Tricia breathed a sigh of relief when she introduced the small cat to gigantic Chuko. Although they never really hung out together, the dog and cat got along peacefully from the first day; fortunately, the giant dog treated the kitten with respect and never chased her. Per her job description, Kochka slept with Tricia and husband the first night, which she did throughout her life.

The little pest-control specialist took her job very seriously. In no time, she had reduced the mouse population to zero. They never returned. Tricia said for years after that Kochka missed chasing mice. Her desire to hunt was occasionally granted when Tricia took Kochka to visit her parents. At least for a short time she got to sneak-attack the resident mice. She seldom came back empty-mouthed.

One night, Tricia feared she'd never see her precious cat again after Kochka slipped out the door unseen. For one long, horrible week she searched for Kochka and called her name. Finally, the tortie returned. She shared no secrets of her wild adventures except for her quickly expanding waistline.

The two ladies, feline and human, bonded over their babies. Kochka slept in the crib with Tricia's infant son, Arvid. The boy's first word was not "Mama" or "Dada" but "Kitty."

When it came time for the cat to give birth, Kochka climbed on Tricia's lap, where the cat's water broke. She carried her cat to the birthing box, where Tricia stroked her throughout her labor. The little mama gave birth to two short-haired kittens with black-and-white markings.

Eventually Arvid went off to boarding school. During school breaks, Kochka would sleep with him. The rest of the time she spent her nights in Tricia's bed. Time moved so quickly. Suddenly Kochka was sixteen. Her kidneys began failing. Fortunately she had a caring veterinarian who worked with geriatric pets. He treated her with a special kidney diet and medication.

In the summer of 1986, Kochka was seventeen and a half, and had become very lethargic. Home on a break, Arvid took her to the vet for what they expected would be just another routine treatment of administering subcutaneous fluids. Tricia was shocked when her son called her at work to break the news: Kochka's kidneys could no longer support her body. The vet had said, "It is time to put her to sleep." She was going fast. To procrastinate meant the possibility of horrific suffering for her beloved pet. Tricia wanted to leave work to come home to hold her, but because she worked so far away from home, there simply wasn't time.

A few weeks after Kochka's passing, Tricia was sitting cross-legged on the living-room rug, playing her guitar. Unconsciously, she looked up, attracted by movement that had caught her eye. Conditioned to see her friend after seventeen long years, Tricia didn't think much about the tortoiseshell cat with tabby stripes and white feet who was trotting toward her. *It's only the cat*, she thought to herself, and started to strum her guitar again. *Only the cat*... until reality settled in and she remembered that she had just lost her friend.

"She walked toward me, between the table and the bookcase, as if she had just come from my son's bedroom," she said. "I will always remember that night." To this day, Tricia laments the fact she was unable to hold her cat as her life slipped away. Maybe that's why Kochka came back: to say goodbye. For that brief moment, Tricia got her precious Kochka back. Tricia said there was nothing scary about it. "I always hoped she would come again."

She added, "I am not a reader of ghost stories, and a belief in ghosts is not part of my religion. I do personally believe in animal souls, however. What would Heaven be without animals to love?"

Since that time she has had several more cats, and some of them have passed on. But Kochka's brief return was the only paranormal visit. "My vet believes our most bonded pets return to us," Tricia said. "He claims his first dog has come back to him in other animals. I have been looking for Kochka in other cats for years. She may be with me now in one of my clowder [group of cats]."

POOR LITTLE PUNKIN

Susan Hamrick of Lewisville, North Carolina, had a big black cat with green eyes whose mother was a Siamese and father was a "traveling salesman." She became heir to the cat after her sister rescued a pair of six-week-old black kittens from the local pound. The mischievous siblings proved to be more than she had bargained for. They zoomed around the house like overheated atoms. Up the curtains, down the hall; pouncing, jumping, and grabbing anything that moved or just looked like it might move at some point. In the end, Susan's mother took the female and Susan adopted the brother.

His middle name should have been Trouble, because he found himself in so many compromising situations. He'd play inside a shirt and get stuck down the sleeve. When he found himself trapped inside a locked closet or a closed cabinet, he'd howl like a coon dog until Susan freed him. He would climb to the top of the shower curtain or jump into the sock drawer when she turned her back. There was little that was beyond his investigation.

When Susan rescued him from each scrape, she exclaimed, "Poor little Punkin." She caught him in so many predicaments, the name stuck. Eventually she shortened it to just Punkin. Susan and Punkin grew very close. When he wasn't tail-deep in trouble, he would sleep in her arms.

For a feline he could carry on quite a conversation—and not just the basic meowing and purring. His Siamese ancestors provided him with a wide range of vocalizations, including specific feline words for specific situations. He called Susan "Mama." He'd call for "Mama" when he awoke from a nap and Susan wasn't around. When she answered his page, he'd run to find her. That Siamese voice certainly could carry, even through closed doors and down hallways. Punkin believed he should always be carried, his feet never touching the ground.

Because of her love for Punkin, Susan began collecting Boyd's plush cats. Soon, she had a wicker laundry basket filled with sixty Boyd's stuffed animals in her living room. Not surprisingly, her favorite was a black cat with a label that named it "Punkin Puss." But although they looked like cat toys, to her relief, over the six years she had her cat basket, her cats never showed any interest in them.

Punkin had the heart of a prankster. He loved going through pocket-books and heisting chewing gum, especially spearmint and peppermint. He'd carry the loot to the bedroom, open a dresser drawer, and deposit his ill-gotten gains until later retrieval for consumption. Yes, he chewed the gum. Susan had to convert her food storage to canisters with snap-on lids to dis-suade her determined diner, because he was able to open containers that had knobs. One of the worst scrapes he got into was when he opened the flour canister by mistake and then proceeded to turn it over. He was covered in flour. You can just guess what happened when Punkin tried to remove the flour from his flour-dusted fur. He looked like a papier-mâché cat. Needless to say, Punkin got a bath that time, much to his disgust! He would eat sugar, and he loved cotton candy. An underage drinker, he'd sneaked sips of beer and even coffee since he was a kitten. He got a huge buzz off those items. His pupils would dilate and he would roll around just like he'd had a big dose of catnip. Susan celebrated his birthday with white cake and icing.

But times were not always that carefree. Susan's marriage had been deteriorating for a long time. She had sunk down into a pit of depression, almost giving up completely. On occasion, she had even considered end-ing her misery—permanently. Looking into those green eyes, she worried about what would happen to her Poor Little Punkin if she were no longer around to care for him. "I realized he would probably go to the pound and that would be the end of him, too," Susan said. "He deserved better than that, and so did I."

So on July 4, she gathered up her courage and guts and declared an Independence Day for Punkin and herself, and left her marriage. They moved from apartment to apartment, but gradually, life only got better for Susan and Punkin.

Punkin grew into a muscular fifteen-pound panther of a cat. He loved to be around people. When someone new would come to the house, he greeted them at the door, as if to ask each guest, "Who are you? Did you bring me something? Is that a beagle I smell on your blue jeans?" Visitors would also get the obligatory breathalyzer and security hand check to see if they had recently eaten anything promising that they could share.

Although Punkin had developed a gourmet palate, he wouldn't pass up good ol' boy vittles, either. He loved hamburgers—grilled, not fried—and he had an affinity for French fries, cantaloupe, tacos, white cake, and, believe it or not, lima beans. As a matter of fact, he rarely turned up his nose at any food.

This feline kleptomaniac would steal Susan's jewelry and pens, and even rummage through guests' purses and swipe their chewing gum too—anything in the mint family. A literary type, he liked to chew on the words of others, or at least the paper they were written on. Punkin was famous for entertaining visitors with an exhibition of Susan's underwear.

A few weeks after Susan met her future husband, David, she introduced him to the cat. "If he didn't like Punkin, or vice versa, well, no great loss," Susan said. "Punkin and I were a package deal."

David had always had dogs until he met Susan. But Punkin not only won David over, he made him jump through several hoops in the process. A match made in Heaven, David provided Punkin with a ready lap for his snoozing comfort, and shared human treats with him as well. David and Susan married, and the three lived happily—for a while. Punkin's muzzle began fading to gray and David, whom Punkin had turned into an avid ailurophile, began to worry about the old cat's inevitable fate. He told Susan that they needed to get more cats so they'd have time to adjust before Punkin left them. They adopted a couple of kittens. Punkin promptly taught them his bad habits of opening cabinets and eating uncatlike foods.

At the time, Susan frequently traveled on business. When Punkin spied the packed luggage, he knew that Susan would be heading out on a trip the following morning. As she packed her clothes, she would find Punkin trying to pack himself, too. He spent the entire night sitting on the luggage, pouting. While she was gone, Punkin would wander from room to room, looking for Susan, calling "Mama." Although he wasn't Mama, David would do his best to fill in.

When she returned, Susan got the cold shoulder from Punkin. He would sit with his back toward her. If she picked up "He Whose Paws Should Not Touch the Ground," he wanted down. It wasn't until she gave him the proper tribute—proper, meaning in the form of Boar's Head oven-roasted turkey, or some shredded cheddar cheese, sharp not mild—that he deigned to let her hold him.

Punkin had reached the age of twenty before his health began to deteriorate. After his weight dropped drastically, the vet diagnosed him with hyperthyroidism, which they treated with Tapazole.

The end started while Susan and David were out of town. Susan began to experience heart palpitations. "I knew I was getting ready to hear some bad news about Punkin, and about a half-hour later, our pet sitter called with the news that Punkin was failing," Susan said.

The trip home seemed macabre and unreal. They drove straight to the vet's office to help Punkin cross over. Susan held him in her arms as the vet gave Punkin the shot to release him from his pain. After he had drawn his last breath, Susan's heart settled back to a normal beat. They cremated him and placed his ashes in an urn shaped like a black cat.

With the passing of Punkin, there was a great empty hole in their lives. Susan and David knew that Punkin's unique personality would be hard to replace. Life does go on, and some days were better than others. Susan had trouble sleeping; she missed cuddling her twenty-pound cat—like missing your childhood teddy bear or favorite blanket.

About six months after Punkin had crossed over, Susan had a dream that she was holding Punkin in her arms and walking through the house, just like she always used to do. But in the dream, instead of looking down and seeing his onyx urn, she saw everything through both her eyes and his eyes—from his perspective. She knew he'd always be with her and be a part of her. The dream was so real that she felt the weight of his body in her arms and the pulsing of his purr.

Susan felt a little strange the next morning. Then she walked into the living room. In the middle of the floor, Susan found the plush black Punkin Puss toy. Why that one in particular?

"I just know that he came to me," she said. "He left me a message and proof of his visit. I really knew right then that Punkin had been there with his old bad self, and in his own way told me to just remember him; he was always close by. So, my feeling is that he is still around. He just wanted to make sure I did not grieve too long about our parting."

A LITTLE BIT OF LOVE

The morning the Drake family left home started just as most trips do. Barbara Drake was trying to get her husband and two daughters packed and ready for a two-week trip to visit her in-laws on Biscayne Bay, Florida. While feeding the cats in the kitchen, Barbara noticed that Little, her elderly Persian mix, had vomited. Having had cats all her life, and realizing that most bodily eruptions are usually due to the occasional hairball, the episode didn't alarm her. Everything would be fine. After all, she was leaving their menagerie of cats and dogs with her oldest daughter, Brittanie, who couldn't travel with them because of her college classes. Barbara cleaned up the mess and continued with her trip preparations. They finally got out the door and boarded the airplane on time for their long flight from Kentucky to Miami.

Barbara had taken to calling her precious cat, Little, "Grizabella the Glamour Cat," the main character from the Andrew Lloyd Webber musical, *Cats*. In the play, inspired by T. S. Eliot's *Old Possum's Book of Practical Cats*, Grizabella had once been an elegant beauty, but her beauty had waned as she grew older. She started looking a bit scraggly and fell down on her luck. Like Grizabella, in her prime, Little had sported beautiful, long, silvery fur and green eyes. Although still beautiful in Barbara's eyes, at twenty-three, Little was showing her advanced age, and was fading away like a gray mist.

When Barbara arrived in Florida, her mother-in-law, Nicole, told her Brittanie had left a frantic message for her to call home immediately.

When she reached her daughter, she learned that Little was really sick— acute renal failure (ARF). She had spent most of the day at the vet's office. Ten years earlier, she had been diagnosed with the early stages of kidney disease. At that time, the vet had recommended managing her condition with a low-protein diet formulated for cats with failing kidneys. It had worked successfully until that day. But ARF translated into the end stages of the disease. Her vet had put Little on IV fluids for the entire day, hoping that lactated ringer solutions would flush the toxins out of her kidneys, allowing her to rally. After a good flush, some cats with ARF can go on to enjoy many more days, weeks, or maybe even months of a reasonable quality of life. With fingers crossed, he sent Little home for the night.

But first thing the following next morning, Barbara received another call from Brittanie. Little's condition had not improved. She had a long conversation with the vet. Little's body was dehydrated. The kitty refused to eat or drink on her own. Her ancient kidneys had given up the ghost. To spare her from further suffering, Barbara agreed that they should help Little pass over.

"That's a decision I wouldn't wish on anyone, even if they were at home dealing with the issue in person," Barbara said.

Little passed peacefully in the loving arms of Brittanie. Shortly after Little passed, around 10:00 A.M., Barbara went out to her in-laws' backyard and sat on the seawall. Nature's beauty surrounded her. Below her, waves gently rolled over the sandy beach. In the distance, the ocean and sky met in a hazy horizon. Barbara saw none of that. She sat alone and cried. Little had been part of their lives and family for twenty-three years.

Homes dotted the beach, but they were spread apart. Despite the distance, Barbara could hear a radio playing popular tunes. One in particular caught her ear; it was "Memory," the haunting song performed by Grizabella in the musical production of *Cats*. She sat there for a long time, grieving her loss.

That first long day and night passed. Barbara tried to enjoy herself in Miami. They had a full schedule with her relatives, shopping and sampling restaurants. They also spent a lot of time in Nicole's backyard pool and on the seawall. The activity was good therapy to treat the gloom that had settled over their holiday. But nothing could fill the enormous hole left in their souls.

The second day after Little had passed, Barbara once again sat alone on the seawall. Again, in the distance a radio played "Memory." The notes pierced Barbara like Cupid's arrow gone awry. Alone, a half a country from home, Barbara wept for her own lost Little Grizabella.

"To hear 'Memory' played at that time of the morning, just like the radio had played it the same time the day before, was just too cruel," she said. "Why was I hearing that song at one of the lowest moments of my life?"

She wanted to jump off that seawall and let her tears blend with the salty water. Sobbing, she returned to the house and told Nicole what had happened.

But Nicole had a different take on it. She said, "Don't you understand? You had a visit from Little. She was telling you not to blame yourself." Referring to Grizabella's ascension to be reborn in the last scene of the play, Nicole said, "She's in a wonderful place now."

"I hadn't thought of it that way," Barbara said. "I was so tangled up in my own grief; I thought this was the Universe's way of punishing me for going on vacation when Little needed me the most." After much contemplation, Barbara adopted her mother-in-law's perspective. "I am somewhat of a skeptic, but I want to believe that Little came back to say good-bye," she said. "While I will never recover from being absent when Little passed away, her loving memory is helping me heal. Every time I think of her, I know that she's feeling our deep love for each other, which will never die."

A SCRATCH FROM THE PAST

Nancy Fulton of Dallas, Texas, always loved and cherished her cat, Trixie. Despite her mischievous streak, the cat was afraid of most people. Nancy never knew the reason. She did know the kitten had never been mistreated because she owned Trixie's mother, a Russian Blue named Gracie, and so had known Trixie since her birth. Nancy had fallen in love with the little kitten with pale gray stripes. In the right light, her smooth coat appeared pure white.

Nancy found the kitten's shyness and vulnerability endearing. From the ring of the doorbell until the intruders left, Trixie would hide under the bed. Although Trixie was timid with strangers, she was bold when she wanted loving. She would sidle up next to Nancy, rub her against her legs, and purr. Like most kittens, Trixie loved pretending to be the great hunter, chasing pieces of string or anything that moved.

Trixie had a long list of charming qualities, but she had one naughty habit. She owned a compete arsenal of sharpened weapons at the end of her paws and she knew how to use them. Despite the fact that Nancy had provided Trixie with a cardboard scratching pad—which she used regularly—whenever she walked past one particular chair in the living room, she loved to give it a thorough ripping. Nancy believes Trixie especially enjoyed tearing into the cloth-upholstered recliner either because it was first "in line," or because she liked the rough fabric.

Whenever Nancy caught her in the act, she'd yell, "No!" Trixie needed no more prompting. She'd stop immediately. There'd be plenty of time to finish when Mama wasn't around. And when the coast was clear, she would return to her chair for a minute and then stop, satisfied that her muscles were toned and her nails honed. With its stringy fabric and exposed stuffing, the chair looked as if it had exploded.

In 1992, Trixie died at the ripe old age of seventeen. One evening about a year after she died, Nancy and her daughter, Jan, were sitting in the living room, talking. Nancy hadn't had the heart to bring another cat into her house, and she certainly hadn't been able to recover, replace, or even move Trixie's raggedy old recliner. The women's conversation paused for a few minutes. With no television or radio to disturb the peace, the home sat absolutely silent. After a few moments, they both heard something that sounded just like Trixie scratching on the chair. Both women stared at the chair and then at each other.

"We didn't know what to think, except that maybe it *was* Trixie and she just wanted me to know she was still around—in spirit."

It appears that Trixie—ever her tricksy self—showed up one last time to give her recliner a final nail treatment. Even though Nancy found the whole incident a "little weird" she felt comforted by the brief visits. Had Trixie continued to show up to scratch the old chair, Nancy would have left it in its place of honor in the living room. She did, after all wait more than ten years to replace the raggedy old recliner with something a little more presentable. Nancy laughed, "Now if Trixie wants to scratch on something, she'll just have to find a scratching post in the sky."

SPOOKY'S LITTLE SCREEN

As a child growing up in Connecticut, Jan Beardsley-Blanco loved her great-aunt's three-panel Chinese screen. The ornately carved teak screen stood six feet tall. Not only did the screen hold great sentimental value, but it was also a family heirloom with a colorful history. Jan's great-aunt had brought it home from China, where she and her husband had worked as missionaries. The piece later went to Jan's mother, and so had been in her family since the mid-1960s when Jan was only five or six.

That was also about the time that Jan's childhood cat Spooky died at the ripe old age of twenty-three. One day in the early 1940s, Spooky had wandered up to their farm as a young kitten, liked what he saw, and stayed with the family for the next twenty-three years. Jan described him as just an ordinary black cat, one of five or six cats in the family. In the morning Jan's mother would put out milk and bread for the cats to eat. The cats would go out and hunt for their meat during the day. Spooky, however, hung out near Middi the dog's bowl, and would raid Middi's food if he hadn't killed enough to satisfy himself.

On a typical day, Spooky had a very full schedule: He ate a hearty breakfast of milk and bread, after which he went hunting. He'd return later in the day, eat the dog's food, sleep, hunt, eat, and go to bed. He worked very hard at being a cat.

In addition to being accomplished in his chosen vocation of rodent control, Spooky was part marriage counselor. Spooky liked anyone who would give him a good neck scratch, but Jan's dad claimed the black cat as his. Unfortunately for the family, Jan's mother was totally consumed by the card game of bridge. One night they couldn't get her to change the subject to anything else but bridge. Dad wanted to discuss his day, but as often happened, the topic quickly reverted back to cards. As Spooky made his way through the kitchen, frustrated, Dad picked up the black cat, and told Spooky all about his day. From then on Dad had an escape from his wife's obsession with cards. His little talks with Spooky probably saved his sanity.

The years passed, and in 1995, Jan and her siblings had to move their mother to a nursing home. As they were dividing up the last items in the apartment, Jan staked her claim to her great-aunt's teak screen from the Far East, and unknowingly, on Spooky.

After they unloaded all of her mother's stuff, Jan propped up her great-aunt's screen in the dining room until she could figure out where she would open it up for display. She could even look at it while she cooked through the screen door that kept the cats out of the kitchen. The teak screen stood in the dining room, undisturbed, for a while. Three weeks after she had propped the teak screen up, Jan was standing nearby, absently looking at it, when she watched a black blob fly out of it. A picture immediately appeared in her mind that the blob was Spooky, and he had moved in for good.

That night, she told her husband Sonny they had a ghost cat named Spooky. Sonny was noncommittal. "Of course, we do."

Sonny still remains skeptical, but Jan's not the only one who sees it. One of her live cats has started going to the door of the kitchen/dining room and talking to Spooky. At least two or three times a week one of the cats will converse with the ghost cat.

One night in February 2004, three or four of Jan's cats came uncharacteristically out of the kitchen fuzzed up and disturbed. Jan soon found out that her mother had just passed away. Jan doesn't know if Spooky hung around her mother's house after he died, but the ghost cat did leave Jan's house for a four-day sabbatical starting with the day Jan's mother died. For the next three or four nights none of the cats followed his or her usual ritual of saying good-night to Spooky. Jan believes that when her mother died, she came by for Spooky. But the black cat was more bonded to Jan and her dad. At the first opportunity he returned to Jan's, where he continues to intrigue her living cats.

Her ebony tortoiseshell cat, Grace, goes to the door and talks to Spooky every night. Jan has no doubt that when the cats go to the screen door and fix their eyes on a single spot, or their eyes track something invisible to humans, they're looking for Spooky.

DYNA-LIGHT

Jerry and Kim Thornton were living in a two-story townhouse in Glendale, Arizona, when what they thought was a cute little female kitten came into their lives. Their townhouse was the perfect home for a family with cats. It had a large enclosed patio where the cat could go and sleep safely in the sunshine and fresh air. Outside the patio, the occasional stray would wander past.

The Thorntons' big, burly construction worker neighbor had rescued the little champagne-and-cinnamon tabby in some bushes outside their home, but couldn't keep her, so he had offered the three-month-old kitten to the Thorntons. Both Jerry and Kim really liked cats, so they took in the little stray. They named her Dinah after Alice's cat in *Alice in Wonderland.*

"We thought she was very tomboyish (for a female)," Jerry said.

He was right. When Kim took Dinah to be spayed, the vet suggested they reconsider. Instead they changed his name to Dynamite and had *him* neutered. Besides, the name Dynamite matched his personality. That was in 1984.

Dyna was a lovable little kitty, and wanted to be around Jerry and Kim all the time. He loved snoozing in their laps. He slept with them, protecting his humans from the evil toes lurking beneath the bed covers. He was a very social cat, and would rub his face against their heads, getting up close to purr in their faces. Jerry and Dyna were especially close "buds." They'd sit together on the couch and watch television, and Dyna often rode around on Jerry's shoulder.

They had lived happily together for a year when Dyna suddenly became ill. Suddenly one night he started having trouble breathing. They immediately rushed him to the emergency clinic. After an examination, the vet uttered those horrible words: "Dyna has a lymphoma." At the time, lymphoma had no cure and no real treatment. It was an utterly hopeless situation. That night, still in a state of shock, they had him euthanized. When they arrived home, Jerry lit a candle in memory of his absent friend.

Later that night as Jerry and Kim watched *Doctor Who* on television, Jerry glanced over at the flickering candle, and noticed a cat with Dyna's exact markings right outside the window. Then the cat turned; for a brief second Jerry saw the tip of the tail as the cat ran away. A strange feeling overwhelmed him, making the hair on the back of his neck stand up. Somehow Jerry knew that the cat in the window was Dyna, coming to say good-bye.

Twenty years have gone by since Dyna's death, and they have lit their memorial candle for every pet they have lost since then—and there have been several. A few of them have even dropped by for just a brief moment to say a last farewell.

SNORKEL'S ESCORT

Karen Commings always loved cats. While she was growing up in Harrisburg, Pennsylvania, her parents allowed her to have cats off and on. After she left for college, she finally got a cat of her own. The woman living in the apartment next to her gave her an eight-week-old black fluff ball. For three months after Karen took him in, the kitten didn't have a formal name, although her roommate used to call him a litany of nicknames, including Snorkel Puss. Snorkel just stuck.

When Karen and Snorkel lived on their own, they developed a special relationship during those quiet moments at home. Like any devoted couple they had conversations at the end of the day. She spoke to him as she would to a friend. He answered her with a multitude of sounds that he would string together in what she imagined to be cat sentences.

Snorkel used to run to meet Karen when she came home. Although he wasn't a lap cat, he slept with her. When she fed him Karen had to stay with him or he would walk away from his food. He played fetch with her. When she had company, Snorkel would sit on the floor in "meatloaf" position and listen to them talk, moving his ears back and forth so as not to miss a single word.

Because she didn't want Snorkel to be alone during the day, Karen tried to find him a feline friend. The pairings never worked out. In those days, Karen didn't know very much about feline behavior, and in retrospect, she didn't make compatible choices. Snorkel, however, was the main problem. Any cat, even one half his size, intimidated him, so he always hid from the other cat, waiting for Karen to come to her senses and find a home for the intruder. When she went away to graduate school, Snorkel stayed with her sister. Karen was surprised to hear that Snorkel actually made friends with his new feline roommate, six-year-old Tigger, her sister's amiable gray tabby. Something else surprised the sisters: chatty Snorkel taught Tigger to talk. Prior to Snorkel's appearance, Tigger couldn't even meow. When she opened her mouth, she emitted only a faint hiss.

After Karen graduated, Snorkel returned to live with her, 400 miles away from from his buddy, Tigger. About a year later, Tigger died. Shortly after his friend's death, Snorkel became gravely ill. During his four-week ordeal, Snorkel endured examinations, tests, and treatments, but vets were at a loss for a diagnosis.

One night during his illness, as Karen drifted off to sleep, something jolted her awake. She looked at the window across from her bed, and up above the curtain rod lay Tigger, curled up in a ball, hovering in midair.

"Tigger!" Karen whispered. Just then the hovering tabby stood up and began walking toward the bed. As Tigger came closer, she simply vanished.

About two weeks later, a scab formed on Snorkel's shoulder. The vet removed it and sent it to a pathologist for testing. The report came back the following week: Snorkel had contracted a rare and debilitating bronchial fungus called cryptococcosis. The condition was contagious to humans, and at the time there was no effective treatment. The vet recommended Snorkel be euthanized and Karen reluctantly agreed. As painful as the decision was, she knew that euthanasia would spare her cat more suffering.

Snorkel and Tigger had the rare opportunity to share a friendship that transcended life and death. To this day, when she recalls seeing Tigger hovering near the window, Karen wonders if Tigger came back for Snorkel, maybe as a guide to show him the way.

PRISSI AND GAIETY

In 1972, Carolyn Vella and her husband John J. McGonagle absolutely fell tail over paws in love with their new blue point Siamese—their first pedigreed cat. They named their new four-month-old kitten Priscilla, and soon shortened it to Prissi.

To Carolyn, there was nothing more elegant than a Siamese with its beautiful, light-colored fur blending into a darker shade on the points. Prissi's lithe, muscular body and her triangular face and shockingly blue, slanted eyes just seemed to define the word "cat." She would curl up in Carolyn's lap, or spoon right up next to Carolyn in bed. Athletic and kittenish, Prissi would perch on top of the fireplace mantle, walking among the statuary without ever harming a thing.

But after thirteen years, the love affair suffered a cruel blow. Their vet uttered those incomprehensible words: "Prissi is suffering from advanced-stage mammary cancer." In a desperate attempt to save Prissi, John called the cancer center at the University of Pennsylvania School of Veterinary Medicine. They scheduled her appointment for the next day. Shortly after the call, her condition began to deteriorate. Again, John called the doctors at Penn State, who instructed him to bring her in immediately. But it was too late for Prissi; she died on the way to the cancer center.

The trip back home with the lifeless Prissi seemed to last forever. When he returned home, John put Carolyn to bed with a box of Kleenex and enough Valium to stun a horse. The next morning, John dragged his despondent wife out of bed and took her to the home of a Himalayan breeder who had a litter of four-month-old kittens.

One of the kittens really tried to convince Carolyn and John to take her, putting on quite a show from her cage. This particular kitten—a seal tortie point Himalayan (a breed created by breeding Siamese to Persians)—was vying for their attention in any number of ways. She climbed to the cage top and hung like a bat; she batted around her catnip toys; the little blue-eyed clown made Carolyn laugh at a time when she thought she would never laugh again. Needless to say, that enthusiastic kitten sold herself. Ironically, they brought home their new kitten on the same day Prissi would have gone into surgery. They gave her the registered name of Priscilla's Bouquet, in honor of Prissi.

John told Carolyn they needed a little gaiety in the house. So they gave the new kitten the call name "Gaiety." Unlike her predecessor, Gaiety has a calm, Persian personality. Gaiety was quieter and less elegant—more a friend than a cat. Once a month or so, she would go nuts and blast around the house. Gaiety grew into a beautiful cat with rounded eyes of vibrant blue. Her long fur, which was creamy in color, ran into brownish-black points with speckled spots of cream and red. She had a short body, short tail, and short, soft ears—not the slightest bit athletic.

John and Carolyn decided to exhibit her in The International Cat Association (TICA) shows as a household pet. Within a few months John and Carolyn took Gaiety to her first cat show to compete in the kitten class. She really enjoyed the show (except for having to endure her show bath), especially the hotel and stealing part of John and Carolyn's sandwiches during the lunch break. She was a real diva in the show hall, and ultimately achieved the highest title of Supreme Grand Master in TICA.

During that first show, John and Carolyn sat front row, center, like proud parents watching their kid's two-line performance in her first play. The judge removed Gaiety from her cage and placed her on the judging stand. At that point, Gaiety turned, found her humans, and maintained eye contact. For that one brief moment, the cat on the judging stand physically morphed into the late Prissi. John said one second she was Gaiety with her long hair and flat face, the next second she had transformed into Prissi—her eyes, her stance, and her short Siamese coat. Shocked, John and Carolyn made brief eye contact with each other out of the corner of their eyes but didn't say anything—at least not right away. Neither John nor Carolyn realized the other had also witnessed the transformation.

"Honestly, I didn't think that Carolyn saw it—but I did," John said. "It took a while for each of us to raise it with the other." John says he often thinks about that moment on the judging stand. "I think Prissi came back to show me that she'll never really leave me, as long as I remember her as being part of my life."

Carolyn says, "I think animals do this sort of thing for their own reasons. I do know that when a cat passes, they do not leave immediately. I have seen a cat from the corner of my eye in another room after it had been gone for a few weeks. I do know that it taught me that our loved ones do not really leave us, but are still with us. Physical death does not make the difference we think it does."

OMAR'S LIGHT

Omar's light and life was a candle that burned briefly but oh, so bright. Sonia Vicknair, from Louisiana, got her kitten when he was four months old, but lost him to heart disease at the tender age of eighteen months. Sonia bought the shaded silver Persian with the intention of showing him in cat shows in the premier class, a special class for altered cats. She showed him a few times, but when she learned he had a heart murmur, she stopped showing him because she didn't want to cause him any undue stress. She figured the trauma of all the bathing and traveling and just being around all those other cats would exacerbate his condition.

Omar was a shy guy. One might even say the shaded silver Persian was a little bit of a coward. When visitors came calling, he'd head for cover beneath the safety of the bed. After Sonia's three-year-old grandson, Aaron, started coming over regularly, Omar would eventually emerge, but only to watch the activity from a safe distance. The minute the guests would leave, he'd return to his place in the living room. Sonia called him a "silly boy."

He was quite the chatterbox and enjoyed talking to Sonia and her husband, Vick. His voice was unique from other felines, akin to a squeaky hum.

Sonia would ask Omar how his day went, and tell him what happened during her workday. Omar always had an answer to her questions, and usually added a point or two of his own. They could carry on a conversation for some time.

Omar loved his comb; when Sonia took it out, the purring began. Unlike most cats, he adored having his tummy groomed. He'd lie on his back, go completely limp, and close those huge green eyes as Sonia combed his belly. He was always up for a petting session. He'd hold his head up so she could stroke him from his little nose to his forehead. He never walked away from an opportunity for some attention.

But all that beautiful, long fur came at a price. He spent hours lying with his belly pressed against the cool tiled floor in the foyer. He liked ice cubes. The sound of ice clinking against a water glass would bring him front and center. Omar just couldn't resist ice water; in Sonia's house it was impossible to drink something cold that hadn't first been baptized by a Persian paw. Whenever Sonia or Vick would bring out an icy drink, Omar would dunk his foot in the water and fish out the ice cubes with his claws. Sometimes Sonia would fill up a plastic bowl with water and a few ice cubes just to indulge him and his passion for his frozen toy.

A mighty hunter at heart, Omar spent hours stationed in front of the window, watching the birds and bugs playing outside. When he spied something he wanted to turn into dinner, he'd come to attention and chatter at his potential prey. After all, he was the most accomplished bug killer in the house. And as any hunter knows, the best hunting spot is the highest point. Rather than leaping from level to level of the five-foot-tall cat tree, Omar would climb to the top level of the tree and lay there on his side, dangling his front feet over the edge.

Since Sonia didn't provide him with live game, he'd while away the hours watching kitty videos. Cat videos were relatively new at the time, and he had a whopping four tapes in his library. He was a big fan of the Animal Planet network; he especially loved watching birds and bugs taking flight. On Saturday and Sunday mornings, he'd station himself next to the VCR, waiting for Sonia to play a tape. Bird- or insect-like movement on television always captured his attention.

After dinner, when the kitchen had been returned to a semblance of order, Omar would wait by the closet until Sonia got a toy for them to play with. He especially loved a toy that resembled a brown striped ferret. He'd toss it up in the air, wrestle with it, rabbit-kick it, and sleep with it like it was a teddy bear. His motto: No play, no peace.

In the morning, when the alarm tried to jar Sonia to life, Omar would ease up alongside of her so she could pet him and wake up a little bit. Always the helpful boy, he'd supervise Sonia as she got ready for work each morning. He'd take over the entire bathroom sink while Sonia attempted to apply her makeup. At breakfast time, he'd jump up on the table to check out what she was eating. Occasionally, he'd surprise her by approaching and giving her a big powerful Persian head butt. Sonia knew he had paid her a high compliment. Other times, he'd rub against her legs (but unlike other cats, he wasn't a leg-weaver).

Eventually, Omar's time and heart ran out. Four years ago, Vick came home from work to find Omar lying on the bedroom floor, the little ferret toy nearby. Before Sonia had left for the office, Omar had had a great final morning—jumping from the floor to the bed and down again, and throwing his little ferret up in the air. Sonia said there was no doubt in her mind that he left this world at the snap of a finger. She and Vick had him cremated, and they keep Omar's urn on the fireplace mantle.

Early one morning shortly after his death, Sonia was standing next to the kitchen table when she felt a cat rubbing back and forth against her leg. When she bent down to pet the cat, she was shocked to find nothing there. She looked around to see if one of her other cats was nearby, but they were spread out around the house. Not one was close by.

She thought, *No, this can't be . . . things like this don't happen to me.*

When she actually checked out where the other cats were, they were sleeping, and looked up at her with bleary eyes. It couldn't have been one of them because they were too relaxed to have just laid down. Some forty-five minutes later, in front of the bathroom sink, she felt the same mysterious sensation of someone's head butting up against her leg. It happened yet again a few days later, while she was putting on her makeup. And again, when Sonia looked down, there was no cat to be seen.

She felt no fear, just a sense of calm happiness. She knew it was Omar, coming back one last time to let her know that he was okay. He never returned for an encore appearance.

SOOZ'S SHADOW

Her registered name with championship titles was GC BW Kiriki Washushe, DM, but Ann Segrest called her Sooz. She was a pedigreed Korat, a breed that originated from Thailand, and Ann's very first show cat. Crowned the Cat Fanciers' Association's Best Korat of 1992, she was everything a Korat should be. She had luminous green eyes and a silver-blue coat that shone like freshly minted silver.

Like most Korats, she was playful and smart, but not always the easiest cat to get along with, especially if you were her feline mom. Like many daughters, she was on the outs with her Korat mother once she became an adult, but she did like her sister. Sooz was not particularly shy; in fact, she was quite willful. She was known to show her displeasure to her human mom as well; Sooz once sunk her teeth into Ann's forearm while getting her claws trimmed. Since Ann had been cutting her nails for years without incident, she concluded that she hadn't been paying enough attention to her while she worked on Sooz's front feet.

While Sooz did well at cat shows, like most Korats, she preferred to be at home, in charge of everything. She tended to hiss at the judges, but she still behaved well enough to earn many awards at shows. Eventually, Sooz retired from the show ring, content to stay home while Ann traveled and showed other cats. Sooz's retirement was simply a life of leisure. She had several litters of kittens. Her daughter, granddaughter, and great-granddaughter were such beautiful Korats that Ann kept them.

When Sooz was only about ten years old, too young for a breed that can live to be eighteen to twenty years old, Ann returned from a cat show to learn that Sooz had died of unknown causes. Shortly after her cat's death, Ann got up in the middle of the night to go to the bathroom. In the hall she spied the silhouettes of three distinct cats. When she turned the light on, she found only two cats there: Sooz's granddaughter and great-granddaughter. The two living cats were simply hanging out together. There was no sign of a third cat.

"When I first saw the apparition, I had not one second's doubt but that it was Sooz," Ann said. "I had other cats around the house, but they were asleep elsewhere."

Ann saw Sooz out of the corner of her eye several times after that. When she looked directly at the apparition, she saw nothing. Sooz continued to appear around the house for several months. About a year and a half later, Sooz's daughter, Mouse, died. Sadly, she was close to the same age that Sooz had been when she passed. After Mouse's death, Ann never saw Sooz's ghost again. Ann believes that Sooz must have waited around for Mouse so they could leave together.

LITTLE JOE'S PORTRAIT

While many may dismiss visits from departed pets as wishful thinking, Anita Morris actually has the pictures to prove it. She operates a feral cat refuge in Oregon. Several years ago, she had a particular favorite cat named Little Joe. A very large smoke-and-white long-haired cat with a Charlie Chaplin mustache, his look was quite distinctive; he was nothing at all like any of the others in the colony.

Little Joe was a feral kitty who showed up in Anita's yard, the product of a cat-collecting neighbor who found himself hip-deep in kittens. A handful of unaltered cats quickly grew into a colony of a hundred. Before long, hungry feral cats showed up in the yard of Anita and her husband. There were so many cats that the Morris family had to hire a professional trapper; once they caught the ferals, they took them down to animal services.

After condemning several sets of wild cats to the shelter, they simply couldn't do it again. They couldn't send any more of those precious animals to their deaths just because they were born feral. Anita did some research and contacted the Feral Cat Coalition. They taught her about a new concept called Trap, Neuter, Release (TNR), in which feral cats are humanely trapped, spayed or neutered, and then returned to their territory. Studies have shown that removing feral cats simply leaves a void that other freely reproducing cats will fill in even greater numbers. Returning altered cats to their territory prevents other cats from moving in, and because the cats can't reproduce, the population reduces itself over time. This humane form of animal control was the way that Anita and her husband wanted to go.

Little Joe was in the first batch of cats trapped and neutered. They also called him "The Mayor." A Maine Coon mix, and weighing in at about twelve pounds, he hefted enough bulk to be a first-class bully, but he wasn't one. He had the gentle heart of the Maine Coon, and easily could have also been called "The Ambassador." His generosity around other cats immediately endeared him to Anita. When a new cat would show up, he'd take them around and give them the grand tour, as if to say, "Here's the food dish. And over there is the water bowl. And they're always full. And this is a safe place. No one will hurt you here."

According to Anita, Little Joe exuded love—and he was also a goofball. He had a habit of stealing acorns from an oak tree a few houses down the road. At home, he'd line them up on the steps like he was bringing Anita a gift. She'd store his nutty little treasures in a coffee can, and when he wanted to play with them, he'd dig his paw around and pull them out with his claws. Then he'd bat the nuts around and try to get the other cats to play with him. Anita called the game "Nutball."

Although he was feral, he had a friendly, trusting soul. Anita could get him so distracted in a game of Nutball that she could reach over and pick him up by the scruff and set him in her lap. She'd hold him and he'd purr as she was petting him, until another feral appeared in the yard. He'd jump down as if to say, "She made me do that. I really didn't want her petting me. "

Every morning and evening Anita fed the cats. Meals consisted of whatever Anita and her husband could afford. The cats always got both dry and wet food. Regardless of what the ferals found on the menu, dinnertime always got Little Joe excited. He would give head bumps, and the cats would rub up against each other, purring and making happy-cat noises, as if to say, "Mom's here with the food." Every day when Anita came home, Little Joe would be right there. He would visit as Anita watered her daylilies.

One May morning in 1999—three years after Little Joe had first shown up—Anita looked across the street. To her horror, she saw Little Joe's lifeless form in the middle of the road. He'd been hit by a car. They buried Little Joe a few minutes later in the backyard under the rhododendrons where he'd loved to sleep. They ordered a marker with the Ecclesiastes passage, "To everything there is a season . . ."

As they stared at the loose dirt covering his new grave, Anita was dismayed to realize that she had never taken any photographs of Little Joe, or any of the other ferals, for that matter. Until that moment, pictures had never been particularly important to Anita. Now she realized how vital it was to have photos of everything and everyone that is special to you. She had mistakenly assumed that Little Joe would always be around. All that was left of him now were her memories.

She grabbed a camera, dropped in a fresh roll of film, and took pictures of everyone, including some of the cats sitting next to the food dish. It took a couple of days to get the film processed, but when the photos came back from the lab, Anita and her husband shuffled through the photographs. They froze as they looked at the first shot of four cats next to Little Joe's beloved food bowls. Although the rest of the cats looked normal and solid, the center cat, a big white-and-gray cat with a Charlie Chaplin moustache, had a crisp outline, but a transparent look. There he was, in living color.

Anita screamed, "Oh my God. There he is! There he is!" It had to be Little Joe, because none of the other ferals resembled him. Through that picture and another remarkable image of Little Joe lounging next to the dishes, he will remain alive forever to Anita Morris.

She wanted an enlargement of Little Joe's photos, but couldn't trust the negatives to just anyone, so she took them to the Kodak lab. The processor called and said they'd discovered a problem with the negative. The woman told Anita that one of the cats looked like a ghost.

"That's because he *is* a ghost," Anita told her.

"Oh."

The conversation ended abruptly.

Anita has since learned that Native Americans believe your soul remains nearby for four days. She believes that could be why Little Joe appeared in the two photographs. Although he never appeared in another picture, Anita occasionally feels his presence. People who have lost pets have been comforted by the proof the picture provides—that Little Joe existed after his death. "Without a doubt, this world is temporary," Anita said. "The spirit is immortal."

MAKING AN IMPRESSION

Andy, a poet and writer living in West Yorkshire, England, believes he was born for many reasons, but among them was to save the runt of one particular litter of kittens. He named her Dolly. He knew from experience that runts usually live much shorter lives. Dolly, however, got the last laugh; she lived to the ripe old age of nineteen.

Andy and Dolly grew up together. Andy was only twenty-one when the tiny tabby kitten entered his life. When he said good-bye to her, he had recently celebrated his thirty-ninth birthday. When the little ball of fur came into his life in 1987, Margaret Thatcher was the prime minister of England, and new episodes of the original *Doctor Who* were still being broadcast on English television. There wasn't a public Internet, and only the rich yuppies could afford box-size mobile phones.

The slender little "moggie," an affectionate English term for mixed-breed cat, was always healthy and well-mannered. She never stole food, and Andy said she didn't misbehave—although she would beg for crisps (potato chips). Dolly was a great listener, sitting in Andy's lap or lounging behind his head on the sofa for hours on end. She seldom meowed, but said everything she needed to say with her eyes or the flicking of her tail. Dolly seemed to know whenever Andy had had an upsetting day, and would sit with him to console him. Andy thought of Dolly as a daughter to him, not a pet.

The alpha cat of six, she disliked her other feline companions. She'd swipe at the others when they did anything she didn't like. Needless to say, the other cats avoided her as much as possible. She preferred the company of her human. She'd venture downstairs occasionally to join Andy and his partner Dave on the sofa. She enjoyed watching television, favoring shows that involved cats. She seemed bizarrely interested in cartoons. She seldom went outside, preferring, especially in her later days, to stick close to the rooms upstairs.

About ten o'clock in the evening Dolly would start demanding that Andy come to bed. At that appointed hour, she'd start pacing at the top of the stairs. When Andy would appear at the bottom of the stairwell, she would elicit a silent meow. But feline words would also accompany the ritual, which Andy assumed to be feline swearing if he didn't head for the bedroom quickly enough to suit Dolly. Once everyone was comfortably in bed, Dolly would settle in next to Andy's pillow.

The week before Dolly died, Andy took her to the vet for a checkup. The vet said she was in amazing shape for a nineteen-year-old cat. She had healthy joints and happy kidneys, but he kept her on her medication for hyperthyroidism. Shortly after she returned from the vet with a clean bill of health, she suddenly went off her food. This time the vet found that her gums had been hiding an abscess. Andy decided to treat her with antibiotics and force-feeding. Sadly, her ancient body simply couldn't fight the infection. As she began to slip away, Andy and Dave took turns holding her. They kissed her and recalled all the wonderful stories they could remember. It was as if they were midwifing her death. She died in Andy's arms at exactly midnight, just as the summer solstice arrived.

About twenty minutes after she died, Dolly began to purr—but the purring came not from the empty shell that had once been Dolly, but instead originated from the empty space a few inches from her body. And she was smiling.

Later, Andy wrapped Dolly in a shroud made from a clean towel, for her final visit to the vet. He chose a casket and worded the inscription for the plaque: DOLLY, 1987–2006, MUCH LOVED & MISSED. Then came the hard part—handing her over to the vet for the cremation.

The weekend after she died a photo was taken of Andy at a friend's house. Although orbs have never shown up in pictures of him before, that night, orbs hovered above his head.

The first time Andy saw Dolly's ghost was the day her body was cremated. He only caught a glimpse of her sitting on the storage boxes at the end of the bed. He burst into tears, told her how he missed and loved her. But as quickly as that moment came, it was over, and she was gone again.

Three days after Dolly died, Andy made the bed flat and perfectly smooth and closed the door to keep the other cats out. When he returned, he found a cat-shaped impression curled up on the bed just below his pillow where Dolly had always liked to sleep. When Dave entered the room, he could even smell Dolly's scent.

Both Andy and Dave still see her, but only with a sideward glance and only for a few seconds. Andy regularly catches glimpses of her at the top of the stairs around ten at night, her traditional bedtime. This is the time she would always start demanding they come to bed. Sometimes they feel her presence like a static charge.

As Andy drifts off to sleep he sometimes sees a nearby orb—a small ball of light. Just as quickly as it appears, it darts off as a blurred line, and then vanishes. The orb is followed by Dolly's feet landing on the bed, and the sensation of invisible paws moving around the bed, settling her heavy body next to Andy, exactly where she used to sleep at night. He has even tickled her ghostly chin. The sensation of her feels like the mild shock you get from touching a television screen, what Andy described as "that hairy sensation of a crackle." In these moments, Andy can also trace her exact shape—an indentation on the bed next to him. Just as with a living cat, Andy could even feel the spirit of Dolly stand up, arch her back, then lay back down and curl up on the bed. He knows that producing this level of manifestation takes a great deal of effort on Dolly's part.

Other people still sense Dolly in her favorite places: under the birdcage and on the back of the sofa. Andy still sees Dolly at a sideways glance or as a tangible electrical pattern in the air, though not as frequently as he once did. Andy believes that is to be expected, since she has things to do or ways in which to evolve and move forward. But she still makes her presence known three or four times a week.

MOUSE'S CAT

Some things are meant to be, and Lynn Yates—or "Mouse," as she is known to her friends—felt adopting Gina was one of those things. Gina, an odd-eyed, white American Shorthair-type, belonged to Lynn's brother. Fortunately for Lynn, the cat didn't get along with one of her brother's other cats. Since she had lost her childhood cat a year earlier, she offered to give the waif a home.

When Lynn first met Gina, the cat marched over to her, flopped right down on the floor, and began to purr, all the while looking straight at her with those hypnotic mismatched eyes. In that moment they bonded—for life, and for death. It was love at first sight. With her right eye a bright blue, and her left eye brilliant yellow, Gina seemed, in Lynn's mind, to be two different cats. It didn't take long for Lynn to get used to it, however.

Although she liked everyone, Gina instantly bonded with Lynn. She clearly preferred Lynn's bed for sleeping, and her lap for lounging. Gina would follow her new mom around the apartment and "groom" her hair. The cat's penchant for starchy foods earned her the nickname "Carbo-kitty." If you had a hamburger and fries, she'd choose the fries first, and you couldn't leave pasta on the table unguarded. She also had an absolute passion for green peas. She would always be at the door when Lynn arrived home from work, chattering about her day and demanding her dinner before all else. Gina woke Lynn in the morning by curling up around her head, grooming her hair and kneading her paws on Lynn's skull. In the evening, they watched television together, with Gina perched comfortably on the arm of Lynn's chair, within easy reach of caressing hands—unless Lynn's significant other, Steve, was there, in which case she usually chose his lap, the better to mug him for some of his ice cream.

Gina had a feisty side as well. The sight of a dog outside the window evoked low growls and a lashing tail. When Lynn's friend Mary dropped in with her toy poodle in tow, Mary expressed concern about Gina's safety.

Lynn warned her that she should be more worried about her little dog, but Mary didn't believe her. When the dog started barking at Gina, the cat marched calmly over to the little yapper and boxed it on the nose (with her claws out), then sauntered back into the bedroom, flicking her tail in disdain, while the dog whimpered and cowered under its owner's chair.

"Your cat's so rude," Mary objected.

"Hey, it's *her* apartment," Lynn answered.

Despite Gina's vibrant life, her days with Lynn were few. Gina had turned ten around the time Lynn adopted her, and looked her age. Her minor skin allergies grew worse; her teeth required frequent cleaning; and soon, her kidneys started to deteriorate. Lynn managed the condition for a few years with a special diet and a daily tablespoon of tomato juice to acidify her urine. Slowly, though, Gina lost weight, slept more, and drank ever-increasing amounts of water. Lynn knew the time was drawing near. She kept hoping she would hang on, just a little while longer, as the summer of their sixth year together came to an end. Gina survived a bout of pancreatitis, followed by another infection and difficulty breathing.

The time had arrived. It was time to say good-bye. Lynn held Gina as the vet administered the shot that released her from pain.

At home Lynn put away all Gina's things, thinking sadly that Gina's chapter was over. However, in typical Gina fashion, it wasn't. At first, Lynn caught the occasional flash of white out of the corner of her eye, or felt the strong sense that Gina would be waiting at the door as she came home. She brushed it off, thinking her mind was filling in the blank spaces that now existed there. Nonetheless, the feeling that Gina was present grew even stronger. Lynn sometimes felt her at night curling around her head on the pillow, or brushing against her legs.

Then Lynn's boss, Cathy, asked her to pet-sit her dog, Muppet. From the moment the miniature poodle stepped in the door, the dog was terrified. She refused to eat in the kitchen, wouldn't go near the walk-in closet, or sleep on the bed—all areas that Gina had favored. Muppet spent most of the weekend cowering under a chair, only venturing out for a walk or to get food and water. When Lynn returned the dog to Cathy, she said she couldn't pet-sit the dog again—the ghost cat wouldn't permit it. Whether it was her fierce determination to live, or the bond they had shared—Gina was still there in spirit.

One evening Lynn stopped in her tracks, shocked and unable to move: Right in front of her was Gina, sitting upright, tail curled neatly around her front paws, staring at her—left eye brilliant yellow, right eye bright blue. Lynn blinked a few times and the cat disappeared. Whether Gina stayed because of love or just innate stubbornness, Lynn knew she was holding Gina's spirit here on the earthly realm. It was time for Gina to move on.

Lynn found the Rainbow Bridge forum on the Internet, where people who have lost pets can find comfort and sympathy from others. The group held an online weekly nondenominational Rainbow Bridge crossing ritual. It was time. The next Monday evening, Lynn pulled up the Rainbow Bridge ceremony, lit a candle, and played a CD of quiet music. As the ritual began, Lynn stared into the flame, recalling how much she had loved Gina. But now it was time for her to go. Someday they would meet again. Lynn felt a slight brush against her ankle, and then the feeling was gone. She never saw or felt even a trace of Gina again.

Lynn believes in the special bond that exists between human and animal, and knows that it can live on even after death. She feels that Gina will be waiting for her on that bridge between the worlds.

STORMY AND LOKI'S MISCHIEF

They say deaths often occur in groups of three. Fortunately for Gwyneth Koberg, a vet tech in Maryland, the Grim Reaper stopped at two. But two is still two too many.

Gwyneth first had to say good-bye to Stormy, a big tuxedo cat who had always acted like he should be dressed in formal attire. While dignified and proper, he had a mischievous and loving side as well. Like all cats, he lacked an opposable thumb, which was probably a good thing.

Even without that most necessary human digit, he still managed to open doors, pull out dresser drawers, and open up the desk. He could infiltrate anything with a round knob and open anything he could pull toward him.

They could have called him Top Cat because he held the alpha position in the home. At his grandest he weighed in at twenty-five pounds. With all that bulk to back him up, he didn't have to be a bully. Not a cat in the house would mess with him.

His weight did present some problems for those around him. He'd lay on Gwyneth's feet—not wholly comfortable. He loved to honor his humans with an old-fashioned head butt. However, being head-butted by a twenty-five-pound cat was like being greeted head-on by a small SUV. He also liked to get a running start as he leapt toward his target, like a linebacker. Since his head happened to be the height of the backs of most people's kneecaps, the twenty-five-pound cannonball, at the right velocity, could literally bring someone to their knees, especially if they weren't expecting to be tackled.

He didn't get to weigh twenty-five pounds without working at it. He'd plunder food right off of people's plates. It didn't matter what appeared on the menu: pizza, chicken, vegetables, sandwiches; once he even made off with an entire steak. What appeared to be a disembodied paw would reach up from beneath the dining-room table. Like a cartoon cat, he'd slip his paw over the edge of the table and feel around. When he'd found something that felt like food, he'd snag it with a claw. Sometimes he pulled down the whole plate. He came by his nickname of Fat Cat honestly. When Stormy walked down the hall it sounded like an elephant stomping around.

The little cat burglar died at fifteen of kidney failure, two years ago.

The other pet the Koberg family lost was Loki, appropriately named for the Norse god of mischief. He belonged to Gwyn's mother, Mary. Loki had a medium coat of sable and dark-brown tiger stripes with a plume tail that he waved smugly with every step. Gwyn said Loki had distinctive footsteps because he pranced everywhere he went. The click of his toenails announced his arrival whenever he entered a room.

Mary lost thirteen-year-old Loki, who *was* a mischievous little soul, to lung cancer just a few months after Stormy died. Unlike his gentle house-mate, Stormy, Loki was the smallest cat, but he had the claws of a bully.

He'd swat the other cats on the butt if they tried to eat first, or if they were sleeping in a chair he wanted. Loki didn't just pick on the cats; he'd pick on anyone no matter how few legs they stood on. Feigning a stretch, he'd use visitor's legs as a scratching post. He'd been known to reach up and stab guests in the rear as he scratched his way up their legs. And woe to anyone who dawdled while opening the canned food. A good nip to the heels usually sped up the feeding process. Age did nothing to mellow his disposition—Gwyneth said he actually got more ornery as he aged.

About three months after Loki died, Gwyn's father, Leonard, heard footsteps down the hall. He was in the kitchen cooking and heard the clicking toenails against the floor. He looked at the doorway and found no cat. He even checked the hallway itself. Despite the fact that he could see all the way down into the room at the end of the hall, he still saw no cat. He found the only nearby cat sleeping soundly in the living-room chair. Leonard asked Mary and Gwyn if they had heard it. They hadn't.

A week or two after her dad's experience, Gwyn had just climbed into bed, but hadn't pulled up the covers yet. She watched as the door pushed open to the accompaniment of thumping and heavy foot-thuds, and then she felt the mattress shift when something heavy settled on the bed. Gwyn stiffened up at first. After all, what she'd just experienced couldn't possibly happen. Finally she relaxed and went to sleep. When she woke up in the morning, the weight was gone.

A few months later the family experienced one final incident. Mary was playing on the computer, and heard toenails moving down the hall-way toward her other daughter Kathea's room. Sitting in her bedroom, Kathea watched the door open, heard the toenails click across the floor, and then felt a cat tug at the blankets and settle to the floor. Her surviv-ing cat was next to her at the time, so it couldn't have been him. Badly shaken by the phantom cat in her room, Kathea ran upstairs and told the rest of the family what had happened.

Kathea's encounter was the last one, and it occurred over a year ago. Gwyn said it might still be happening, but they can no longer be sure because they have added new cats to the household, making it a bit harder to discern phantom cats from living ones.

FLUFFY'S GUIDE

Fluffy lived a long and interesting life in the loving care of Amanda Slavik. A Turkish Van mix, Fluffy wore a long coat that felt like cashmere and sported Van pattern markings. That meant she had a few spots on her head and a tail that looked like whoever put her together ran out of white and gave her a calico appendage instead. Fluffy had originally belonged to a woman who couldn't keep her any longer. When Amanda took her to a vet for a checkup, the vet estimated that Fluffy was about five years old.

Turkish Vans are very dedicated to their chosen people, and Fluffy found the transition to a new owner difficult at best. The cat rejected her new surroundings for almost a year. Whenever Amanda approached her, Fluffy would hiss, and she never let Amanda pet her. When it served Fluffy's purpose, she would occasionally sleep with Amanda. Because of this rough start, Amanda almost found another home for her, but her patience won out. When Fluffy finally came around, she really loved her new mom. She'd follow Amanda from room to room. Once she decided Amanda was okay, everyone was okay.

Other animals, however, were a whole different story. The feisty cat wouldn't tolerate other pets at all. One afternoon a friend of Amanda's visited with a full-grown Labrador. Like a scene out of a TV sitcom, Fluffy brought all teeth and nails to bear and attacked the dog. Amanda had to pull her off of him. Amanda herself did not come away unscathed; during the confrontation she found herself wearing Fluffy—the cat's claw was imbedded in her forehead, and for a moment Fluffy dangled from her forehead like a piece of pierced body jewelry.

In 1991 Amanda moved in with some roommates who owned three cats, including a gentle cat named Sugar. Sugar, or Toogs as he was sometimes called, was an overweight gray tabby. Shaped like a football, he weighed more than twenty pounds. Although he was the alpha cat, he was a funny kind of guy; his belly swayed from side to side when he ran across the house. With momentum behind him, nothing could stop him except a wall or a piece of furniture. The house had wooden floors, so Sugar slid everywhere, and when he didn't slide, he sounded like a thundering herd of rhinos.

Fluffy was not kind to her feline roomies. She'd attempt to starve them by guarding the food bowl. The best she could do with another cat in the house was put up with them in the room without growling at them. Of course, there were those times when tensions would escalate and frays would explode. Poor gentle Sugar wasn't immune to her bullying. Eventually Amanda graduated and got her own place. Because of her cat's dislike of anyone wearing fur, Amanda eventually decided she couldn't have other pets while she had Fluffy. Fluffy lived out the rest of her life as Amanda's sole pet—at least, until her last two weeks.

Fluffy had lived a good life, but in her last few years her health began to deteriorate. A blood test determined she suffered from hyperthyroidism. The vet decided to treat her with medication. Amanda tried to hide the pills in her food, but Fluffy always found them. When the meal was over, every speck of cat food had been eaten, except for the pill at the bottom of the bowl. Amanda had to give it to her like the vet had shown her: by popping the pill in the back of her mouth and rubbing her throat so she would swallow. Her health progressively declined. Before long, Fluffy lost control of her bladder. By the time Fluffy turned twenty, she had started fading away.

In October 2004, about two weeks before Fluffy died, Amanda was in the kitchen, cooking. Out of her peripheral vision she saw a gray blur moving along the floor. Another time she saw it in the kitchen, just hanging out. When she managed to get a good look at the gray shape, she realized it was a cat. Amanda knew it wasn't just any cat by the sheer size, the football shape, and the way it moved along the floor. Amanda knew the ghostly blur was Fluffy's old roommate, Sugar. Before her eyes Sugar vanished. He lived to be twenty-five, but had died of summer heat and old age ten years earlier.

Amanda called out to him, "Hello, Toogs! You came to visit again!"

"Energy-wise it felt good to me," she said. "He was happy to be visiting, and he also felt like he was here for a mission—like he was saying, 'I'm not here for long.'"

"It had a friendly feeling. Sugar was so friendly and the ghost's presence felt very good." She instinctively knew he was there for Fluffy.

One night a few weeks after Sugar's first visit, Fluffy suffered a stroke. She quickly lost much of her motor function. Walking became a struggle. Eventually, Fluffy lost the ability to walk at all, and eating and drinking became impossible. Amanda knew it was time to let her go. She took her in to the vet's office for the inevitable. She petted Fluffy and spent a few last loving minutes with her old cat. When Amanda left the room, they put her to sleep.

Amanda believes that Sugar Toogs came back to greet Fluffy and show her the way. Sugar did it simply because he knew her, and perhaps somewhere beneath Fluffy's gruff disposition, they had been friends after all.

MIKEY'S MESSAGE

In October of 1992, Ginger Buck decided that her kitten, Angel, could use a companion, so she trekked down to the local humane society in southern California and went through the arduous task of screening the many cages of candidates. Naturally, she wanted to take them all home, but at the time she had room for only one. One little gray tabby with a distinctive "M" on his forehead caught her eye. He was about six months old, with short, soft fur. That day she brought home Mikey Mouser, so named because the gray highlights in his coat were the same shade as a mouse's fur.

Her plan worked. Angel and Mikey hit it off right away. Mikey was such an outgoing guy; he eventually earned the title "Ambassador of Goodwill," because as Ginger gradually added cats to the household, he welcomed them into the family. But serving as household greeter was just one of his jobs; the other was his role as the Rock of Gibraltar. He always listened patiently to Ginger's problems. After a good purr session with her tabby therapist, Ginger always felt better.

When he reached his fifth birthday, Ginger noticed Mikey needed some kitty breath mints. Since she knew healthy cats should never have bad breath, in June 1997, she left him at the vet's office for a cleaning. Neither Ginger nor the vet expected the procedure to be anything but a routine dental cleaning, so neither of them saw any reason to spend money on a preoperative blood workup. After all, Mikey was a vigorous five-year-old. However, unbeknownst to everyone, Mikey was already suffering from renal failure as a result of congenital kidney deformities. Anesthesia from the dental work pushed him over the edge and sent him into acute renal failure.

The once-exuberant Mikey now had to visit the animal hospital every few days in order to receive lifesaving fluids. He'd go home feeling better, but in another few days he'd become weak again when his body filled with toxins. He'd have to return to the vet for another round of fluid therapy.

In July, Ginger dropped him off for his treatment, expecting the same old routine. She would pick him up later that afternoon. That evening when she entered the clinic, the receptionist told Ginger, "The vet wants to talk to you." Not a good sign. The vet didn't need to say a word; Ginger already knew that Mikey had left his body. As soon as she saw the vet, she asked, "Mikey died, didn't he?" The veterinarian nodded, explaining that they had called but hadn't been able to reach her.

Mikey Mouser still lay in his cage with a towel draped across him when she went in to see him. She spent some time alone with her "Mr. Congeniality," telling him how much she had loved him, and how very sorry she was that she hadn't been with him before he passed.

She left the empty shell that was once Mikey at the clinic. It wasn't until later that she realized with much regret that she should have had him cremated so she could have brought him home. She also still regretted not being there for him when he'd needed her most. But Ginger knew she had given him a chance to live, short as it was. Had she not adopted him that day five years before, his life would have been much shorter.

Before Mikey's passing, Ginger had already made plans to adopt another cat. Her new pet had large ears and hopped like a rabbit, so Ginger named her Bunny Girl. She stuck to her plan and picked up her new kitty as scheduled. The little brown tabby had many of Mikey's characteristics; she was both outgoing and affectionate.

About a month after Mikey's death, Ginger was driving home from work when she felt the presence of Mikey Mouser inside the car. He was curled up warmly around her neck like a collar. She got a message from Mikey that he was okay and that it was all right to love her new kitty. He let Ginger know he was passing the "cat-love torch" to Bunny Girl. The new cat would pick up where Mikey left off.

When Mikey visited her a second time, Ginger actually felt Mikey around her shoulders again. She felt the softness of his fur against her neck. Again, Mikey let her know he was "all right," and that he would always be with her in spirit.

And he is. She continues to feel Mikey Mouser's presence.

THE RETURN OF SUMMER SOLSTICE

T. J. Banks, from Connecticut, couldn't have chosen a more appropriate name for her ruddy Abyssinian than "Solstice." She chose this name because the Summer Solstice/Midsummer's Eve is traditionally a very magical time. The frail kitten, who was so tiny T. J. had to hand-feed her by breaking up food and offering it to her on her fingertip, had an enchanting affect on everyone who met her. Besides, her very survival was miraculous; she came through a potentially fatal affliction and two risky operations to remove throat polyps. She was transformed from a very skinny, sickly kitten to a sleek little cougar-cat. Her very presence was a miracle to T. J.

Although her throat healed, she seldom ever used her voice, not even for soft meows. Most Abys aren't all that vocal to begin with, and their meow tends to be very soft and plaintive.

When Solstice was a year old, T. J. nicknamed her "House Blessing" because of her complete recovery from her throat surgery, and because the kitten's arrival marked the end of a sad, dark time when T. J. had lost several beloved family pets. Instead of using her voice, Solstice talked to T. J. with her expressive amber eyes. Depending on the light and her mood, the hue of her eyes could shift from honey to greenish amber and back again to honey.

A busybody, Solstice had to know what T. J. was up to at all times. When T. J. and her twelve-year-old daughter, Marissa, sat at the back-yard picnic table, Solstice could be seen spying on them from the kitchen window. Solstice made it clear that she was a one-person cat, unusual for the ordinarily gregarious Abyssinian breed; and T. J. was that one person. Solstice would follow T. J. up and down the stairs, as well as perform push-paws on T. J. when they laid down for a quick rest together.

For almost five years, Solstice had a hearty appetite to fuel all that nonstop Abyssinian activity. When her desire to consume vast quantities of food faded, T. J.'s vet began treating the cat for a badly abscessed tooth. Things looked promising when Solstice appeared to respond to the antibiotics. And when T. J. found a cat fang lying on her daughter's bureau, she figured that it was the end of Solstice's problem tooth.

But it was really the beginning of the very end. T. J. soon noticed that Solstice had lost her cougar sleekness. That beautiful ruddy coat with its apricot underbelly suddenly felt loose and wooly. A trip to the emergency veterinarian clinic revealed the underlying problem: acute kidney failure, the bane of so many Abyssinians—and nearing the final stages. An experienced writer about cat health, T. J. didn't need the vet to explain what that diagnosis meant. A disease by any other name is just as deadly. This time, there would be no miracle for Solstice.

T. J. brought her home. Working as a team, T. J. and her daughter, Marissa, gave Solstice subcutaneous fluids to help flush the toxins from her failing kidneys. When Solstice no longer wanted cat food, T. J. coaxed her to lick baby food—sometimes from a spoon, sometimes right off of her fingers. With all the TLC, Solstice rallied a bit. But hope of recovery was a tease. The ruddy little cougar soon resembled a ghost, still breathing for the moment, but a mere shadow of the lively cat she had been only months before.

On the last morning of her life, T. J. brought Solstice to the vet to be put to sleep. When he couldn't find a vein, he gave her a slow-acting abdominal injection. He wrapped Solstice gently in a towel and left the room so that T. J. could spend the remaining time—maybe ten minutes or so—alone with her cat, to hold and talk to her.

Solstice squirmed at first. Affectionate as she was, like most Abys, she didn't care much for being held. Finally she settled down in T. J.'s arms. T. J. talked to her precious little companion and prayed a little, until Solstice was finally gone.

About a week after she had said good-bye to Solstice, T. J. was outside in the middle of the morning, raking her backyard, when her eyes caught something strange—yet somehow friendly and familiar—sitting at the edge of her meditation garden. It was Solstice, her ruddy coat once again vibrant in its autumn color. Her reborn image could have been a painting by one of the masters, so perfect was it in hue and form. T. J. could even see the silky apricot underbelly that she loved to have stroked; it no longer appeared saggy or wooly. Her tail was daintily wrapped around her paws. She simply radiated love and happiness. She appeared very solid, and she stayed for a long time, several minutes, before slowly dissolving like the Cheshire Cat. The image continued to return regularly for weeks, appearing stronger and stronger each time. And for the first time since she'd learned her beloved friend was dying, T. J. felt happy.

Solstice's other visitations have lasted from a few seconds to a couple of minutes, but her presence has become increasingly stronger. T. J. usually sees her when she's outdoors, where she's less apt to be distracted by extraneous things like the phone ringing. T. J. believes Solstice appears to her while she's in her garden because it's quiet; T. J. is more in tune with (super)natural rhythms, and can enter a meditative state.

Sometimes T. J. sees Solstice while she's taking a walk; once or twice Solstice even appeared on the car's dashboard. T. J. has lost track of how many times Solstice has dropped in. Although Solstice doesn't come as often anymore, she seems to appear most frequently when T. J.'s in a meditative state, feeling a bit low, or in need of spiritual guidance. She's also apt to show up when something significant is about to happen. T. J. looks at Solstice as something of a spiritual lodestone. If she's not sure of a particular step she's about to take, Solstice appears, and T. J. knows she's moving in the right direction.

Like a message from Heaven, T. J. understands the verse from the Song of Songs—that love is as strong as death. T. J. believes that Solstice's visits are meant to remind her that some connections are indestructible and eternal. "The miraculous is always around us; it's just that the nature of the miracle changes," T. J. said. "We only know they're miracles because of that feeling of 'unexpected grace' that they inevitably bring with them . . . the way they stop time and reveal the soul of things."

T. J. feels that her "House Blessing" is still with her, as miraculous as roses in November. The body is gone, but the spirit is more than willing. We think miracles have to be big and flashy, and sometimes they're not. A miracle can be as quiet and understated as an amber-eyed Abyssinian, watching her owner from the kitchen window. Sometimes they can be as simple and as beautiful as an old friend coming back to light the path we need to take.

GRUNGY'S GREETING

Dr. Wanda Neely is a chaplain at the Medical Center of Lewisville, Texas, and a retired ophthalmologist. In her work as a chaplain to the terminally ill, she has witnessed the death of human patients and helped families deal with the passing of a family member. In 1998, she found herself providing that kind of comfort to her own family.

Wanda traveled to Oakland, California, where her son's mother-in-law, Dorothy, was dying of uterine cancer. One respite during the emotionally difficult time was at the home of Wanda's son and daughter-in-law, David and Pam. They had a very friendly and personable cat named Grungy. Grungy was a five-year-old gray tabby cat and a beloved member of the family. He was neutered, had vivid stripes and long gray hair, and was well fed. Grungy was especially close to Mariah, David and Pam's nine-year-old daughter. He slept with her every night.

To Grungy, a stranger was simply a friend he hadn't met yet. He'd jump into any available lap, expecting a throat scratch, and would reward the person with a rumbling purr. Grungy went outside at will—the advantage of a cat flap—and although they had a fenced-in yard, he could easily climb over the fence.

In her healthier days, Dorothy had frequently visited Pam and the family, and, of course, her good friend, Grungy.

Finally, Dorothy's condition deteriorated. They moved her into the Intensive Care Unit. Dorothy was a frightening sight, hooked up to machines and tubes. She had slipped into an unconscious state. Nurses were preparing to do a tracheotomy when David asked Wanda if they should let Mariah see her grandmother now, or wait until she was gone and had been cleaned up by the funeral home. Wanda said she should be allowed to see Dorothy while she was alive and warm.

Dorothy had been unconscious for four hours when the little girl climbed into the bed and curled up next to her grandmother. Dorothy opened her eyes and said, "Hi, Mariah."

Pam ran up to her mother's bed. "Mom, where have you been?" she asked.

Recalling some pleasant memories, Dorothy said, "I was having tea with Edith."

Pam reminded her mother that her sister, Edith, had died two years earlier.

"I'm sorry," Dorothy insisted. "I was having tea with Edith, and Grungy was there."

Again, Pam corrected her mother. "Edith is dead and Grungy is very much alive. We fed him just before we left for the hospital." Despite her mother's resolve, Pam felt the need to get the facts straight.

Finally, after a long, emotional roller coaster of a day, the family went home. When they rolled up the street they were shocked to find the body of a long-haired gray cat in the middle of the street. Grungy had been dead for several hours.

Two days later, Dorothy joined her sister and her feline friend on "the Other Side."

SILVER'S STEREO

In 1978, longtime friends and roommates Leah McGrew and Connie Crouch lost their cat "Flirt" to feline leukemia. They were devastated. Their Austin house simply wasn't a home without that black cat hair on the couch and a set of innocent golden eyes waiting to be fed in the morning.

They decided they wanted something positive to come from their loss. Since they couldn't bring Flirt back to life, they wanted to save a cat who would otherwise be put to sleep. Their next cat would come from the Town Lake Animal Shelter. No-kill shelters were rare in those days, and Town Lake put down homeless animals every day.

Leah and Connie found a gray cat at the shelter, and they named her Silver. She'd been looking at them through the bars of the cage with those huge copper eyes. They knew she was unspayed since her breasts were still swollen from a recent litter of kittens. Leah thought Silver was one of the least adoptable of the cats there, because spaying was very expensive at that time, and in 1977, shelters didn't help pay to fix the cats that were adopted. Despite these facts, Silver was very pretty with her beautiful blue coat; they knew they'd found their new pet.

When Silver arrived at her new home, she was frightened. One of their other kitties, a black cat named Sab (short for Sabbath) wanted to play with her, but Silver cowered away. Sab stopped, looked at her, then came over and licked her on her head. From then on Sab and Silver were friends.

After researching her blue cat, Leah discovered that Silver resembled a Russian Blue more than a British Shorthair. She was a shy cat, as is common with Russian Blues. She loved her humans, but she didn't sleep with either of them. Leah also read that Russian Blues aren't necessarily known to be friendly to other cats. Silver accepted Sab, but their high hopes for feline harmony in their home crashed when Silver made the life of their other cat, Zucchini, one of sheer torment.

Silver often trapped Zu under the couch in the corner and wouldn't let her out. In fact, the only thing that would lure Zu out of her corner prison was an offering of potato chips. Fortunately, Sab and Silver loved a rousing wrestling match, which was a blessed reprieve for Zu. They would leap into the corner, where Silver liked to trap Zu, and the games would commence. Her view was obscured by the couch, but Leah could see them flipping around and hear them thumping against the wall, the floor, and the couch.

The two cats sometimes played chase. They'd wrestle and play king of the mountain, defending the highest place they could get to. They would also lie down and groom each other. When Sab would try to cuddle and groom Zu, Silver would go into a rampage with Zu as the target of her ire.

Leah and Connie loved all their cats, but they didn't know how to deal with the discord. In a sad way, the situation took care of itself. The following year, Silver grew ill, and with a sense of déjà vu, they learned that she too had feline leukemia. The ladies noticed that Silver appeared lethargic, and uncharacteristically, she started sitting on top of the stereo. The only time she stirred from the stereo was to come to the kitchen for her special feedings. Most noticeable, Zu started coming out and sitting in plain sight without getting the slightest rise out of Silver.

Silver declined slowly at first, sometimes sitting on the couch and then sometimes sleeping on top of the stereo. She laid on top of the turntable/amp that was kept in a tall metal bookshelf. She went from not feeling well to barely hanging on in about four months.

Still aching from their loss the previous year, the women put Silver to sleep. By that time she was so sick that death was a release for her. Almost immediately after her death, Leah noticed their cat, Sab, playing alone, accompanied by flashes of black fur and thumping sounds, similar to those of a feline wrestling match. Still later she did a double take a time or two when she thought she saw Silver sleeping on the stereo, just as she had during the last few weeks of her life. When she looked back, she saw no cat. Leah figured the vision was just the product of an overactive imagination or wishful thinking. She believed her eyes were just playing tricks on her.

Leah kept her hallucinations to herself for about two months. Then one evening both Connie and Leah watched as Sab crept up on the stereo, staring as if watching another animal. She slowly sniffed the area until she finally sniffed the top of the stereo. She then relaxed and jumped down. As they watched Sab stalk the stereo, Leah said, "Sab acts like she sees Silver." Connie agreed.

They looked at each other. After all these months of each of them fearing they were going crazy, they both confirmed what the other had seen. Both women admitted to seeing Silver playing with Sab behind the couch. They had both witnessed her sleeping on the stereo where she had spent so many of her last days.

"I guess we've got a ghost," Leah said. Connie agreed.

Leah had seen Silver about fifteen times over a period of four months before they both witnessed Sab "playing" and started talking about it. But Leah began to think it was wrong to keep Silver with them, even though they missed her very much. She wondered if they should release her completely from this life, like they had released her from the agony of her disease. They finally decided they should help her move on.

The women discussed how they should go about setting Silver free. It took them a couple of days to decide what to do, but they finally concluded they needed to talk to her.

Leah sat by the stereo with a bottle of holy water in her hand.

"Silver, I know you loved us and we loved you, but you need to go on now. There's a better place for you, with everything you need. There are people to love you, toys to play with, wonderful things to eat, and you won't be hurting anymore. I know you were happy here, but you'll be even happier there. I love you Silver."

Connie added, "I love you too, Silver."

Leah used the holy water, making the sign of the cross on top of the stereo and invoking the name of the Holy Trinity. She knew this would be her last conversation with her precious Silver. Tears ran down their cheeks; in a sense, it felt like they were losing Silver anew.

They never saw her again.

chapter 5

One Last Good-bye
BEDTIME VISITATIONS

Cats come and go without ever leaving.
  —MARTHA CURTIS

Many of us who love our cats have had the trauma of losing our lifelong friend unexpectedly. Who of us wouldn't give almost anything to have a chance to say good-bye, or a final "I love you"?

The psychological nature of cats leaves the potential for an ocean full of unfinished business. In the wild, cats, being such small predators, live on the precipice of personal extinction every day. Cats are masters at disguising disease. Unlike humans, cats bear up to suffering with amazing stoicism. I have heard people say that cats don't feel pain the way humans do, because in the face of traumatic injury or horrific disease, they maintain a quiet dignity. Suffering the same illness or injury, humans would most likely howl with a volume that would reach the moon, or maybe at least a few houses down the street. However, the cat's instinct discourages him from drawing attention to pain or discomfort, often to his detriment. In nature, hiding disease keeps him alive. He's a helpless little predator living at the lower end of the food chain. When he feels ill, his instincts tell him, "Don't show that you're sick, or something bigger will eat you." So cats hide their illness and mask their symptoms, often until it's too late to save them. Many people, not realizing their cats are sick, are suddenly faced with their imminent death. They find themselves robbed of the chance to fight the illness, or even to prepare for the inevitable. People are also denied closure when their cats become lost or simply vanish.

Sometimes our feline friends can take the matter in paw and give us a special final gift—a chance to say good-bye, an opportunity to receive forgiveness for our human failings, and finally, closure.

For years I believed my experience with Maynard to be unique. Once I started doing research about cat spirits, I learned that was not the case. I also discovered that the bedtime visit was by far the most common encounter with ghost cats. People would often preface their stories with "You won't believe this, but . . ."

Yes, I did believe them. While many of these experiences entailed nightly rituals of cats and their people that went on for years, if not decades, a good number of them only happened once, as if the cat just wanted to say good-bye—like adult children calling their parents to say that they made it to their destination safely. "I got here fine, and am having a great time. Don't worry about me. I love you. I'll see you again . . . someday."

CINDERS

Karen has always loved animals, especially cats. She got her first cat when she was ten years old. Her entire adult life has been surrounded by animals; first, working in a dog and cat grooming shop; then as a veterinary assistant at the local humane society; and then back to grooming, with other types of non-animal-related jobs thrown in. Today, she owns four cats and a Pomeranian.

About twelve years ago, Karen brought home a medium-haired black-and-white cat named Cinders from the vet clinic where she worked. When Cinders was ten years old, he developed a lower urinary tract infection. Karen gave him antibiotics to manage it. One day after Cinders' infection began to improve, Karen found him walking in circles. She needed no psychic to tell her a trip to the neurologist was in his immediate future. However, feline specialists cost a king's ransom, in addition to the battery of tests they usually want to perform. Her budget simply couldn't afford the expensive CAT scans or MRIs; reluctantly, she passed on all the expensive tests and opted to treat the problem with drugs. The vet suspected

Cinders had a tumor or brain lesion. With the help of the medication, Cinders lasted another eight months.

When the dreaded day arrived, Karen took Cinders to the vet and stayed with him through his last breath. She felt his spirit leave his body, and sensed that he was happy he was going to be free of pain and discomfort.

A week or so later, Karen had just gone to bed. She was relaxed, lying facedown with her eyes closed, when she felt something jump up on the bed, walk across her body, and up to the pillow. All that time she didn't open her eyes. The pressure felt just exactly as if Cinders had hopped up on the bed, and was saying hello. Karen had put out her hand and felt the head and the shoulders of a cat. The sensation was so familiar, so comfortable, that it took her a few minutes to remember that her beloved Cinders had died.

She never felt his presence again after that single incident, but she was at peace, knowing that Cinders had come back to say a final farewell.

T AND E.T.

Donna Wilbanks's show cat, a national award-winning Exotic Shorthair (a short-haired Persian) named T, passed away recently. When the kitten, T, first opened her eyes, she saw Donna's face. Likewise, Donna's face was the last thing T saw as she left this life. The kitten's registered name was GRC GRP NW Starship's Magic Fire. In the beginning Donna referred to her as "The Tortie"—short for her tortoiseshell color. She later shortened it to T, and it stuck. T lived to be seventeen years old.

T was the boss, and all the other cats recognized her for that. As a young cat she was constantly harassed by one of Donna's older female cats. The wily little tortoiseshell learned that Donna would protect her from the bullies. Then the tables turned when T grew up and became the tyrant. She believed she could get away with anything, especially when her human mom was around; and she did. The tortie had a special place in Donna's heart.

Whenever Donna stretched out to watch television on the couch, T would jump up beside her. After Donna had lavished love on her, T would target the first cat she encountered and club him over the head with her paw, as if to say, "Mom loves me the best!"

And she did. Despite her other wonderful cats, Donna looked at the tortie as her child, and her soul mate. She said they were like E.T. and Elliott from the Steven Spielberg movie. And like the movie character, Donna could actually feel it when T started to feel sick from severe anemia. It turned out to be lymphoma.

Even on her last day, T could make that jump to the couch. The evening after T died, Donna was lying on the couch, watching TV. Out of the corner of her eye, she saw T walk up to the edge of the couch. T paused for a moment, just as she would have in life, and then leapt up. When Donna looked straight at where the cat should have been, she saw nothing.

It didn't matter. She felt so happy that T had come around one final time.

HARRISON

In 1999 Cindy Willoughby lost the feline love of her life—her first Maine Coon show cat named Grand Premier Purricoon's Harrison. She named him after actor Harrison Ford, and called him her love bug, her constant shadow, and Big Boy—after all, he was an old-style Maine Coon, a hefty seventeen pounds, with big feet, big chest, and a big head. The huge brown mackerel tabby cat followed her around like a puppy. At cat shows, when other exhibitors had to watch their cats closely to make sure they didn't get loose, Cindy would leave his cage door open while she read so Harrison could lay with his head outside the door and watch her. That way she could pet him more easily. If the chairs were high enough he would lay with his head on her knees.

The night he passed was like any other evening. After they had supper, Cindy checked her e-mail. As was their ritual, Harrison always had to sit on her lap for a little while and would then go lay on her feet while she read her messages. He even put his two cents' worth in on a couple of responses by putting his big old paws on the keyboard. Later, Cindy stretched out on her bed to watch television. As always, Harrison stretched out full-length alongside her leg, with his head by Cindy's hand so he wouldn't miss out on any scratches or head rubbing. Often when he crawled in bed with her, he'd get that bedtime expression, a dumb look he assumed just before he went to sleep. He'd lay there with his tongue sticking out a little from his mouth.

That night, Cindy had dozed off when suddenly something woke her. Harrison had moved off of the bed. Something made her sit up and look down. He lay motionless on the carpeted floor, moaning the way cats do when they are dying.

Cindy immediately became hysterical. She grabbed the phone and called Janine, a nurse friend (and also a Maine Coon breeder) who lived just down the road. Between sobs, she told her friend that Harrison was dying. She wrapped Harrison in a blanket and drove like a crazy woman to her friend's home. Before she'd traveled more than a block from home, Harrison passed on to the Rainbow Bridge. From the time she'd discovered him on the floor until the time he passed hadn't been more than a few minutes.

She stood at her friend's front door dressed in pajamas, holding her dead cat wrapped in a blanket, crying uncontrollably. Janine checked Harrison over. She believed that eight-year-old Harrison's heart had just given out. Cindy stayed with Janine for about forty-five minutes. She left Harrison with Janine so she could bury him in the kitty graveyard next to his uncle, who Janine had owned.

Cindy's home seemed different without her Big Boy there. She had a Yorkie and her three other cats, but no Harrison. Physically worn out and emotionally exhausted from crying, Cindy finally returned to bed. She had just about fallen asleep when she felt the side of the bed give and something stretch out against her leg where Harrison always used to sleep. She looked, but she saw none of the other animals nearby. There was nothing there.

She told Harrison goodnight, and went to sleep. She has never felt him again since then. Cindy believes that her Harrison came back to tell her that he was okay and to say good-bye.

The Mystery Kitty

Karen Duban was eleven years old in the late 1960s. Her family lived on a suburban street in Austin, Texas. The family had always had cats, and often kittens, too, since it wasn't popular to spay them back then. Her favorite, Girl Cat (named by her younger sister), had several litters of kittens, for which they always managed to find homes. The cats usually stayed outside, but came inside on especially cold nights. Young Karen thought it was cool when one of the cats slept with her. Sometimes she even snuck them into her bedroom before going to bed.

One evening Karen's parents went out for the evening, leaving the girls in the care of a teenage babysitter. The younger kids had already gone to bed. Karen wanted to stay up and watch that new rock 'n' roll group, the Beatles, on her family's black-and-white television. She loved the Beatles, and had looked forward to the television concert all week. But the babysitter insisted that Karen go to bed just as the show began. Karen bargained that she would go to bed if she could leave the bedroom door open so she could listen to the music. With door ajar, Karen could hear the music and see the glow from the TV, but she couldn't see John, George, Paul, or Ringo. While they sang, Karen stayed awake, angry that she had missed her heartthrobs and hurt that she'd been sent to bed like her younger sisters.

Soon she felt an adult-size cat jump on the bed, take a few steps at the foot of the bed, and curl up to sleep next to her feet. She got some little comfort knowing that a cat had come to sleep with her when she was so unhappy. After a little while, she looked up to see which cat it was. She stared, shocked to discover there was no cat on the bed. She saw no indentation showing that a cat had been there recently. She got up out of bed and searched her room and closet, thinking the cat had jumped down. There was no cat in the room. Then Karen remembered that she hadn't seen a cat come through the doorway—or leave, for that matter. She had, after all, been watching the glow from the television, hoping to see the Fab Four.

She got up and asked the babysitter if she had seen a cat either come into her room or leave it. The teen said she hadn't seen any cats at all.

Shaken, Karen returned to her room. After eliminating all the logical possibilities, Karen concluded that a ghost cat must have joined her on the bed. She lay in there and stared at the ceiling that night, unable to sleep.

Karen didn't recall losing a cat, so she didn't know who the ghost cat was. Perhaps it belonged to the previous owners of the house. She believes cats are sensitive to moods and often comfort their owners when they aren't feeling well—as if "comforter" is in their job description.

SAPPHIRE

Sandra Toney lost Sapphire when he was only ten years old. In an age when inside cats can often live fourteen, even eighteen years, ten was much too young—especially when he had always been so healthy.

One spring afternoon in 1994, Sandra discovered a mother cat nursing her lone kitten in the garden shed. Sandra immediately fell in love with that precious little wad of fur, a little male wearing a blue fur coat and with piercing blue eyes. What name could she give him other than Sapphire? Anytime she noticed that the mom cat had left for a hunting expedition, Sandra would go to the shed and play with little Sapphire. She wanted him to learn to trust humans and get used to being handled. Although Sandra fed the mother cat, the conscientious queen started bringing dead mice back to the shed for her baby. Like any good huntress, she eventually brought live ones so he could learn to make the killing bite when the time came for him to fend for himself.

Of course, he would never need to. Once the mother had weaned Sapphire, Sandra brought him into her home. Outside, she trapped the feral mom, had her spayed, and released her back into the neighborhood.

Despite Sandra's handling, little Sapphire had already picked up his mother's innate distrust of people. Sandra knew it would take patience to bring her new baby around. She and her husband socialized Sapphire by holding him and playing with him every day. Even with all the handling, the blue kitty always maintained a bit of the "wild" in him. Sandra knew that earning his trust was a great compliment—as well as a privilege.

For his whole life, Sapphire slept at the end of Sandra's bed every night. He always let her know when it was time to go to sleep because he would meow loudly, demanding his canned food, and then once he'd finished, he wanted "lights out" right away. A few minutes after Sandra climbed into bed, Sapphire would pounce—almost fly—gracefully up to join her. She felt the oh-so-gentle landing at her feet. He would stretch out on her legs, like someone had dropped a sandbag on her feet. Naturally, Sandra couldn't turn over or get more comfortable because she couldn't disturb Sapphire. An achy back was a small price to pay for a happy cat.

Sapphire lived in the Toney home for a decade. He fell ill very suddenly and, within a month of his cancer diagnosis, he passed away. It was one of the hardest things Sandra had faced in her life. He'd only lived ten short years; she had wrongly believed he would always be there, or at least for another six or eight years.

Nothing seemed the same without her blue cat shadowing her steps. Evenings were the worst. He had been such an important part of her nighttime ritual. Sandra didn't want to go to bed because it seemed so empty. What she wouldn't give to have a Sapphire-induced achy back! For two or three nights she cried herself to sleep. One night she had just settled in to her sleep mode when, all of a sudden, she felt that familiar pounce at the end of the bed. She thought her heart had stopped beating. She quickly turned on the light, expecting—hoping—to see Sapphire at her feet, where he had spent nights for the past ten years. Of course, she saw no cat.

To Sandra's surprise, that comforting feeling of Sapphire jumping onto the bed continued nightly for a few weeks. During the first few visits, she turned on the light to look for him, disappointed when she didn't see him, but still comforted knowing his spirit had returned. Over those two weeks, the visits grew less frequent, until they finally stopped. To this day, Sandra believes it was indeed her beloved Sapphire calling on her from the Great Beyond. In fact, there is no doubt that Sapphire was saying good-night, and, finally, when he thought she was ready, good-bye.

CUPCAKE

When Karen Commings lived on Maryland's Eastern Shore, she took care of a black-and-white stray cat she named Pepper. Before she'd had a chance to trap Pepper and have her spayed, the cat became pregnant and gave birth to five kittens under a neighbor's house. Before Karen even saw the newborns, a neighbor girl had adopted two of them. Of the remaining three, the largest kitten, a solid-black female, was the outgoing one who loved people.

The other two kittens—a solid-black male and a gray-and-white female—were shy and preferred to hide under a bush or behind the woodpile when Karen brought them their meals. In the evening, the three ventured out, following their mother in single file wherever she went.

In addition to the mother and three kittens, Karen was also feeding another stray, an energetic orange tabby she'd named Sparky. Sparky had taken to exploring a two-story hotel that was being renovated across the street from her home. Every night before going to bed, Karen gave Sparky a nighttime snack.

On one of Karen's nightly Sparky excursions, Pepper, along with the three eight-week-old kittens trailing in single file, followed Karen across the street. She had no idea Pepper's little shadows were behind her. After Sparky got her dinner, Karen headed back across the street to her house. That's when she noticed a tiny dark shape lying in the middle of the street. Only then did Karen see Pepper sitting on the sidewalk with the two kittens, the third one obviously missing.

As Karen approached the dark shape, she realized it was the smallest black kitten, the shy one who always walked at the end of the line behind his mother and sisters. A neighbor helped her pick the kitten up off the street so she could bury his tiny body in her flower garden. As Karen shoveled dirt out of the ground for the kitten's grave, she felt especially sad that she hadn't named any of the kittens. Believing that no kitten should die without a name to recall its memory, she decided to call him Cupcake.

That night as she lay in bed trying to drift off to sleep, she became aware of the weight of Cupcake's little body curled up on her shoulder. As she whispered his name, he disappeared. Karen believed he had returned for a brief moment to say, "Thank you."

Nashua

In 1989 Maryellen Miranda bought an eight-week-old seal point Siamese from a breeder in Nashua, New Hampshire. Maryellen's five-year-old cousin, Julie, thought she should name the cat "Nashua." Maryellen shortened it to Nash.

At night, the twelve-pound Siamese slept on Maryellen's pillow. When her car pulled up into the driveway, Nashua would sit in the window and scream, "ma, ma, ma," until Maryellen opened the front door. Nash would play fetch until his human pitcher tired of the game. Needless to say, when guests came to call, Nashua would amuse them with his antics. He was a seal point shadow. Wherever Maryellen went, he followed. After the birth of Maryellen's daughter, Nashua would sit next to the baby carrier, protecting her. If anyone tried to touch the baby, he would try to lay on her.

Sadly, Nashua was diagnosed with Feline Infectious Peritonitis (FIP), a virus for which there is not only no cure, there's not even a treatment, or a definitive blood test. FIP is always fatal. In 1991, Maryellen left his body at the vet's office. She was so heartbroken by his death, she couldn't bear the thought of replacing him. So she decided to remain catless.

One very early morning three years later, Maryellen felt a cat walking on her back. Since she lived with no other cats at the time, she knew she couldn't really be feeling a cat on her back. "The covers were over most of my head," Maryellen said. "My heart was beating out of my chest when I lifted my head to look—and there was nothing there."

She knew Nashua had returned for a visit.

"It was then that I was able to let go and get another cat, because I knew that no matter where I am or what cats I do have, he is and will always be watching over me."

Who Was that Cat?

Ghost cat hauntings are not isolated to people who have just lost a pet or live with a house full of cats. Jason Karolczak-Konen had a very odd experience one morning. It was especially odd because he knows nothing about the cat who visited him.

Jason loves cats and has been surrounded by them for almost his entire life. When he was five years old he used gift money to pay for a kitten. He loved her for sixteen years. He missed having cats during his college years because the dorm didn't permit pets. However, once he graduated and got an apartment of his own, he adopted another kitty. One morning in May 2005, Jason was lying in bed with his eyes closed when he felt a cat jump up on his bed, near his feet. Motionless, he opened his eyes. He saw nothing but he could feel the cat walk behind his back. It stepped softly onto his pillow. Jason turned his head, but there was no cat next to him. He didn't expect to see one, because at that time he was catless. The visit only lasted a minute or so before the presence disappeared.

Although he has no idea who his little ghost cat is, it has visited on several occasions since that morning.

Junior Ray

Junior Ray was blue, a Russian Blue wannabe, with white on his feet, belly, and on his upper lip. He had wonderful green eyes with a faint ring of blue around the pupils. Denise Dorton got him, literally, by accident. In the winter she always banged on the hood of the car before starting her car. But in the August heat, she had never dreamed there would be anything hiding under a scorching car hood. When she turned the key in her ignition, she heard the unforgettable thump of a creature being hit by the fan blade.

Under the car she found a little gray-and-white kitten. The fan blade had broken his left front leg up by his shoulder—a compound fracture—and the fan belt had worn the hair off his tail in a barber-pole pattern. He had a little blood coming out of his mouth, which she later learned was from a nick he had bitten out of the edge of his tongue—a nick he still had the day he died.

She took the kitten to the vet, had him patched up, and decided to keep him. For the next seven years, Junior Ray lived in the newspaper office where Denise worked until she changed jobs, moved to a different city, and made him a house cat.

Because he had started life as an outdoor kitty, he always yearned to spend time outdoors. To indulge his craving, yet keep him safe, Denise walked him on a harness and leash. She would ask, "Junior Ray, you want to go outside?" He'd rush to the door and patiently stand while she harnessed him.

He never played all that much. He was more of a sit-back-and-observe-the-world kind of guy. He loved to lie on Denise's chest and watch TV with her. He was a man's-man kind of cat. After all, he loved to watch sports and *The Three Stooges*. The first time she caught him watching TV, he was standing on his hind legs watching a bicycle race, biting at the bike tires. He also had a special "birds and squirrels" cat video he liked to watch. Like his bike-tire assault, he'd try to "catch" the birds on the screen.

During their bedtime ritual, Junior Ray jumped up on the bed and crawled into the crook of Denise's arm. She'd pet him while he purred them both to sleep.

He was seventeen when Denise had to let him go because of kidney failure and diabetes. He had been in ICU for a week, and wasn't getting any better, when she decided she couldn't put him through any more. In the last couple of weeks of his life, he was too sick and weak to jump on the bed; that, and he was also keeping his distance because so many of their interactions had involved her poking a pill down him.

But on the Sunday night before she let him go, he summoned his strength and managed to jump up on the bed as he had always done. Denise had promised him earlier in the evening that she wouldn't take him back to the vet, and she wouldn't put him through any more treatments. She believed his jumping on the bed that last time was his way of thanking her for the decision, and he wanted their last night together to be a memorable one. He lay with her and purred while Denise cried herself to sleep.

The next day, she shared her final moments with Junior Ray.

After three catless months, she finally adopted two feline companions, Taboo and Auggie. Shortly after she brought them home, she felt a cat jump on the bed and lay down. She was very surprised to look down at the foot of the bed and see no cat. She knew immediately that Junior Ray was visiting.

Rather than being scared, Denise found great comfort in his visits. She would say, "Hey Juray. I still love you and miss you. You'll never be replaced. Thanks for coming to visit." The visits happened with some regularity—a few times a month—for that first year, but they have tapered off over the years.

Junior Ray even haunted one of her new cats—the one who "took his place" as her lap kitty. Often, Taboo would run around the house, yowling like something was after her. Denise would say, "Junior Ray, you behave yourself," and Taboo would soon settle back down.

Two years ago, Denise adopted a little black kitten, Stanley James, who is so much like Junior Ray she often wonders if it's JR reincarnated. Sometimes she takes Stanley's little face in her hand, looks into his eyes, and asks, "Juray, are you in there?" So far, Stanley/Junior Ray isn't admitting anything.

CASPER

Casper had a long, pure-white coat and stunning green eyes. Unlike the cartoon character, this Casper couldn't hear. His owner, Kathy, used hand signals whenever she wanted him to come to her. Like many deaf cats, he feared almost nothing.

In some ways he acted very doglike; for one thing, he loved riding in cars. The family lived in the country, so on special occasions, whenever Kathy allowed him outside, he'd protect his territory against much larger and more dangerous intruders. Casper chased deer into the woods, and ran raccoons up trees whenever they strayed into his dominion.

At night, he jumped on the foot of the bed and lay down to snooze. A restless sleeper, he'd hop off the bed for a while to grab a bite to eat or use the litter box. A while later he jumped up on the bed again. This ritual continued several times throughout the night, every single night. Casper's invincible spirit saw him through many difficulties in his life, including a bout of cancer when he was younger. In 1999, at the age of sixteen, Casper grew ill. Reluctantly, Kathy put him to sleep.

Shortly after the cat's passing, Casper took up his old nightly ritual of jumping on the bed and then off again several times during the course of the night, just as he had all those years before he crossed. Kathy understood it was Casper's way of showing them he was okay. Kathy found his continued nighttime activities comforting.

His restless late-night visits continued for about a year.

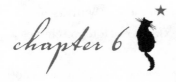
A Room with an Unusual View
HOTELS WITH CAT SPIRITS

There is something beyond the grave; death does not end all,
and the pale ghost escapes from the vanquished pyre.
     —SEXTUS PROPERTIUS

It's late. You're exhausted. The first day of your vacation seemed to fly by. You've got a full belly, and now you'd just like to go to your room for some rest. As you're dropping off to sleep, you feel the comforting and familiar sensation of a cat leaping onto the bed. He takes a few steps, circles a couple of times, and drops down next to your feet. Who'd have thought: a hotel with all the comforts of home—even the furry ones.

In the morning you compliment the innkeeper on her well-mannered hotel cat. She smiles, as it's praise she's heard many times before. There's only one problem: She doesn't have a hotel cat. Not a live one, anyway.

I've found some fascinating hotels and B&Bs that happily admit to having permanent pets, and a few who said, "No comment."

Get out your skeleton key and put it in the keyhole. We're going to visit some hotels where the spirits have four feet and whiskers, and you never have to worry about cat hair showing up on your clothes. It's time to meet the feline spirits with rooms to rent.

MORRIS THE CAT
High atop East Mountain, in the northwest corner of Arkansas, the Crescent Hotel stands over the town of Eureka Springs, Arkansas, like a sentinel on watch. The five-story, sixty-eight-room hotel was built of

eighteen-inch-thick native white magnesium limestone. With its aristo-cratic arches, turrets, and chimney spires, the Crescent Hotel resembles a European castle.

In the nineteenth century, Eureka Springs became a boomtown—not due to gold or oil, but because of the healing springwater bubbling up from deep beneath the limestone. In the mid-1850s, Dr. Alvah Jackson discovered a long-sought-after legendary healing spring. In those years before antibiotics, sick people flocked to Eureka Springs to drink and bathe in the area's healing waters.

The Crescent Hotel, completed in 1886, was built to attract the more elite clientele from around the country. It cost $294,000 to construct, as the *Eureka Springs Times Echo* put it, AMERICA'S NEWEST AND MOST LUXURI-OUS HOTEL.

At the hotel's grand opening on May 20, 1886, the newspaper also re-ported, "The magnificent structure was then furnished in the most exqui-site manner. It is lighted with Edison lamps, furnished with electric bells, heated with steam and open grates, has a hydraulic elevator, and is truly a showplace of today's conveniences."

The hotel thrived for almost fifty years. However, the Depression hit the Crescent Hotel hard. People could no longer afford such opulence, so they simply suffered at home. During those meager days the hotel opened for guests in the summer. In the fall and winter off-seasons, the Crescent Hotel operated as the Crescent College and Conservatory for Young Women. Eventually, the Crescent was forced to close its doors, but not for long. A few days after its closing, Norman G. Baker purchased the grand building for $30,000, a fraction of the original construction cost. It would become the new Baker Hospital and Health Spa for the treatment of can-cer and other noncommunicable diseases. In 1940, Baker was imprisoned for mail fraud, and once again, the Crescent Hotel stood vacant.

Several years later the Crescent Hotel reopened to guests once more, and has remained in continuous operation ever since.

According to porter Boyd T. Pyle Sr., in 1973 an orange tabby kitten with yellow eyes ambled up to the hotel entrance. The staff let him come in, and he stayed for twenty-one years. They named him Morris because he looked so much like the 9Lives Cat Food spokescat. (Some people say he was the second Morris TV cat, but that's doubtful.) Before long, he'd been promoted to hotel general manager. A message board behind the reservation counter displayed Morris's name and position along with that of the bookkeeper.

Morris would sit around in the lobby and greet people as they came through the front door. The tabby spent his days surrounded by elegant antique furniture resting on hardwood floors. He would follow people he fancied back to their rooms to help them pack and unpack.

Morris could come and go as he pleased. When he first showed up, someone installed a cat door. He couldn't see through the original wooden door, so they replaced it with a window he could peek through. The only time he ever went off the property was to visit the St. Elizabeth Catholic Church, which adjoins the hotel property. Car-savvy Morris would always look both ways before crossing the street, said Boyd.

Morris followed people he liked everywhere, including all the way down to the basement. Since he was such a heavy guy, twenty pounds in his heyday, you could hear his footsteps behind you, Boyd says. He would jump up in the laps of guests sitting around the lobby, preferring mature guests to rough and noisy little kids. He was usually pretty patient with people.

Like Morris, little Vickie Beason loved sitting on the antique couches in the lobby on her many trips to the Crescent. Putting aside his usual dislike for youngsters, Morris would come over to her and climb onto her lap. He'd crane his neck so she could scratch him behind the ears. With his claws fully intact, he'd sometimes get a little carried away and dig his nails into her legs as he barreled out deep purrs.

As he grew older his bulk made it harder for him to do the things he had done easily in his younger days. He stopped jumping into people's laps. When he started having difficulty getting through his cat flap, the maintenance man constructed a set of wooden cat steps so he could come and go more freely. Because of his advancing arthritis, the staff had to put up signs that read PLEASE DO NOT PET THE CAT. Morris's once-impressive volume shrunk down to a mere orange shadow.

Finally, after his old joints had begun to ache and he could barely walk, the manager put up signs asking guests not to pick up the cat due to his arthritis. Even then, Morris always recognized Vickie and somehow managed to hop up into her lap. The teen garnered dirty looks from the clerk at the registration desk when they caught her with the cat in her lap. She always explained that Morris had jumped up there, but doubted that they believed her.

When Morris passed away in October 1994 at the age of twenty-one and a half, the hotel staff buried him in the hotel's rose garden where he had traditionally sunbathed. The maintenance people built a wooden casket and lined it with red velvet. They ordered a granite headstone marker. The priest from the Catholic church next door even came over and said prayers over his grave. More than fifty people showed up for Morris's funeral.

Today, near the couch he so loved, an elegant color portrait of Morris, framed in a golden oval, hangs in the lobby in his honor.

During a visit in the mid-1990s, Vickie Beason was once again enjoying the beautiful furniture of the Crescent lobby. Immediately, the ghost of Morris recognized her and, as he had always done, leapt up into her lap. Warily, she glanced toward the desk and saw that no one was paying any attention to her, so she scratched behind his ears as she had always done. It surprised her that all of the DO NOT PET THE CAT signs had been taken down.

After a few minutes, Morris jumped down, disappearing underneath one of the other couches. Vickie stood up and went to find her family, when she noticed an obituary displayed at the front desk: "Our beloved cat, Morris . . ."

That was the last time she ever saw him. Even today when she stays at the Crescent Hotel, she sits on that couch just to see if he'll show up again.

"I guess he just wanted one more scratch before he went on his way," Vickie said.

Vickie isn't the only one who has seen the late general manager. Carroll Heath, one of the operators of The Crescent Hotel Ghost Tours, saw Morris's ghost from the cat's more rotund days.

"I saw this great big orange tabby cat in the garden for just a brief second," Heath said. "There he was, sitting in a flower bed. He was quite fat. I turned around and, *boom*, he was gone."

He also witnessed the kitty spirit around the turn of the millennium. At first, Carroll said it didn't register that he was looking at Morris until he did a double take, and the cat had disappeared. A few weeks after Carroll's Morris sighting, one of the workers in the laundry told Heath that after his death, she had seen him three or four times down in the laundry, where she used to feed him scraps.

No one has reported him lately.

Crescent Hotel
75 Prospect Avenue
Eureka Springs, AR 72632
479-253-9766
877-342-9766
www.crescent-hotel.com
www.eureka-springs-ghost.com

THE ALLEY CAT APPARITION

Pride House in Jefferson, Texas, is a perfect getaway for a cat-loving ghost hunter. Although the ten-room Victorian inn has no house cats of its own, it offers pet-friendly lodging. In the breakfast room, a sign prominently displayed on the wall depicts the silhouette of a black cat with a caption that reads ALLEY CATS RESCUED HERE. The sign is sincere. It's a delightful omen of things to come when guests see a colony of feral cats dart from bush to bush.

This recorded Texas landmark was the first official bed-and-breakfast in Texas. Sawmill owner G. W. Brown built Pride House in 1888 as his own home. The official Texas Historical Marker next to the door reads BROWN-BENDER HOUSE. The two-story house, heavily embellished with gingerbread trim, has thirteen-foot ceilings and king- and queen-size beds. Nine-foot-tall windows with stained-glass panels can be found in every room, and door inserts hold original glass that is wavy and bubbled. With construction standards unheard of today, Pride House boasts heart-of-pine floors and triple-layer cypress construction—a whopping 100,000 board feet of lumber.

The building has been through several owners since 1888. In the 1960s, a fire damaged one room of the building, and the establishment was forced to close. The state's first bed-and-breakfast stood vacant for fifteen years. In the mid-1970s, Sandy Spaulding and Ruthmary Jordan purchased the inn. The building's age had clearly caught up with it. After a year of reconstruction and renovation, the Brown-Bender House opened as the Pride House, named after the new owner's son.

That's when the alley cats came into the picture, according to today's owner, Sandra Reisenauer. "Cats have been hanging around here for thirty years," Sandra said. "Bonnie, the innkeeper before me, took care of them."

Sandra said that Jefferson, Texas, has no animal control. Ruthmary started feeding the strays that would come begging for a meal. They weren't allowed inside the inn, but the cats were welcome to set up housekeeping in the shrubs that surround the property. The tradition of caring for the ferals continues with Sandra today. She and another neighbor feed them. She wants to spay and neuter them, but can't afford the expense, and Jefferson has no low-cost neuter clinics. Although the ferals add a homey touch to the B&B, they aren't pets. She's never been able to touch them.

Two years ago a high-school student named Laynii (pronounced *Lane-y*) Patrick worked at the B&B as a weekend maid. As she made up the bed in the Royal George Room on the second floor, she glanced out of the corner of her eye and saw a full-grown black cat standing in the open door, eyeing her.

"I knew Sandra didn't have any inside cats," Laynii said. "It creeped me out because black cats are supposed to be unlucky. A chill went down my back."

She went to the door, but the large black cat had vanished. Shrugging it off, Laynii went back to straightening the room. Again, she saw the cat in the hall. It was a solid but foggy shape. She could definitely see the feline form. Laynii turned off the vacuum and went back into the hall. Again, she found nothing there. Although she wasn't afraid, she felt disturbed by the fact that something was in the hallway that wasn't supposed to be there—and she could feel it watching her. Her uneasy feeling came not from the cat's color, but because it wasn't supposed to be there.

Sandra thinks the azalea bushes and the free meals make Pride House a happy place for the ferals, including those who have passed on. "Some of them must enjoy hanging around." Sandra believes she may have seen a cat spirit herself. "We have zillions of cats," she said. This may be a bit of Texas embellishment, but there certainly are many alley cats at Pride House. Although the colony's population varies, Sandra said there are usually ten kitties on the block, plus or minus.

She recalled one particularly striking calico cat who had hung around since they bought the place. Every day she would see the tricolored queen dart out of the bushes or nibble at the bowl of food, or snooze in the shade of the fig tree. Suddenly, she disappeared. She wondered what had happened to the poor little mama kitty she had so enjoyed. Then, as suddenly as she'd disappeared, she returned, but only once, as if to say, "So long, and thanks for the food." Sandra believes that the mother kitty who reappeared was a ghost.

Now she wonders whenever she looks at her elusive ferals which ones are real and which ones are spirits.

Pride House Bed & Breakfast
409 E. Broadway
Jefferson, TX 75657
800-894-3526
www.jeffersontexas.com

Catnip and the Faust Hotel

Despite its ominous name, the Faust Hotel has nothing to do with Mephistopheles, ancient German literature, or the occult. It has more to do with a Texas banker named Faust, his family homestead, and a small Texas city's desire to encourage tourism.

Following the end of World War I, the city leaders of New Braunfels, Texas, wanted to have a world-class hotel in order to attract tourists from around the globe. The city of New Braunfels is located between Austin and San Antonio, conveniently situated along a route well traveled both before and after the advent of the horseless carriage, and therefore, a perfect place for an upscale hotel.

In the 1920s, The Travelers Corporation set out to raise the funds for the project. Walter Faust Jr., who was the vice president of the New Braunfels Chamber of Commerce and president of the First National Bank in New Braunfels, was instrumental in procuring the money to build the hotel. Standing just a block off of the historic downtown square in New Braunfels, The Travelers Corporation built the hotel on property offered by Walter Faust—the Faust family homestead.

Shortly before the great Stock Market Crash of 1929, the spanking new hotel opened its doors under the name of The Traveler's Hotel.

Faust loved the four-story art nouveau Spanish Renaissance–style building so much that he purchased it from the The Travelers Corporation. He lived there with his family until his death in 1933. Three years later, the hotel was renamed "The Faust." Today's Faust Hotel has been renovated to provide modern amenities, but contains the antique-style decor and ambience the hotel had when it first opened. Guests can step back in time and find themselves surrounded by fine antiques. The hotel lies just a block from the New Braunfels' town square.

The front lobby is decorated with a 1930s motif. It even has a 1929 Model A Ford parked next to the antique grand piano in the lobby. The rooms have been renovated, but still boast original furnishings and period photos, including a photo of famed bank robbers Bonnie Parker and Clyde Barrow. Another photo hanging just outside Room 306 is supposed to be an image of Christine, one of Walter Faust's ancestors who grew up on the family homestead on which they built the hotel. In the picture the little girl is holding a white kitten.

There are reports that a hotel housekeeper working on the third floor observed the ghost of a little girl about four years old playing in the hallway. Occasionally a white cat accompanies her.

My husband Weems Hutto, who's a noted cat photographer, had heard about the Faust Hotel when he'd first moved to Texas in the early 1980s. He even dropped by to book a room while on a weekend trip to New Braunfels in 1990. When he walked into the elegant lobby, it was filled to capacity with former soldiers and sailors who were attending a World War II veterans' reunion. Seeing the very dapper gentlemen in their vintage uniforms and the ladies in their elegant evening gowns made him feel like he had stepped back in time.

Twenty-something years after his initial introduction to the Faust Hotel, Weems read a book about haunted Texas vacations. On the Internet, he read other stories of furniture moving around on the upper floors, the contents of rooms being rearranged, and for the first time, he learned about a phantom cat. The prospects were quite irresistible.

On Christmas Eve several years ago, Weems and I booked a room on the third floor, which is reputedly where the hotel ghost cat hangs out. Fortunately, it was a slow night and there weren't any other guests on that wing. We came equipped with video cameras, digital cameras, laser thermometers, electromagnetic field meters, and an irresistible collection of cat toys, balls, teasers, and freshly dried catnip buds.

After unpacking our gear, I went into the hall to try to entice the ghost kitty out into the open. I must have taken almost fifty lovely digital images of only catnip, fur mice, and little cat balls in exactly the same spot. A few minutes later Weems brought his video camera out into the hall and was extending the tripod legs when he saw one of the cat balls roll several inches on its own across the carpet, as if a paw had swatted it.

"It moved."

Naturally I had turned around to ask him a question and missed the show.

He excitedly pointed at the cat ball, which had moved a few inches away from where it had sat for more than half an hour. I immediately snapped the shutter and captured a small white orb hovering over the cat ball. Weems captured another appearance in the form of an unusual cat-face reflection in the hall end-table mirror with his own digital camera.

For the rest of our two-night stay we experienced no more kinetic activities with the cat toys nor captured anything else with the camera. We guessed that the kitty had tired of the toys as kitties often do—in a matter of minutes.

As Weems can well attest, it doesn't matter whether they are alive or not; cats seldom cooperate when it comes to taking their pictures. But they will come out for a whiff of good catnip and a chance to play a little ball.

The Faust Hotel
240 South Seguin Avenue
New Braunfels, TX 78130
830-625-7791
www.fausthotel.com

Mamma Kitty

The Tokeland Hotel, which was built in 1886, is the oldest resort hotel in Washington State. Located in the seaside village of Tokeland and surrounded by meadows, the hotel, a large gray building, draws people to—well—the middle of nowhere. But it is the perfect place to get away from it all. Built on the Tokeland Peninsula overlooking Willapa Bay, it takes just a few minutes to drive to Pacific Ocean beaches. The Tokeland Hotel operates the only full-service restaurant in the area. Hotel guests can unwind with some nearby adventure, whether it's fishing, whale watching, surfing at Westport, clamming or crabbing, beachcombing, or biking.

Guests can relax surrounded by turn-of-the-century charm. Just off the hotel's lobby, a moose head dominates the mantle and brick fireplace (original to the building), making the room a toasty place to read or relax. You can almost picture a cat warming herself next to the golden embers, giving off a welcoming glow that might even entice a feline back from the dead.

Hotel owner Scott White said he has heard apparition reports of both a cat and a ten-year-old boy named Albert. When Scott and Katherine White bought the property in 1990, it came with a hotel cat—an orange tabby. They appropriately called the feral cat "Mamma Kitty" because she had given birth to several litters of kittens down in an old nearby pump house. Scott was able to befriend Mamma Kitty, as much as anyone can befriend a feral. He could pet her on rare occasions. Once she even let him remove a barbless hook that had become embedded in her lip. The hotel fed her well, and she kept the mouse population down. She never came in the house; being feral, she never had the desire.

When Mamma Kitty was about fifteen years old, she simply disappeared.

A short time later, Scott began receiving reports of a cat in Room 3. Although Scott has never experienced the hotel's ghost cat personally, he has heard from different guests that an orange cat sometimes appears in that particular room. Guests have been awakened in the middle of the night by the distinct sensation of a cat's feet landing at the foot of the bed, then walking over and lying down next to them. He never heard guests in other rooms mention the phenomenon—only Room 3. None of the guests was frightened by it.

Scott believes that the ten-year-old boy's ghost and Mamma Kitty are the protectors of the hotel. They have even scared off people who were trying to vandalize the building.

Appropriately enough for a hotel visited by cat spirits, living pets are also welcome.

Tokeland Hotel & Restaurant
2964 Kindred Ave.
P.O. Box 223
Tokeland, WA 98590
360-267-7006
tokeland@comcast.net

THE FOUR-FOOTED SPIRITS AT THAYER'S

Some hotels are tight-lipped about their hauntings, even when it comes to spirits as inoffensive as a cat. Not Thayer's Historic Bed 'n Breakfast. Thayer's touts itself as the Victorian bed-and-breakfast with a "haunting personality." Located in Annandale, Minnesota, just an hour from the Twin Cities, the B&B is decked out in Victorian style, with plenty of charm and grace. This haunted jewel is listed in the National Register of Historic Places.

Originally built as the Rail Road Hotel in 1895 by Gus and Caroline Thayer, this rare balloon-framed building has been beautifully restored by its current owner, Sharon Gammell, and her late husband, Warren.

There's always something interesting going on at Thayer's. Available by prior arrangement, the hotel offers Ghost Hunting Weekends, Murder Mystery Dinners, and even readings by Sharon, who is a gifted psychic. For your paranormal pleasure, Thayer's resident ghosts include the original owners, Gus and Caroline, and Warren Gammell, Sharon's husband, who passed away in 1996.

The B&B also boasts a number of four-footed ghost spirits. Sharon talks a little about her little furry phantoms, but not too much. She doesn't want to taint her guests' otherworldly experiences with too much info. But the B&B's website gives up a few secrets.

Among the feline spirits are Ghost Kitty (GK for short), a short-haired gray kitty who likes to play and chase things. He was the first kitty to introduce himself from the Other Side. He likes to sit on the beds, leaving an indentation where he lays. Some of the guests have seen him in the living room. Sharon explained that Tennessee, her Maine Coon who hasn't yet crossed over, has a collection of cat balls with the little bells in them. GK also loves to play with these toys. It's not unusual to hear the ball bells jingling even when nothing is seen near the toys. GK and Tennessee play together as well, playing tag and chasing each other around the house. Thayer's guests report actually seeing GK in the flesh—well, similar to the flesh, anyway.

Kimmie Cat and Clyde Kitty are Sharon's little Angels of Death. Kimmie and Clyde came to get her other cat, Professor Herald, when it was time for him to cross over the Rainbow Bridge. She said they show up to help cats cross over to the Other Side, escorting them out of this life. As Professor Herald lay dying in Sharon's arms, Kimmie Cat stationed herself on one side of him and Clyde Kitty on the other until the Professor passed away.

Kimmie Cat sometimes pushes all of Sharon's papers off of her desk onto the floor when she thinks it's time for her to quit working. Fellow angel Clyde Kitty gives kisses to people he likes.

One member of the Ghost Hunter 101 class on her Ghost Hunting Weekend captured a photo of Professor Herald in Room 207. Sharon said you always know if it's Herald who joined you in bed. He sleeps with his paw on the guest's shoulder and a loud purr rumbles from his invisible throat.

Cocoa Bear, a Maine Coon who died in 1996 of a urinary-tract ailment, has been seen and felt by a number of guests, and he isn't shy in front of the camera, either. Recently, a mother came in with her four-year-old son to buy a gift certificate. The boy saw Tennessee and Sharon's other living kitty, Miss Sadie, and asked if he could play with them. After a while he returned and asked how many cats she had. "I have two," she said.

Defiantly, the little boy folded his arms across his chest and said, "You have three kitties." He added, "Cocoa Bear said he's fine. And how can you miss a big kitty like that? And he's really soft."

The boy was right on all counts, including the cat's name, which Sharon had *not* shared with him. Cocoa Bear was a not-so-subtle cat, weighing in at about forty pounds with a big fluffy tail.

The B&B's most recent fluffy ghost kitty is a walk-in; Sharon had never seen him before. Nothing is known about him except he's a very fluffy, medium-haired cat. Sharon said one guest described him as a medium-gray kitty with a little random white. A week later, Sharon was outside cleaning up the yard and found the body of a cat that fit that description.

Last but not least, Thayer's also has a Ghost Mouse whom Tennessee and Miss Sadie love to play with. Sharon says all he does is run around and drive Tennessee crazy.

Thayer's Historic Bed 'n Breakfast
60 West Elm Street
P.O. Box 246
Annandale, MN 55302
320-274-8222
800-944-6595
www.thayers.net
slg@thayers.net

THE PHANTOM LITTER BOX

Tom and Kathy Johnson own the Ivy House Inn, a roomy 1916 Cape Cod–style bed-and-breakfast in Casper, Wyoming. Ivy House was chosen as the country's eighth-best bed-and-breakfast for catering to travelers' needs in the Arrington's Bed & Breakfast Journal "Book of Lists 2002." The inn offers three rooms and two suites.

Not only do they have immaculate accommodations, but they also have special guests who checked in long before the Johnsons bought the place, and may live there for many years to come. The guests are feline in form and otherworldly in nature.

The Johnsons have lived at Ivy House for ten years. Before that, the property belonged to Mrs. White, who owned several cats. In 1995, Mrs. White passed away in her home at the age of ninety-three. She's still there, and so are some of her pets.

Tom, Kathy, and son, Erik, began experiencing the cat spirits shortly after they moved in. The first time, Tom and Kathy watched two Siamese cats running down the hall. Tom and Kathy had a bit of an argument, each accusing the other of accidentally letting their three pet cats into the public area. On closer inspection, they found all of their cats sleeping on different beds in their living quarters. Of course, none of their pets bore any resemblance to two "scrawny, pencil-tailed Siamese" cats.

The middle part of the house where the ghost cats spend most of their time was built in 1941. In the ten years they've lived there, Tom and Kathy have actually seen the Siamese cats twice. Most of the time they appear as shadows, but even when they can't see them, the Johnsons know the ghost cats are around. They often feel the cold spots that are frequently associated with ghosts.

Once, their son, Erik, was lying on the couch watching television when he felt a cold spot on his legs. His dad took a digital photo, and there was a distinctive orb right where Erik had felt the chill. Erik has also taken pictures from the outside that show two individual cats between the window and the curtain. Once in a while the curtains rustle as if a cat was moving around behind them. Like mischievous living cats, they've been known to knock over vases and candles.

"You can't stop them from getting onto the counter," Kathy laughed.

The Johnsons recently adopted a nine-week-old Gordon Setter named Claire, and while their own cats didn't have a problem with the new dog, Mrs. White's cats did. Kathy said they could hear a cat hissing at Claire. The dog returned the favor by barking at the invisible cats. Claire wasn't the only dog annoyed by the phantom Siamese cats. Their old Sheltie would avoid certain spots in the home. Kathy believes his reluctance to go to those places was ghost cat–related.

In the winter of 2006, the B&B held scrapbooking weekends. Scrapbookers like to come to Ivy House to work undisturbed. A lady attending the event told Tom that one of his cats got out. She knew the inn didn't allow pets, and thought he'd want to know that she saw a Siamese climbing the stairs. Tom tried to assure her that, while they do have some cats of their own, they are confined to their private family apartment, and never allowed to go into the main part of the B&B. He paraded every one of their pets in front of all of the ladies so they'd know what the ghost cats *didn't* look like. Then he told them about the Siamese specters who live in the hotel. The ladies were delighted.

In the Blue Rose Room, guests have said that a cat spent the night at the end of the bed. In the morning the cat wasn't there anymore. One morning a guest with a headache was still in bed, and felt a cat nudging the small of his back.

Guests have mentioned that they've felt cats rubbing up against their legs, and Kathy has also experienced that sensation. When she was outside working in the garden, a cat rubbed around her legs. When she looked down, she saw nothing there. Two other ladies described the Siamese cats; specifically, a slender short-haired Siamese and a heavier-looking long-haired Himalayan.

Kathy said you can hear cat noises and the *thumpety-thump* of them playing. The Johnsons' cats often see the ghost cats. Kathy has even watched their pets wrestling with cats that aren't there. However, the ghost cats aren't confined to any one particular area, as are the living cats. Occasionally in a public hallway, an invisible litter box emits a noxious aroma—and like any box, the smell dissipates in a few minutes on its own. After all, the family hasn't been able to locate an ectoplasmic litter scoop.

Ivy House Inn Bed & Breakfast
815 South Ash
Casper, Wyoming 82601
307-265-0974
www.ivyhouseinn.com
ivyinn@yahoo.com

But We Don't Have a Cat at the Stephen Daniels House

The Stephen Daniels House has stood for over 350 years. It is one of the few three-story homes from that era to survive in Salem, Massachusetts. Captain Stephen Daniels built it in 1667, and the house is Salem's longest continuously operated inn.

Two large walk-in fireplaces warm the common rooms, while canopy beds, wood-burning fireplaces, and antique furnishings adorn the guest rooms. Down comforters and creaky wide-plank floors add to the old-world ambience. Like many other old inns, guests feel like they have stepped back a century or so in time. Guests can relax in the huge original kitchen, the parlor, and the dining room, or in the pleasant English garden filled with flowering shrubbery and colorful blossoms.

Despite all the antique grandeur, the inn welcomes children and well-behaved pets. If you don't travel with your own pet, you might run into the tabby who makes the inn his home. Innkeeper Kay Gill, who has owned and run the inn for forty-five years, said the tabby is different from most cats; this one is a ghost. The specter cat and a woman's ghost abide in the house. According to Kay, the cat's manifestation assumes many forms. One guest heard the mewing of a cat. Others have mentioned seeing a cat-shaped indentation on the bed. Still others have seen a shape running through the hall. One lady, thinking it was alive, actually brought it some milk.

The cat spends most of its time in the Rose Room on the 1756 side of the house. However, one online report said that the cat went from room to room, sometimes walking, sometimes darting. When it jumped into each bedroom, it acted like it was looking for someone. The person who wrote the report thought it was a living cat because it had such a presence about it. When the guest spoke with Kay, she learned the inn had no cats.

Another person said that their entire four-person party saw a black-and-gray tabby "ectoplasmic display."

Other people have described a slightly different cat. In 1996, Goldie Browning and her family stayed at the Stephen Daniels House. They were fortunate enough to have the entire second floor to themselves. A very friendly brown-and-white tabby cat wandered in and out of all three of their guest rooms for the entire night. He acted like any other cat, sitting casually, watching the activity around him, and giving himself a bath. With typical feline curiosity, he followed the Brownings around. Goldie and other family members even petted him. The next morning they, too, mentioned the cat to Kay and she told them, "People are always telling me about the cat. I've never seen him."

Kay believes that she was destined to have her ghost cat. Back in 1953 she painted a picture of a cat. Many years later she realizes the painting looked exactly like her guests' description of the ghost cat.

"It's a tabby," she said. "The cat knew I was coming here before I did."

Stephen Daniels House
1 Daniels Street
Salem, MA 01970-5214
978-744-5709

THE MILE-HIGH GHOST CAT

Jerome, Arizona, sits on the side of the mountains, over 7,000 feet above the Verde Valley. Founded in 1876, Jerome was a copper-mining town. It didn't take long before hotels, bars, brothels, opium dens, and pool halls began to spring up. By the middle of the twentieth century, Jerome's once thriving population had dwindled down to fifty—a ghost town, literally and figuratively.

Today, shops and galleries have replaced the brothels and opium dens in Jerome, but there are still hotels and bars that offer a place to lay your head down or order a cold one. This former nearly deserted ghost town does have the genuine article—a few ghosts of people who once struggled to survive here, plus one ghost cat.

The newly remodeled Mile High Inn and Grill, built in 1899, was originally called the Clinkscale Building. Other buildings constructed on this piece of property kept burning down. Built on the ashes of past infernos, this fireproof replacement had eighteen-inch-thick walls of poured, reinforced concrete.

Until recently, locals had known Mile High Inn as the Inn at Jerome. In an even earlier life, it housed a bordello owned by madam Jennie Banters. Some legends claim that Madam Jennie haunts the hotel, as does her cat. But one of the new owners said that the spirits belonged to an older woman and her cat, who died when the previous structure built on the same spot burned down in 1897. At the time the ground floor held a store and the upstairs rooms were rented as apartments.

The current owner says that evidence of the cat is seen throughout the building, noting that people don't actually *see* the cat; it is usually heard meowing around two or three in the morning.

In the past, guests and paranormal investigators have reported a wide variety of activity, including the apparition of a cat walking through the halls. Both guests and employees have reported a friendly feline rubbing up against their legs and others have heard the sound of a cat sharpening its claws. A cook claimed to have witnessed a cat strolling through the kitchen and then disappearing. The invisible cat also takes naps in different rooms, leaving cat-shaped indentations on the beds. As one guest described it, "It looked like someone plopped right down in the middle of the bed."

The nice thing about the cat at the Mile High Inn and Grill is when he cries in the middle of the night, you won't have to drag yourself out of bed to let him out. He can just walk through the door himself.

Mile High Inn and Grill
309 Main Street
Jerome, AZ 86331
928-634-5094
www.milehighinnandgrill.com

HOTELS WITH RUMORS OF CAT SPIRITS

ARIZONA

Hotel Vendome DR
230 South Cortez Street
Prescott, AZ 86303
928-776-0900
888-468-3583
www.vendomehotel.com

This 1917 historic inn combines the warmth of a bed-and-breakfast with the privacy of a hotel. Hotel Vendome, located just off the city's Courthouse Plaza, is a ninety-minute drive from Phoenix. During the golden age of silent moving pictures, cowboy star Tom Mix lived at the hotel. He rented his room for a year at a time while filming westerns on location in Prescott.

The hotel has early-twentieth-century touches such as an old-fashioned claw-foot tub, transom windows, iron radiators, oak furnishings, original woodwork, period wallpaper, handmade patchwork quilts, and pull-chain toilets. It also has modern conveniences like air-conditioning.

The hotel also has both two-legged and four-legged spirits. Room 16 has one of each.

Abby Byr and her cat, Noble, spent their last days in their room at the top of the stairs. Abby moved to Prescott for the treatment of consumption (now called tuberculosis) when she was in her late teens. At the time, the warm, dry climate was considered a potential cure for tuberculosis. She recovered from her illness and married Mr. Byr. In 1921, the couple purchased the four-year-old hotel. It seemed like a good idea at the time, because the health benefits of Arizona's climate were being promoted worldwide. Claims were even made that the extreme Arizona heat sterilized the air. Sanatoriums and retreats were inviting new business opportunities. But Abby and her husband found no pot of gold at the end of the consumption rainbow. Financial times were tough, and they lost the hotel due to unpaid taxes.

However, the kindly new owners hired the struggling couple to manage the hotel and allowed them and their cat, Noble, to live in Room 16 at no charge. One evening, when Mr. Byr went out to get Abby some medication, he simply disappeared. No one knows if he abandoned her or if he had been murdered. Abby continued to merely exist in her second-floor room, refusing to eat. She died in Room 16, along with Noble. A 1984 séance revealed that Noble died in the closet. Abby and her cat have been spotted haunting the hotel ever since.

Internet reports claim that some guests have heard the ringing sound of a cat toy; other guests have felt Noble. Another guest mentioned being awakened by a cat's meowing. Whenever she tried to approach the source of the sound, "It seemed to move."

TEXAS

Plaza Marriott
555 South Alamo Street
San Antonio, TX 78205
210-229-1000
800-421-1172

This hotel sits next door to San Antonio's famed HemisFair Tower of the Americas. One of the most unique hallmarks of this hotel is that it utilizes four circa mid-1800s buildings listed on the National Register of Historic Places. An 1850s German-style home contains the health club, which is reportedly haunted by one of the former owners of the old home. She was so distraught over her husband's death that she hanged not only herself, but also her cat in her living room. It is now the exercise room. According to some reports, the woman wearing a long white dress strolls through the upper levels holding her cat and stroking his head. Sightings have also been reported in the employee corridors in the basement as well as in the garden.

VIRGINIA

Cavalier Hotel (Formerly Cavalier on the Hill)
Oceanfront at 42nd Street
Virginia Beach, VA 23451
757-425-8555
800-446-8199
www.cavalierhotel.com

Opening its doors in 1927, the Cavalier Hotel was the spot for the pre–jet-set set. Beer magnate Adolph Coors, owner of Coors Brewery, died at the hotel, falling to his death from the sixth floor. No one believes Coors' death was accidental, but the debate rages as to whether he committed suicide or was pushed to his death. Regardless, rumors abound that his ghost still inhabits the hotel. Some people have compared the hotel's style and decor as reminiscent of the hotel in the movie *The Shining*.

This hotel is reputed to have a number of ghosts, including a cat. When asked, hotel management would not comment. There are reports that the cat is seen roaming the halls. His meow is also heard. A former hotel worker says the Cavalier has spent a lot of money over the years trying to catch the mysterious cat, but with no luck. Another worker says the cat drowned in the hotel pool and the cat's owner, a nine-year-old girl, also drowned while trying to save it. There haven't been any reports of the child's ghost.

Public Phantoms
Out and About with Feline Specters

*The boundaries which divide life from death are at best
shadowy and vague. Who shall say where the one ends
and the other begins?*

—Edgar Allen Poe, The Premature Burial

In times past, people have often had cats at their place of business, both
for rodent control and for companionship, to keep them company on
those slow days. Railroad stations and even military outfits enjoy having
a cat to break the monotony of a difficult and isolated life. Even today, li-
braries, bookstores, boutiques, and vet clinics often have a friendlier,
more inviting feel because the official greeter is a cat.

But some cats take their jobs very seriously. Like their dedicated
human counterparts, sometimes these devoted creatures never leave their
jobs—even a century after their deaths.

You may catch a fleeting glimpse of black darting in and out of the
ruins of a southern outpost, or hear the pitiful cry of a store cat perpetu-
ally waiting for her breakfast. You may even feel her rub up against your
legs while you wait to pay your vet bill.

Get out your library card and put on your reading glasses. We're going
to check out some very special public servants and faithful office cats.

In a Blu Mood at the Cat Hospital
In death, Blu, a clinic cat, comforted broken hearts just as he had in life.
In 1992, the big guy's career in veterinary medicine began on the wrong

side of the examination table, when his former owner left him at the Cat Hospital of Las Colinas, a cats-only clinic in Irving, Texas. The man had asked Dr. Patricia Hague, the clinic owner, to deliver the two-year-old cat to the pound because he'd been peeing outside the litter box. He had a nasty case of ringworm, too.

Since there's not much demand for cats who pee on carpet, Dr. Hague treated his bladder infection and then shaved and shampooed him to treat the fungus. Somehow Blu managed to maintain an air of dignity despite the fact that he looked like he'd had a run-in with a barber-school dropout. Once his coat was restored to its former beauty, the clinic staff discovered Blu was a majestic, Siamese-mix blue point with long legs and dynamic blue eyes.

"We knew right away that Blu was extraordinary," Dr. Hague said. "He had such a kind and gentle spirit." She hired the cat on the spot, giving him the title of "Official Clinic Greeter." Blu exceeded expectations. He never shied away from a stranger, and thought nothing of jumping up on a client's lap and asking for affection while the client and his cat waited to see the vet. While Blu was a goodwill ambassador, he also worked as a feline philanthropist, and literally gave his blood, sweat, and tears for the good of other cats. (Okay, he just gave his blood.) In addition to being the hospital's official blood donor, he helped the office staff file charts, among many other duties.

One of Blu's most remarkable talents was his compassionate perception, which enabled him to see feline patients, as well as their owners, through difficult times. Blu took it upon himself to welcome the cats who were awaiting their appointments in their carriers. Oddly, few of the visiting cats objected to his greetings. He was the clinic therapist and grief counselor. People have commented to staff members that he intuitively sought out cat owners who had received tragic news and sat next to them, offering them silent comfort and consolation. He just had an instinct as to what people needed. Never a stranger, he would greet clients and staff alike, occasionally rubbing up against their legs in greeting.

But life wasn't a bed of catnip for Blu. After that initial bladder infection, he was plagued by repeated lower urinary tract and kidney infections. Fortunately, his job came with a good medical plan.

In 1997, versatile Blu expanded his duties to include surrogate mom to Amazing Grayce, a six-week-old kitten who was found abandoned near the clinic. They became best friends, sleeping together all the time and grooming each other. As they cuddled, Grayce would knead her paws on Blu's belly. And of course, neither cat could resist a good game of tag.

Then, in late 2005, at the age of sixteen, Blu's health problems caught up with him and he lost his fight. On October 14, Blu passed on his position as goodwill ambassador to his protégée. But Grayce simply wasn't up to the job. Immediately following Blu's death, Grayce appeared fine, acting as she always had, but a short time later, veterinary nurse Julie Starry noticed that Grayce's behavior had changed. She must have finally realized that Blu would never return.

"She seemed sad all the time," Julie said. "She wasn't coming out to see us. She quit greeting people like she used to."

Despondent, Grayce pined for her companion. She refused to sleep in the cat bed that she and Blu had shared in the back of the clinic. Julie said they brought the bed up to the office area, hoping she'd use it, but she didn't. The staff felt powerless to help Grayce though her grief. But, even in death, Blu couldn't let his inconsolable best friend pine away.

Julie Starry recalls the night she went into the clinic to check on patients and boarders. As she walked toward the front of the hushed clinic, she encountered an odd sensation. "I felt something rubbing up against the inside of my right leg—just like a cat would do. At first I paused, thinking I had bumped my leg on something. I looked down, but there was nothing and no one there." No one, not even Grayce, was nearby. Clearly, something unexplainable had happened. At first Julie felt uneasy about the presence, but relaxed when she realized that Blu must have returned for a visit.

Julie soon learned she wasn't the only one who had encountered Blu. Some of the other nurses had felt a "presence" as well. "It was a sense. You catch something out of the corner of your eye but you don't see anything," Julie said. "I'd get that sense when I was by myself, when I was doing animal care at nights and on weekends. I was never that close to Blu," Julie admitted. "I feel he came back here until he was sure that Grayce was okay."

Blu's grief-counseling sessions must have worked. Toward the very end of December and early January, Grayce started returning to her more gregarious self.

"I noticed she started coming up front more," Julie said. Now Grayce once again greets clients and lies in her basket. Julie said Blu's presence no longer stands vigil over his younger charge. In early January, that feeling of "someone there" seemed to vanish.

"Grayce is better now, playing and more active," Julie said. "I felt he was staying behind to comfort her. He didn't come back for us; he came back for her."

TOM CAT'S LAST BATTLE AT FORT MCALLISTER

An old military motto proclaims that an army marches on its stomach. But even with full bellies and fine weaponry, hardship and death combined with a yearning for home can cause even well-fed soldiers to succumb to low morale. Throughout the history of war, animal mascots have often served as a magic pill for homesick troops.

In the mid-1700s, the Royal Welsh 1st Battalion traveled with a royal goat named Billy, while poodle mascots were all the rage during the Napoleonic Wars. In the American Revolutionary War, the military showed compassion for the mascots, even those of the enemy. A British dog was captured by Americans—sort of a doggie prisoner of war. General George Washington ordered a short truce so the dog could be returned to the British general who owned him.

During the Civil War, when men literally took up arms against their neighbors, or even their brothers, that special bond between soldier and animal was all the more important. Regimental mascots came in both two-legged and four-legged varieties. Dogs and horses, for obvious reasons, were the most common animals found with the troops, but other more exotic animals also earned the respect and affection of the regiments. Eagles, bears, chickens, and camels traveled with their units—even the occasional feline showed up on the battlefield. Just as there was massive loss of human life in the War Between the States, the mascots often perished alongside their human counterparts.

Although dogs and horses appeared to be the preferred mascot of the soldiers in the field, cats were often found on ships and in forts, where they performed utilitarian mousekeeping chores as well. One such cat was a black tom appropriately known as "Tom Cat" who served alongside Confederate soldiers at Fort McAllister, near Savannah, Georgia.

Today the site doesn't look like much, but more than 150 years ago the soldiers of Fort McAllister, with the help of its feline mascot, staved off Union assaults for three years. Built in 1861 of bricks made of bottom mud from the Ogeechee River, Fort McAllister helped create a protective perimeter around the strategic city of Savannah and its harbor. The massive earthen walls almost completely protected the fort's seven gun emplacements, as well as its 230 defenders plus one cat.

Tom Cat was Fort McAllister's cherished mascot. According to sketchy historical records, this black cat was adored by the men. During the fury of his three battles, Tom Cat would run back and forth along the fort's ramparts as cannonballs and musket rounds were ringing overhead. According to an official report sent to famed Confederate general, P. G. T. Beauregard, Tom Cat's eight lives ran out on March 3, 1863. During seven hours of shelling, the fort's shortest soldier became another casualty of the war when an exploding shell fired by Major General Quincy A. Gillmore's artillery landed near Tom Cat, ending his corporeal life.

The fort endured seven hours of bombardment that day, but did not ultimately fall to Union general William T. Sherman until December 13, 1864, completing the general's March to the Sea. But the loss of Tom Cat that March day warranted its own mention in the report of the day's combat to higher headquarters.

Tom Cat's sacrifice was so significant that the state of Georgia raised a historical marker in his honor in 1963. Located at the fort, it reads:

Tom Cat
Garrison Mascot

The sole Confederate fatality after seven hours of intensive bombardment on March 3, 1863, by the monitors PASSAIC (Capt. Percival Drayton), NAHANT, and PATAPSCO, supported by the MONTAUK, the WISSAHIVKON, the SENECA, the DAWN, the FLAMBEAU, the SERBAGO, the C.P. WILLIAMS, the NORFOLK PACKET, and the PARA was the garrison mascot. The death of the cat was deeply regretted by the men, and news of the fatality was communicated to General Beauregard in the official report of the action.

GEORGIA HISTORICAL COMMISSION
1963

The stray round that brought an end to Tom Cat's brilliant military career only claimed his eighth life. He's still working on his ninth. Park staff, visitors, and Civil War reenactors at Fort McAllister State Park have reported to park police that they have had otherworldly encounters with the ghost cat.

Although park administrators are tight-lipped about Tom Cat sightings, there have been numerous published reports and eyewitness accounts about the four-footed phantom who still stands sentinel at the ruins of Fort McAllister. Witnesses have reported seeing a black cat hanging out inside the fort's bunkers or running along the fort's earthwork fortifications. Other people swear they have felt a cat rubbing up against their legs. Naturally, when they look down, they see no cat. One park official mentioned that one of the park managers had an orange tabby, also named Tom Cat. Ironically, Tom Cat II died in 1981 (or in 1982, no one is really sure) on the anniversary of the original Tom Cat's death.

Fort McAllister State Park
3894 Fort McAllister Road
P.O. Box 394-A
Richmond Hill, GA 31324
912-727-2339

THE ANTIQUES STORE'S PITIFUL LITTLE CAT

In July of 1983, the Texas sun would have quickly parched the body of a full-grown man. It would have taken no time at all to kill an eight-week-old kitten, but somehow this one managed to survive. There she cowered, a pitiful tortoiseshell, raising herself under the claw-foot bathtub in the back alley behind two antiques stores in Jefferson, Texas. The tub had been filled with soil and planted with oleander. Under the shade of the tub, green St. Augustine grass offered a cool oasis from the blistering summer rays. The little stray barely subsisted off of whatever prey she could scrounge, mainly crickets and lizards.

Bob Haynes, owner of River City Mercantile Antiques, felt sorry for the tiny orphan. He convinced his business neighbor, Dee, to put out some water. The following day food appeared. Once her livelihood was assured, the wily kitten wanted more. By watching people coming and going, the kitten figured out that the antiques shop had something her bathtub didn't—air-conditioning. The kitten learned she could open the door by pushing it with her paws. Without warning, the kitten would burst into the shop and jump into Dee's lap.

Now, Dee had a big heart, but no real love for cats. She complained to her husband, "Do something about that pitiful kitten."

In one move, good neighbor Bob rescued both Dee and the orphan by taking the pitiful kitten into his fine antiques shop. The moniker of the "pitiful little kitten" stuck. He shortened it to Pitiful, or Ms. P. That was the beginning of their twenty-year adventure of growing old together.

Pitiful's job was to hold down the chair at the front of the store and to keep the elephants away. She performed her job beautifully. After all, Bob never saw any bull elephants in his china closet or in his 5,000-square-foot shop that had once been a pre–Civil War cotton warehouse.

Pitiful's other job was to make snap character judgments by biting people she didn't like, "Especially," Bob added with a mischievous smile, "unruly children."

In her twenty-year tenure as elephant guard, she only broke one thing—a complete china dresser tray with powder box. Of course, she was a rookie in the antiques business at the time. She'd only been there a few weeks when she jumped up on a table and caught the edge of the tray, sending china and herself flying in all directions. Preferring Pitiful's company to that of small unruly kids, Bob wrote the $150 mistake off to inexperience. Soon Pitiful perfected her antiques vaulting skills. She was famous for jumping up on a table full of expensive breakables and pussyfooting through the fine crystal.

Bob lost far more revenue to well-meaning customers who would try to grab her off the table. "I had to tell the customers, 'Leave her alone. She knows what she's doing.' "

Bob and Pitiful had a morning ritual that they observed from 1985 right up until the time she didn't have the energy to make the effort. Bob would enter through the back door where his faithful little security guard waited. He'd pick her up, put her over his left shoulder, and carry her to the front of the store. She'd jump down onto the bookcase next to his front counter and desk where she'd receive a treat because there was no evidence of nighttime elephant activity.

Like any other cat, Pitiful had an affinity for upholstered chairs. Toward the end of her life her kidneys were failing her, and people would complain to Bob that the cat was going to ruin her favorite chair. "You won't be able to sell it," more than one person chided him.

His response was short and definitive. ". . . And?"

It wasn't long before he came to his shop one terrible summer morning in 2002 and found her on the floor, dying. He scooped her up and took her to the vet. In just a few minutes it was all over. He returned home with Pitiful in a cardboard box, wrapped in a towel. Bob's companion, David, knowing that Pitiful's remaining days were few, had already hand-made a wooden casket with a cushioned velvet lining. They placed white Mardi Gras beads around her neck like a collar and buried her at their home.

When Bob next opened the shop, there was no one there to greet him. "It felt weird," Bob said. "I felt disconnected in my life."

Then periodically, he would hear her distinctive voice, calling several meows in a row, from the back of the building where Bob had kept her litter pan.

"The first time I heard it, I thought, 'How can that be?' " Over the next three months, he heard her crying six times. Bob never saw her, or even felt her presence, beyond hearing her voice.

Today Pitiful no longer cries from the rear of the store. A new cat, a black bruiser named Chippendale, has assumed her spot near the bookcase. The elephants are still at bay, and the chair held down, in a legacy that the town of Jefferson will not soon forget. You can visit Chippendale and Bob Haynes at River City Mercantile Antiques.

River City Mercantile Antiques
111 Austin Street
Jefferson, TX 75657
903-665-8270

THE LITERARY GHOST CAT

For ages literature and cats have gone together. Some of the world's most famous authors have also been ailurophiles. When Ernest Hemingway lived in Cuba, it was said he had thirty cats, one of them a polydactyl. (Polydactyls have more than the usual number of toes.) Today the Hemingway house in Key West is full of descendants of those cats, many of them polydactyls. The list of literary cat lovers includes Charles Dickens, Edgar Allen Poe, T. S. Eliot, Sir Walter Scott, Samuel Clemens (better known as Mark Twain), Paul Gallico, H. H. Munro,

Walter de la Mare, Thomas Hardy, Lewis Carroll, Beatrix Potter, H. G. Wells, W. B. Yeats, and H. P. Lovecraft. Samuel Clemens once said, "If a man could be crossed with a cat, it would improve the man but deteriorate the cat."

With this strong association between cats and books, it seems natural that in a place with an endless supply of books, there should be a perpetual cat.

The Doris & Harry Vise University Library at Cumberland University in Lebanon, Tennessee, has a ghost cat who oversees the checking out of books and the people who come and go. No one really knows where he came from. Although the university itself dates back to the mid-1800s, the Vise Library has no long or colorful history; in fact, the building was built in 1987. But it's what has happened since the new millennium that makes it colorful.

On March 5, 2001, at approximately 9:45 P.M., serials librarian John D. Boniol was in his office at the Cumberland University Library. There were other people in the library, and John was preparing to close up. He had just stood up from his desk to make his nightly rounds when he saw a cat-like form sail across the room and disappear. He described it as gray and willowy, but he couldn't make out its features. The long-haired gray ghost cat floated across the office floor and disappeared among the boxes stored under the table behind John's desk. He said the cat hovered just above the floor and appeared to be gliding. He saw no legs or paws and detected no movement like that of a normal cat walking on a floor.

John wasn't sure whether it had come in through the door or from under his desk. He said the appearance of the phantom feline was an interesting phenomenon but it didn't scare him.

Library employees speculate that the cat may belong to a little girl who also haunts the library. The former library director, Roger Karl, used to see the little girl all the time. Before Dr. Karl died, he even played hide-and-seek with her around the checkout desk. Dr. Frank G. Burns, Cumberland's archivist, has also seen the ghost of the little girl in the library, and reports that she is dressed in white. Dr. Burns once took a photograph in the library in which the ghost cat appeared. In the photo the cat also appeared to be white.

John Boniol said he'd like to see the cat again. Besides, what could more natural to the world's future writers than the presence of a perennial cat muse?

Doris & Harry Vise University Library
Cumberland University
One Cumberland Square
Lebanon, TN 37087
615-444-2562
800-467-0562
www.cumberland.edu/library
info@cumberland.edu

STONEHENGE'S POOR PUSS

In the early 1990s, British Heritage, the organization that oversees conservation of English landmarks, granted access to the Stonehenge inner circle to journalists and VIPs only. The regular tourists, mere mortals, stood behind a fence over a hundred feet away, and watched with envy as a security guard escorted photographer Ruth McClure from Dallas into the historic Druid holy place.

It was a cold late afternoon in February. The sun was beginning to cast a golden glow across the huge monoliths of Stonehenge. Ruth wandered in and out of the inner circle, biding her time for just the right instant when the light would be perfect for that photographic masterpiece. She stood among the immense towering stones with her camera in hand, loaded with a fresh roll of film and brand new batteries, just waiting. The sun dropped lower in the sky. Finally, the moment came; she had only minutes to shoot in this perfect light before the sun slid behind the horizon and left her in darkness.

All too soon, the last rays of sunlight had faded, replaced by the light of the moon. Ruth replaced the AS100 film with infrared film and changed her lens to an expensive one that permitted her to view her surroundings bathed in infrared light. The huge lintels glowed in the lens with their own eerie white light as if they had a life force all their own. Viewing the monoliths through the infrared viewfinder was like stepping into a photographic negative. Objects reflecting more heat appeared whiter and cooler objects looked darker.

As she shot in infrared, Ruth wondered what stories the stones could have told had they had a voice.

Her guide, tall, slender, and in his late thirties, seemed fascinated by the Texan's traditional cowboy hat and her Dallas accent. He told her she could take all the time she needed since the site had closed for the night. He added that if she had any questions, she should feel free to ask them.

Through her viewfinder Ruth panned the circle, snapping the shutter. Then, something extraordinary caught her eye. At the base of one of the pillars, somewhere between the outer megaliths of the sarsen stone circle and the inner horseshoe of stones, an eerie black shape appeared in her viewfinder. It didn't have a definite shape the way trees, people, or even the vertical stone slabs did. It appeared—well, roughly cat-shaped, as well as cat-size. It seemed to shift back and forth. She moved closer to see what could be causing this, scanning the area with her flashlight.

Her guide asked if she had seen something usual. She turned to him and said that she'd seen something strange in the viewfinder. The next moment, something brushed against her pant leg. She looked down. There was nothing there.

Seeing the startled look on her face, the guide laughed and said, "I see that Pussy Cat has found you." He proceeded to tell her the story of this ill-fated cat.

Before the circle had been fenced off, present-day Druids would try to sneak in and make sacrifices. One morning a guard found a poor black cat who had been maimed and left to die. They nursed him back to heath and gave him a place to live. He had one bad leg and a lot of scars, but seemed happy to live with the kind people at the Stonehenge visitors' center. About two years later the Druids managed to sneak back in and catch poor Puss.

They killed poor Puss in sacrificial fashion.

When the caretakers found his body the next day, they buried him there at the foot of the very stone where Ruth had seen the cat-shaped dark spot. The guard said to Ruth, "You are not the first to feel his presence. I guess your special film picked him up."

Poor Puss brushed up against her leg as if in agreement.

THE RAILROAD STATION CAT FROM MARS

The Chesapeake & Ohio Railway is known affectionately as the Chessie Railroad System. Today, the C&O is probably best remembered for its advertising mascot. In 1933, the railroad adopted a new advertising campaign to promote their new air-conditioned sleeping cars. They came up with the slogan, "Sleep like a Kitten and Wake up Fresh as a Daisy in Air-Conditioned Comfort." The company's advertising agency conceived an ad blitz around a kitten and chose the name "Chessie" from the railroad's nickname. Naturally, they needed an adorable kitten to illustrate the magazine ads. An artist came up with the painting of a tiny tabby kitten peeking out from beneath her Pullman blanket. With the termination of Chessie passenger service in the early 1970s, the Railroad Kitten disappeared from advertisements. But the Chesapeake & Ohio Railway's charming little feline wasn't the only timeless Chessie.

The Mars Railroad Station in Mars, Pennsylvania, also has a Chessie who has been a railroad cat for about a century. According to legend, this Chessie first appeared in the early 1900s. At that time, when the station was relatively new, a small cat worked alongside his owner, the stationmaster. It wasn't uncommon for stations to have cats to kill rats in the storage rooms. One day, this little cat inexplicably vanished. He wouldn't turn up for a hundred years.

Mars resident Bill Swaney was on the Mars town council in 1980 when Chessie Railroad officials decided they were going to tear down the obsolete railroad station. To save the station, concerned citizens formed the Mars Historical Society (MHS). The Chessie Railroad donated the building to MHS for removal and restoration. The only caveat:

the historical society had to move the building so the Chesapeake & Ohio Railway could utilize the valuable property on which it sat.

In 2000, MHS volunteers cut the twenty-by-seventy-foot railroad station, comprised of three major rooms, into six sections, and moved the pieces 600 feet across the tracks to city property. In August 2000, they were moving the section that contained the storage room when volunteers made an upsetting discovery. They found the hundred-year-old mummified body of a cat in the building's foundation, under the mail-storage room.

Bill Swaney, who has been actively involved in the station's preservation, said they believed the little cat had become trapped under the railroad station and suffocated. He said it looks like he was brown with little tiger stripes, just like the original advertising mascot.

The old station now sits on the other side of the tracks from its original location. After finding the remains of the cat, Bill said they have taken special care to animal-proof the structure. They have patched all the holes, making it impossible for any cats to sneak inside the structure today.

MHS volunteers named the deceased cat Chessie after the railroad system and its heartwarming mascot. They have carefully preserved the cat's remains inside a shadow box, which they keep on display in the former mailroom. For now, the storage area doubles as makeshift woodworking shop, which is now covered in a layer of sawdust generated by the power saw. Since they moved that section across the tracks, members of the MHS have experienced strange happenings in the old building—especially in the storage area, which is a completely sealed room.

"Every now and then, when volunteers enter the building early in the morning, they find paw prints in the sawdust," Bill said. Since this was Chessie's domain, some have wondered if perhaps the cat is still protecting the mail and cargo from vermin. Paw prints have never appeared in any other room. According to the Chessie legend, the cat can occasionally be seen, although Bill has never eyeballed the ghost cat himself. Bill has never heard the cat crying either, but one little girl said she heard a cat meow.

A self-admitted skeptic, Bill usually doesn't believe anything unless he's seen it with his own eyes. But even though he *has* seen the paw-shaped patterns firsthand, he still isn't quite ready to acknowledge that this is anything but a local legend.

Nevertheless, while Bill is not afraid of the railroad station's specter, you won't find him working there past midnight.

Mars Railroad Station
Mars Historical Society
Box 58
Mars, PA 16046

THE MAGNOLIA MOUND PLANTATION MYSTERY CAT

Magnolia Mound Plantation is located in an area that has become quite an urban setting in Baton Rouge, Louisiana. When the small settler's house was first built in 1791, the 900-acre plantation had frontage on the Mississippi River. As success and prosperity increased, the house expanded both in size and grandeur. Today Magnolia Mound Plantation is a museum that opens its doors and remaining sixteen acres to the public. Museum guides conduct tours of the property and perform demonstrations of what life was like in the 1700s and 1800s.

Not long ago Laura A. Gallagher of Saginaw, Texas, went on a tour of the main plantation house. The tour guide had taken the group into the master bedroom. The guide kept a close eye on guests and required everyone to stay on the plastic floor runners laid down to protect the aging wooden floors.

As the guide discussed details of the antique furniture and artwork, Laura suddenly noticed that there was a cat in the room. He was a typical cat—grayish-brown with vivid black stripes. Everything about the cat was ordinary: he was medium-size, short-haired, and well fed—obviously not a stray. The cat wandered across the floor and sidled up to an old wooden chair and desk. In typical feline fashion, he rubbed his cheek up and down the leg of the chair. Laura didn't bother to look closely at the cat because he was, well, just a cat.

Laura laughed and commented to the lady standing next to her that the cat didn't have to follow the plastic floor runner. The woman gave Laura a strange look. She didn't see the cat. None of the other folks on the tour made any remark when the cat arrived. There was bound to be at least one other cat lover in the room, or even a cat hater complaining about cat dander. They asked other questions, but on the subject of the tabby cat, the audience remained as silent as a tomb. Laura didn't think to ask the guide about the cat until she was on her way home.

The cat had looked so real, and had acted so normally that it didn't occur to Laura until later that the museum would never allow a cat inside the house. After all, cats have their own rules—especially ghost cats; they do what they want to do, and the museum wouldn't be able to control where they went.

Despite Laura's encounter with the feline entity, Magnolia Plantation officials strongly deny the presence of any ghosts at all. Laura assumes that the cat was associated with the house; maybe he belonged to a child who lived there long ago. The tabby acted as if he owned the place. And with all his cheek marking of the chairs, maybe he did.

Magnolia Mound Plantation DR
2161 Nicholson Drive
Baton Rouge, LA 70802
(Between downtown and the LSU campus)
225-343-4955
information@magnoliamound.org

THE UNSINKABLE CAT AT THE MOLLY BROWN HOUSE MUSEUM

Most people are familiar with the 1960s musical, *The Unsinkable Molly Brown*. It was based on the amazing life of Margaret (Molly) Brown in the years after she survived the sinking of the RMS *Titanic* in 1912.

Her friends and family actually called her Maggie, not Molly. It's believed that the nickname "Molly" was just poetic license on the part of the press and Hollywood. Long before she set foot on the doomed cruise ship, she and her husband, J. J., bought a three-story Victorian home on Pennsylvania Street in Denver. Today the 7,600-square-foot house serves as a tribute to her courageous spirit. When the Browns purchased it in 1894, it had electric lights, a telephone, indoor plumbing, and hot and cold running water. It even had an indoor bathroom and forced heat and air—talk about luxurious!

Molly was a philanthropist. Many charities benefited from her generosity. She even founded Denver's Dumb Friends' League, a term commonly used to describe a person or animal who couldn't speak for himself. Since she loved animals, it's not surprising that her cat would be waiting for Molly. Nothing is really known about her cat except what has been observed by museum staff and visitors. But this kitty has been waiting for a century.

In a 2003 interview by Anna Maria Basquez of *The Coloradoan,* Kerri Atter, director and curator of the Molly Brown House Museum, said, "This time of year (Halloween) people always see a black-and-white cat here." Visitors to the museum sometimes notice the cat in or near the pantry.

Today, Molly's home is said to be haunted by several spirits, including the cat and her husband, J. J.

The Molly Brown House Museum DR
1340 Pennsylvania Street
Denver, Colorado 80203
303-832-4092

LOCATIONS THAT MAY HAVE GHOST CATS

Remember that many places listed here require permission to visit or investigate. If you trespass, you may be prosecuted. This list was compiled from many sources, including books, Internet sites, and articles—none of these haunted locations have been confirmed in any way.

CALIFORNIA

The Hart Theatre
Ferndale Repertory Theatre
447 Main Street
Ferndale, CA 95536-0096
707-786-5483

The Hart Theatre was one of the first theaters built in the Eel River Valley of Northwestern California specifically for the showing of motion pictures. It opened on December 8, 1920, with a showing of *The Molly-coddle*, a silent adventure comedy with Douglas Fairbanks. The theater hired a pianist for the movie's musical accompaniment. Admission fees were a quarter for adults and fifteen cents for children. The Hart Theatre showed movies and hosted vaudeville companies for almost forty years.

Marilyn McCormick, Ferndale Repertory artistic director, says that the theater has a late-night spirit named Bertha. There are reports that the Hart Theatre also has a ghost cat who occasionally roams up and down the aisles during performances. Marilyn couldn't confirm the presence of the cat's spirit, but said they have had cats, and maybe some of them have returned for an afterlife appearance.

HAWAII

Waianae, Maili Coralsands
O'ahu—Honolulu, Hawaii

This area across from the Maili 76 Gas Station is reportedly haunted by animal spirits that were buried there since the 1980s. Supposedly visitors can hear the meows of cats and howls of dogs. Human voices can also be heard.

KENTUCKY

Loudoun House
Lexington Art League
209 Castlewood Drive
Lexington, KY 40505
859-254-7024
800-914-7990

Loudoun House was originally built to be a residence for Francis Key Hunt in 1850. It's considered one of the grandest and finest examples of Gothic Revival architecture in the state of Kentucky. The Loudoun is owned by the city of Lexington and is the home of the Lexington Art League. The Lexington Art League office hours are Monday through Friday 8:30 a.m. to 5:00 p.m. There are unconfirmed reports of a black ghost cat and other apparitions inside this home.

MISSOURI

Doniphan Cemetery (downtown district)

Doniphan, MO

There have been unconfirmed reports of a woman in the back of the cemetery walking out of the wall of a mausoleum and wandering through the headstones. She holds a headless white cat in her arms, and cries mournfully. The story says they lived sometime in the 1920s. She was holding her cat when they were both run over by a beer wagon.

NEVADA

Boulder City Pet Cemetery

Boulder City, NV

The Boulder City Pet Cemetery was established in 1953. Rumors claim that the ghost of a white cat hangs out there at night. If the cat takes a liking to a visitor, it will follow that person throughout the cemetery.

NEW YORK

Jacksonville Cemetery

Baldwinsville, NY

Legend has it that a black ghost cat with glowing green eyes watches everyone who enters this cemetery.

NORTH CAROLINA

The Biltmore Estate

Asheville, NC

800-624-1575 or 828-225-1333

The Biltmore Estate was once owned by millionaire George Vanderbilt. This historic three-story home boasts 250 rooms and sits on a sprawling 8,000 acres. Considered America's largest home, the Biltmore is even larger than the Hearst Castle. Tours are given daily. Allegedly, a headless orange cat roams the area between the gardens and the bass pond.

Shoals Creek
Shoals, NC
The word is that a large cat roams the creek and chases people who are wandering the area late at night. Witnesses report that all they see is two eyes coming after them.

OHIO

Sinclair Community College
Blair Hall
Dayton, OH
In Blair Hall cats can be heard meowing in the walls. Administrators say that this legend dates back to a Halloween haunted house they created several years ago, but said they do have other ghosts around the college and in the dorms.

OKLAHOMA

City College Inc., or Oklahoma Health Academy
Berg Anatomy
Moore, OK
A biology classroom is purportedly visited by the spirits of cats who were used in scientific experiments conducted by a Ms. Berg.

OREGON

Little Crater Lake
Mt. Hood National Forest, OR
Campers have reported seeing a white cat that vanishes whenever it is approached.

PENNSYLVANIA

Marianna Cemetery

Marianna, PA

It is said that the ghost of a woman floats through the field and then into the cemetery, where she sits on a fence with a black ghost cat.

SOUTH CAROLINA

White Wolf Hollow

Blacksburg, SC

There have been reports of a huge cat-like animal with eyes that shine red instead of the normal fluorescent green.

Kiawah Island

Kiawah, SC

In the nineteenth century a plantation existed on this island. During a stay in 2002 in one of the homes on the island, one witness described the ghost of a small boy, who it is believed was killed while looking for his missing cat. The boy has been seen with his cat running along beside him inside the house. Sometimes he and the cat run right through the walls.

TEXAS

The Old Police Station

Laredo, TX

After the station was closed, people reportedly performed ritual sacrifices of animals here. Witnesses claim to have seen a headless cat inside the station building.

UTAH

Old Arrowhead Swimming Resort

Benjamin, UT

There are stories of a ghost cat who wanders around the back of the house near the place where she was buried.

WISCONSIN

The woods on Church Street off of Rinden Road

Cottage Grove, WS

There are reports of a ghostly cat figure roaming those woods.

GREAT BRITAIN

The Beehive

The Village, Great Waltham

Chelmsford CM3 1AR

Tel: 01245 360356

www.beehivegreatwaltham.co.uk

enquiries@beehivegreatwaltham.co.uk

Rumors have circulated that on several occasions a gray cat has been seen running down the hallway of this country pub. The cat disappears into the wall in the bathroom. Linda, the new owner, has never heard stories about the cat, but doesn't discount them.

Chingle Hall

760 Whittingham Lane

Goosnargh, Lancashire PR8 2JJ

In the village of Goosnargh stands Chingle Hall, the oldest inhabited brick building in Britain. Built in 1260 by Knight Adam de Singleton, it was originally called Singleton Hall. It's considered one of the most haunted locations in Britain. Many of its past residents were either murdered in the house or executed.

Internet reports describe cold spots in the chapel despite warm weather outside. In the same area, people have felt an invisible cat weaving in and out of their legs. Other people report petting a black cat that no one else can see. There have also been reports of an unseen cat meowing loudly and pitifully, and mention of a gray-and-white cat with unclear features simply vanishing in the priest's room.

Gatehouse Restaurant

Battle (Sussex)

A small house cat supposedly floats down a hallway before vanishing into a wall.

King John's Hunting Lodge

The Square

Axbridge, Somerset

Tel: 011 44 (01934) 732012 (Call for tour times)

This restored Early Tudor merchant's home is now run as a local history museum by Axbridge and District Museum Trust, in cooperation with Sedgemoor District Council, Somerset County Museums Service, and Axbridge Archaeological and Local History Society. According to legend, a tabby cat ghost has been seen trotting around the first floor. He vanishes when he sits down. There is also a human apparition that appears in the lodge.

Yarwell Tunnel

Nene Valley Railway (13 miles west of Peterborough)

Wansford, Cambridgeshire

01780 784444

The ghost of the stationmaster and his cat, Snowy, haunts the one-hundred-year-old Yarwell Tunnel. The deaf stationmaster was looking for his cat when he was struck and killed by a train. The white ghosts can occasionally be seen breaking through the mist that accumulates at the tunnel's entrance.

selected works cited

Alexander, John. *Ghosts: Washington's Most Famous Ghost Stories.* Arlington, VA: Washington Book Trading Company, 1988.

Basquez, Anna Maria. "Phantom Cats and Shadowy Visitors Lurk in Downtown Neighborhood of City's Past." *Fort Collins Coloradoan Online.* 11 October 2003, www.coloradoan.com/news/coloradoanpublishing/ Ghosts/101103_capitolhill.html (accessed 9 September 2006).

Bayless, Raymond. *Animal Ghosts.* New York: University Books Inc., 1970.

Bhattacharya, Shaoni. "Black Cats May Be the More Fortunate Felines." *NewScientist.com news service,* 04 March 2003, www.newscientist.com/ article.ns?id=dn3459 (accessed 13 September 2006).

Boroff, Paula. "The Sacred Cats of Burma." *Cat Fanciers Association Website,* 13 September 2006, www.cfa.org/breeds/profiles/ articles/birman.html.

Browne, Sylvia and Chris Dufresne. *Animals on the Other Side.* Cincinnati: Angel Bea Publishing, 2005.

"Chingle Hall Investigation." *Ghost-Story.co.uk.* June 2003, www.ghost-story.co.uk/stories/chinglehallvisit1.html (accessed 20 July 2006).

Clutterbuck, Martin R. *The Legend of Siamese Cats.* Bangkok, Thailand: White Lotus Press, 1998. As appears on *ChitPaDe's Burmesen* 13 September 2006, www.burmese-cats.de/catbook.htm.

Conway, D. J. *The Mysterious Magical Cat.* New York: Gramercy Books, 1998.

"Crescent Hotel Opens Today." *Eureka Springs Times Echo*. May 20, 1886. As appears on *History—Step Back in Time*. "Crescent Hotel and Spa." 17 September 2006, www.crescent-hotel.com/history.htm.

Dixon, Jean. *Do Cats Have ESP?* New York: Aaron Publishing Group, Inc., 1997.

"Domestic Cat's Wisdom." *Shamanism: Working with Animal Spirits*. 4 November 2006, www.geocities.com/rainforest/4076/index34.html.

Falwell, Lisa. *Haunted Texas Vacations*. Englewood, CO: Westcliffe Publishers, 2000.

"The George Washington Papers at the Library of Congress." Library of Congress American Memory. 11 August 2006, http://rs6.loc.gov/ammem/gwhtml/1777.html.

Goodwin, Dave. "Fort McAllister: The Phantom Feline of the Savannah River Defenses." *Military Ghosts*. 2003, 11 October 2006. www.militaryghosts.com/mcallister.html.

Hartwell, Sarah. "Cats and Babies Can Coexist." Messybeast.com, 1994, http://www.messybeast.com/cat_baby.htm (accessed 21 November 2006).

"Haunted American-District of Columbia-Senate." Left-Field Paranormal Studies and Investigations. 13 September 2006, www.leftfield-psi.net/ghosts/haunted_places/usa_d.html.

Hayes, Deborah Childs, PhD. "Turkish Vans Rediscovered: A Living History: *Cat Fanciers' Almanac*, October 1994.

"Hotel History." *The Faust Hotel*. 21 August 2006. www.fausthotel.com/history.html.

"How Did So Many Animals Escape?" *Tribune India Online Edition*. 06 January 2005, www.tribuneindia.com/2005/20050106/world.htm#4 (accessed 15 October 2005).

"King John's Hunting Lodge." *National Trust for Historic Preservation.* 20 July 2006, www.nationaltrust.org.uk/main/w-vh/w-visits/w-findaplace/w-kingjohnshuntinglodge.

Lane, C. H. *Rabbits, Cats and Cavies.* 1903. As appears in Van Vechten, *The Tiger in the House.* New York: Alfred A. Knopf, 1968.

Lehr, Lisa J. "Cats, People, and the Black Plague: Those Who Kept Cats Survived." *Petlvr.com-The Blog.* 8 April 2006, www.petlvr.com/blog/2006/04/cats-people-and-the-black-plague-those-who-kept-cats-survived (accessed 13 September 2006).

Lovelace, Wicasta. "The Mallefus Maleficarum of Heinrich Kramer and James Sprenger." 13 Septtember 2006, www.malleusmaleficarum.org.

Malek, Jaromir. *The Cat in Ancient Egypt.* London: British Museum Press, 1997.

Miller, Joan. "Breed Profile: Abyssinian" *Cat Fanciers' Association Website.* 24 July 2006, www.cfainc.org/breeds/profiles/abyssinian.html, (accessed 14 September 2006).

Mott, Maryann "Can Animals Sense Earthquakes?" *National Geographic News,* November 11, 2003, http://news.nationalgeographic.com/news/2003/11/1111_031111_earthquakeanimals.html (accessed 1 September 2006).

O'Donnell, Elliot. *Animal Ghosts or Animal Hauntings and the Hereafter.* William Rider & Son, 1913. As found on *Horrormasters,* www.horror-masters.com/Collections/SS_Col_OD2.htm.

Ozduzen, Nezihi. *Adiyamanli.org Agency.* 17 February 2006, www.adiyamanli.org/vangolu.html (accessed 1 October 2006).

"Plague and Public Health in Renaissance Europe." Institute for Advanced Technology in the Humanities University of Virginia. 28 October 1994, www3.iath.virginia.edu/osheim/plaguein.html (accessed 13 September 2006).

Radford, Edwin, and Mona. A. Radford. *Encyclopedia of Superstitions*.
New York: The Philosophical Library, Inc., 1949.

Rowe, Jeremy. "A Photographic History of Arizona 1850–1920."
Jeremy Rowe Vintage Photography, 2002. 15 September 2006,
http://vintagephoto.com/reference/azphotohistory.htm.

Sayahda. *Animal Totems-Cat Sayahda*. 1997. 4 November 2006,
www.sayahda.com/cyc1.html.

"Siamese Cat Breed Information and History." *Schimmel Felines*.
13 September 2006, www.schimmelorientals.com/
information_siamese_breedinfo.php.

"Some Famous Ghosts of the National Capitol." *Philadelphia Press*.
13 September 1896. As found in Reeve, Arthur. *Some Real American
Ghosts*, 1919. www.web-books.com. 13 September 2006,
www.web-books.com/Classics/Stories/BestGhostStories/
BestGhostStoriesC14P1.htm.

"Tom Cat Historical Marker." *Carl Vinson Institute of Government*.
17 August 2006, www.cviog.uga.edu/Projects/gainfo/
gahistmarkers/tomcathistmarker.htm.

Travis, John. "Feline Finding: Mutations Produce Black House Cats,
Jaguars." *Current Biology* (Vol. 13, p. 448) March 8, 2003; Vol. 163, No.
10, p. 147. *Science News Online*. 8 March 2003, www.sciencenews.org/
articles/20030308/fob2.asp (accessed 13 September 2006).

"Turkish Van Cat Folk-Lore" *Classic Turkish Van Cat Association*.
1 September 2006, www.vantasia.org/turk_folk.html.

"Turkish Van Cat History" *Classic Turkish Van Cat Association*.
1 September 2006, www.vantasia.org/turk_hist.html.

Turville-Petre, E. O. G. *Myth & Religion of the North: The Religion of
Ancient Scandinavia*. New York: Holt, 1964.

Van Vechten, Carl. *The Tiger in the House*. New York: Alfred A Knopf,
Publisher, 1968.

von Muggenthaler, Elizabeth. The Felid Purr: A Bio-Mechanical Healing Mechanism Fauna Communications. 2006. 18 September 2006, www.animalvoice.com/catpur.htm.

Weir, Harrison. *Our Cats and All About Them: Their Varieties, Habits, and Management, and for Show, the Standard of Excellence and Beauty.* New York: Houghton, Mifflin and Company, 1889.

"What Are Applehead Siamese?" *Miller's Shoobox Traditional Siamese & Balinese Cattery.* 13 September 2006, www.siamesecats.com/ siameseNature.htm.

Why Do Cats? Part II" Pawprints and Purrs Inc. 1 September 2006, www.sniksnak.com/cathealth/whydo2.html.

Winslow, Helen M.. *Concerning Cats.* Ann Arbor, Michigan: Lowe & B. Hould Publishers, 1900.

Young, Stephen. "The Domestic Cat and the Law: A Guide to Available Resources." *LLRX.com.*

Zanetti, Aida Bartleman, Elinor Dennis, and Mary E. Hantzmon. "Journey from Blue Nile." *Abyra Abyssinians,* 22 January 2003. 10 September 2006, http://ourworld.compuserve.com/ homepages/Harry_Blok/journey.htm.

Dusty Rainbolt is an award-winning cat writer and the author of *Kittens for Dummies*. She also writes humorous science fiction and fantasy, including her novel *All the Marbles* and the *Four Redheads of the Apocalypse,* which she coauthored with Rhonda Eudaly, Julia S. Mandala, and Linda L. Donahue. She is the product editor for *Catnip,* the magazine published by Tufts University Cummings School of Veterinary Medicine. In a past life, she worked as a reporter for several North Texas community newspapers. Her monthly columns appear in *City + Country Pets,* www.stickypaws.com, and www.hartz.com. Her articles appear regularly in *Cat Fancy Magazine.*

Dusty is a member of the International Association of Animal Behavior Consultants. She and her husband share their unhaunted home with their living, breathing cats. Involved in kitten rescue for two decades, she has raised more than 250 surviving orphan kittens. Unfortunately not all of the bottle babies made it. One in particular changed her life. A former card-carrying skeptic, Dusty started investigating paranormal phenomena after her recently passed foster kitten named Maynard returned for a brief one-time afterlife experience.

Check out her Web site at www.dustyrainbolt.com. She'd love to hear your cat, dog, and horse ghost stories.